THE Dazzling Darkness

PAULA CAPPA

CRISPIN BOOKS

Crispin Books is an independent press based in Milwaukee, Wisconsin. With its sibling imprint, Crickhollow Books, Crispin publishes a variety of quality fiction and nonfiction titles for discerning readers.

For a complete list of books in print, visit:

www.CrispinBooks.com

The Dazzling Darkness

ISBN-13: 978-1-883953-61-4
(ISBN-10: 1-883953-61-8)

First Crispin Books Edition

Cover design by Gina Casey

Also by Paula Cappa:

Night Sea Journey

Both *The Dazzling Darkness*
and *Night Sea Journey*
are also available in eBook editions.

for more information:

http://paulacappa.wordpress.com

For my darlings,

Gina and Jon-Paul,

with love.

Contents

There is a God, some say,
A deep but dazzling darkness, as men here
Say it is late and dusky, because they
See not all clear.
O for that night! Where I in Him
Might live invisible and dim!

"The Night"
by Henry Vaughan (1621–1695)

Prologue

Old Willow Cemetery, Concord, Massachusetts

Elias Hatch is an old soul who spends each day trusting the dead.

Midnight at his heels, Elias walks the paths through the gravestones in the deepening night of a moon-splashed cemetery. He stops and gazes straight up at the sky. The constellation of Perseus glimmers right next to Aries. Magnificent. Brooding autumn leaves sail down one by one with breathy sounds. A chill is present. At the gates of Old Willow Cemetery, the twisted vines choke the bald ironworks, their thorny cords crisscrossed into images of wrinkled faces and hoodwinked eyes. Trust. *Be brave, old man.*

Elias Hatch is the keeper of Old Willow Cemetery, a scientist who imitates the medieval art of alchemy transforming not metal into gold, but hidden reality into clear perception. At least that's how he would tell it. *These secrets.*

Inside the dark hollow of the surrounding woods, he lives like an old cat, prowling here and there for a patch of sunlight, pawing through books each day as if they were his only reliable friends. He does have one friend, a man from Italy, whom he calls loyal. Teenagers tease Elias, calling him Old Saturn, likening the grave keeper to a lion-headed dragon with his stringy mane of white hair, bearded face, and black-ice eyes that are constantly guarding the cemetery.

Twelve weeping willow trees stand outside this walled garden, their trunks bulky like wild muscular men ready to charge should anyone venture inside. The cypresses within the walls are like trees of light, sun trees and moon trees. And there is a blackthorn tree that sheds in autumn, leaving its bony branches to hook over a quarry stone.

Of the abundant trees hovering in this graveyard, there is one long-lived silver birch whose branches extend above a row of small headstones where three babies are buried. Elias, never having had children, sits by the babies' graves, deep in thought. At the back of the yard, he has a favorite trembling lilac tree. A nervous sort, the tree likes to hug the obelisk carved with two hands raised in benediction. And sometimes, that old wild-hearted pine at the corner swipes at the satin moon as if to snatch it down. *Nature growing conscious,* Elias might say.

There are pieces of sculpture here among the headstones: the usual doves in flight, angels with curly feathers, a star of David. What cemetery doesn't have some patron saints—St. Helena of the Cross, St. Agnes with hand over heart. And there is the unusual: a flat stone fresco of the birth of Venus, a kneeling woman draped in flowing veils as she hugs a cross. Elias enjoys petting her bowed head as he passes by.

Deep in the center of the cemetery, another statue draws the eye upward: a petal-thin woman beneath the drape of a thick cape. Her face is barely visible within the folds of the hood: her arms hang loose at her sides; fingers fall limp; a shy ankle peeks out from the hem and exposes delicately carved marble toes. As old stories have gone around the village through the years, the statue is said to weep human tears. Someone named her the Weeping Woman of Old Willow, and children still try to squeeze their faces between the gate irons to see if her tears are real or rain.

Elias Hatch, he knows her tears are not rain.

GREVE, ITALY 2005

The man in a thin black suit strolled along the noisy Piazza Matteotti, searching for the associate. He threaded his way past open shops selling local produce and ceramics, the walls festooned with long salamis, cheeses, red peppers. At a crude street oven, a young woman chopped mounds of garlic and red-hot cherry peppers on a wooden board and slid them into a hot skillet of olive oil. A quick stir, then she added a handful of jumbo shrimp. The smoky fragrance stimulated his appetite as she tossed the seafood over a bowl of steaming linguine. She lifted her exotic eyes to him. He gave her a wink, and she returned a flirty smile.

Each time the man visited the associate in Greve, they would feast on the most astonishing cuisine. This Sunday in July, the man anticipated another delicious meal. In the distance, on a sunny café balcony, he spotted the associate sitting where a white tablecloth blew in the noonday breezes.

"We meet again, sir." He greeted the associate in English and sat down.

The associate wore a tan fedora and a white gauzy shirt as wrinkled as his face. His beard was a scruffy grey. Thick tufts of chest hair showed at his neck where antique Roman medals hung on a gold chain. Completely absorbed, the associate ate a bowl of pasta with black olives and juicy tomatoes, pausing only to take a drink of a clear thick liquid.

The man removed the envelope from his jacket pocket, laid it ceremoniously on the table.

The associate half smiled. "Tell your boys in Rome I'm grateful."

"That's the full payment, in advance, for this last job."

"*Excellente!* Lola will like that."

"Lola? Who's that? What does she know?"

"*Nada.* I've not come this far by being stupid." His pale blue eyes shining, he flipped a small photograph to the man. "My new bride."

The man held the photo. Lola was about twenty with streaming black hair and the bosom of a goddess.

"I've ordered you the *Fave con Pecorino.* Very creamy. Cooked all night in a flask with olive oil. *Vino?*" He signaled the waiter.

"*L'aqua minerale.* Do you have the location yet?"

"Aaaaaah." The associate made circles with his forefinger as if confused in the head. "Maybe America."

"That's unusual. Where?"

"Massachusetts, we think." He lifted a small leather briefcase.

"What's this?"

"Dossier. For you."

"Me? What are you saying? You're not going to complete this last job?"

"*Como si dice questo . . . forse?* Maybe. If not, you will do it."

The man shook his head. "I don't know the first thing about your business. I can't do your work. You can't expect—"

"'By this sign, conquer.' Constantine of Rome won his battles by such words. Have a little faith."

"I'm just the messenger here, remember?" Then he whispered, "I don't even know your name."

"You'll know when I'm dead. Doctors say by Christmas." The associate swallowed another slug of the thick liquid.

"You keep drinking that grappa, you won't make September. Tell me your name."

He smacked his lips. "Emilio Perucca."

"Don't you want to know my name?"

"What for? You're just the messenger."

The waiter appeared, placed down a steaming dish of white beans, crisp pancetta, and thick shavings of Pecorino cheese. Intoxicated with the aroma, the man dived in with his spoon.

Perucca placed a small black velvet pouch on the table.

"What's this, now?"

"*Chiave.*"

"What key? You mean—?"

"*Si.* To the underground hatch."

Sweat broke on his neck. "The hatch. I know nothing about that! This is your responsibility, isn't it? I don't even know where it is." He pushed the pouch away.

Perucca snatched the pouch and placed it hard on the table. "Pass it on to Cavallo to keep safe. When the time comes, he will contact you through Cordone." Perucca poured himself another glass of grappa, drank it in thirsty gulps. "We should agree on a place to meet. After it happens."

The man calmed his nerves with a deep breath. "Where . . . do you think is best?"

Perucca took off his hat, exposing thin grey hair. "*Cimitero.*"

"In the cemetery?"

"*Si,* where else? On Via Cassia in the woods. Look for me on the banks of the Greve River."

"How will I know . . . when?"

"Cavallo will call."

The man's hands began to shake. "I've not done this before."

Perucca laughed, his pale blue eyes sparkling. "Ah, neither have I. Eat your beans."

Book One

March Rain

Alchemy, which sought to transmute one element
into another to prolong life, to arm with power—
that was in the right direction.
All our science lacks a human side.

Ralph Waldo Emerson,
The Conduct of Life, Beauty, 1876

Chapter One

Concord, Massachusetts, March 20, 2010

Antonia Scarlatta Brooke opened her oak front door and gave her son a call. The front gable of the nut-brown house zoomed high in a triangle over her petite frame. Sunlight leapt on three old crows screeching from the chestnut tree that leaned dangerously low over the rooftop. Lined up on one branch, these blackbirds shouted their crackling trills and kept their bald eyes on Antonia below.

"Henry? Where are you?"

Quickly she shot her dark eyes to the old cow path beaten down with dried witch grass that led into the woods beyond. Antonia squinted to see the Red Sox baseball cap and blue jacket, but her five-year-old did not come skipping down the path.

She went down the brick walk. "Henry? Answer me."

A gale roared up as if to snap the old crows off their shivering branch. They flew up suddenly and carved the sky with feathery black circles.

"Oh, honestly, where is that boy. Laura, were you holding his hand? I've told you time and again to hold your brother's hand when you're walking home."

Laura, with her sweetheart face, Alice-blue eyes, and blond zigzagging hair, appeared from the narrow foyer of the house, her hand inside a bag of chocolate-chip cookies. Antonia stood on the weathered lawn in black jeans and a thin turquoise v-neck sweater that left her vulnerable to the cold March winds.

"We do hold hands," Laura said. "But sometimes he lets go. He thinks he's a big shot kindergartner now."

"And you, of course, are a big shot third-grader."

"Well, eight years old is more than five." She threw her arms around her mother's waist. "He's such a kid, you know, Mom?"

Antonia wrapped her daughter into her arms. "Chilly today and so windy."

"I love the wind. I wish I could drink it." Laura spun around, letting her bright curls fly out like corkscrews, then dramatically arched her back to one side with both arms waving. "How's this for a ballet pose?"

Antonia looked back at the cow path. "Was he ahead of you or behind?"

"Behind me. We were collecting blue jay feathers. Mom, look."

She glanced at Laura. "You walked the cow path, right? Not in the street?"

She muttered a yes, arms lifted over her head, swaying on tiptoes as ballerinas do. "Henry loves the cow path. He thinks the trees are people. Says they tell him secrets. When are we going to have teatime?"

"As soon as I find Henry. I'll be back in five minutes exactly. Sit on the bench in the foyer and wait for me." She directed Laura into the house, grabbed a shawl from the closet, and locked the door behind her. With a quick look into the hedged backyard, she shouted twice more for Henry, made a quick scan of the yard, then headed to the cow path.

It certainly was convenient having this woodsy path parallel to Eastwick Road so the children could walk home safely. Antonia followed the path curving into the woods where the pines retreated into their shadows. Not far away was Old Willow Cemetery. The high black iron fence, the heavy gate with so many hanging chains and padlocks, and the massive rock walls looked more like a fortress than a quiet garden for the dearly departed. She continued on the path until she came to a thicket of pine trees Henry usually found irresistible.

"Henry?"

He was likely sitting in a mess of pine twigs, searching for mica stones and not at all aware he'd wandered off. Couldn't blame him, for she too might want to sit in the grove and just be. The delicious scent of pine surged and drew up a string of words. *The melted snow of March, the willow sending forth its yellow-green sprouts; for spring-time is here.* Walt Whitman. For Antonia, such lines of poetry rose inside her as often as she might feel hungry during the course of a day; even lines of her own poems would spill out with no warning.

But now, a fearful cry gathered in her belly. "Henry!" He'd never delayed this long before. She hurried back to the path and ran to the main gate at Old Willow Cemetery, adjacent to the school bus stop at the corner.

"Henry?"

Only the wind gave off a low cry. A sob caught inside her throat. *Dear God, please, where is he?*

"Mom?"

Antonia spun around.

"He's not here?" Laura said, panic in her voice.

Antonia tried to hide her own rising panic. "I told you to stay in the house."

"I want to help. He's not in the backyard. I looked."

"Is he hiding somewhere?"

"I looked in his favorite place in the hedges."

"Did he take that turn off the path, do you think?"

"No. He was right behind me. I heard him doing all that silly stuff with the rocks. You know, listening to them hum. We were playing follow-the-leader."

"Oh Laura, you didn't run up ahead of him very far, did you?"

"Yeah, but, I mean, you have to get way ahead or it's no fun." Her lips quivered. Tears rose. "Oh, Mommy!"

Antonia knelt down, placed her hands on Laura's head, her hair in strings of thin curls across her shoulders. Always tangled, this child's hair. "Henry's okay. He's wandered off, that's all. We'll find him." She wiped the tears away.

"Mom, maybe Old Saturn has seen him." She pointed to the cobblestone cottage in the distance.

"You mean Elias Hatch, don't you? And it's Mr. Hatch."

"Misstaahhh Elias Hatch. That's how Henry says it."

"And what do you mean, maybe Old Saturn knows? Have you two been poking around his property?"

She looked away. "Sometimes we wave hello." Laura swept her curls out of her eyes, then tossed the strands behind her as if she were swatting flies. "I hate my hair. I saw that girl with the braids again over by the linden trees."

"You did? When?"

"When I looked in the backyard for Henry. Oh, Mommy, her braids are way down her back and with ribbons. When can I wear braids? Tara wears braids every day."

During the rushed morning routine, there was no time to braid her little mop. "Laura, please. On Saturday, we'll do braids."

"I asked the girl to come over and play, but she ran away. I wish I knew her name. Can you find out her name?"

"Never mind that now. Let's go see if Mr. Hatch has seen Henry."

The Hatch cottage was deep inside the pine grove, which discouraged the most determined light of day. Elias often lit the house with candles, even in the middle of the afternoon; one white candle would be lit in each window. Antonia thought this candle lighting was just the ritual of an eccentric old man who lived alone until she caught him pocketing a bag of Hershey's kisses at the market one morning. He likely was on a small pension and cutting a few dollars off his electric bills. But on this day, Antonia saw no candlelight in the windows.

They hurried to the cottage and rang the doorbell. "Mr. Hatch? Hello? It's Antonia Brooke." After a minute, she peeked into the arched black-leaded windows.

"Are we snooping?" Laura drew circles with her finger in the dirt on the window ledge.

"Of course not. Snooping is rude, you know that." Antonia cupped her hands over her eyes to block the light and see inside. She couldn't make out much: a few shadows, a grey puddle, a stream of dull light. And then a shadow abruptly shot up—a scowled face with monkey eyes and cavernous nostrils. She jumped away.

Laura jumped too. "What? What happened?"

"I thought I saw someone." She looked inside again. The view was too dark to see anything except her own reflection in the glass, her dark pixie-cut hair blown out like wings.

"Is it Mr. Hatch?"

"I don't think so." Antonia quickly raked down her hair, then rapped at the door.

"There's nobody in there." Laura cupped her hands at the window as her mother had done.

"Come on, Laura." She grabbed her daughter's hand. They ran the cow path again, to the bus stop, to the brook, and once more into the pine cove. A sick wave tumbled Antonia's stomach as they approached the grim woods where the blackbirds flocked in a series of odd circles. What were they doing? She shook off a chill.

* * *

On this Friday afternoon, Adam Brooke inhaled the moist spring air as he strolled up the bluestone gravel driveway to his brown clapboard house sitting among deep stretches of oaks. The house wore its multi-paned windows and four gables pointing sharply like a tribute to the sky. At the far end of the backyard, he especially loved the row of great linden trees. These old German trees stood a hundred feet high, six of them with broad winding trunks, forks of fissured bark, and tree hollows so deep that Henry could crawl inside pretending to be a rabbit.

By far, though, Adam's favorite tree was a remarkable weeping willow. It framed the view outside the back kitchen windows, hung its branches down like dozens of arms letting go to the gentle breezes. The image calmed Adam's mind at the end of every day.

Adam thought this a perfect home in a perfect town. Concord remained the soil of the first battle of the Revolutionary War and home to giants like Emerson, Alcott, Hawthorne, Thoreau, and now his own family. Who cared that the windows jammed or the closets were too small or even that the floors sank slightly in the center—it all made wonderful creaky music beneath everyone's feet.

With the front door left wide open, Adam hesitated before stepping in. He suspected Henry left it open since the boy was constantly running in and out of the house. In the living room, Vivaldi played on the CD player. From the narrow pine-paneled foyer, he entered the kitchen. A freshly baked loaf of bread sat cooling on the wood table in the sitting nook. What an aroma, all yeasty and hot.

"Mmmmm. Vivaldi and bread baking. It must be Friday." He waited for a delighted scream of surprise from his Laurie or a jumping down the stairs from Henry.

With a pull at his red tie, eager to strip off the navy suit, Adam pounded up the staircase. Normally his footsteps brought everyone out with shouts of "Daddy's home." But not today.

On Fridays, Antonia didn't go to work at the Brooke Bookshop. As the owner, she deemed it stay-at-home-day to attend to family needs, and it had become the most important day of the week since the move to Concord in August. Friday afternoon teatime had been on Adam's mind all day. He visualized his daughter munching away on her slice of bread slathered with raspberry jam. And Henry, with eyes big as pennies, tea-spooning his tea because he preferred his cup filled to the brim and relished the challenge of not spilling a drop.

"Antonia?" The house had an unfamiliar quiet. "Hey, where is everybody?" In the master bedroom, he found her notebook left open on her lounge chair by the back window. Lots of cross-outs and scribbles on several pages until he found a few lines of her poem in her crisp printing.

I walk naked into your arms, like the faithful violet and the lusty oak leaves, an equinox, equal in night and day. Somewhere an eagle screams. I melt into your light.

He groaned. "Yes, well, you'd better stick to being a bookseller." But what did he know about poetry anyway? He really didn't get it. All that metaphorical drama of words—truth be told, Adam would take the business of numbers any time. Debit and credit, and the beauty of a balanced sum spoke perfection. Who could argue that the multiplication tables didn't have unimpeachable truth?

He looked into Laura's room and flinched: the war zone. Pink tights lay about like atrophied legs, sweaters and nightgowns dumped in heaps, books and Barbie dolls scattered everywhere. Will she never learn to pick up anything?

In Henry's room, all five of his colorful baseball caps hung on wall pegs; a perfect line of airplanes, basket full of mica stones, and blue jay feathers decorated his desk. He even had his beloved action figures lined up in V-formation, and woe to anyone who moved one out of position. Adam tossed Henry's foam football into the air, then placed it under the bed pillow, right where Henry kept it along with his favorite storybook, *The Miracle of the Stag.*

Out the hallway window, Adam spotted Antonia's blue Honda parked in the driveway. *They can't be far.*

He changed into jeans and a pullover, dialed his office from the bedroom phone, listened to his tedious voice mail, then sank onto the unmade bed with its massive white pillows. The smell of their lovemaking still clung to the cotton sheets. His mind drew a picture of Antonia, those serious cheekbones ruled by huge deep-set black eyes with silky lashes, her great creamy breasts. He buried his face in the linens. Just as he was dozing off, he heard Laura come screaming up the stairs.

"Daddy, come quick."

He bolted up.

Antonia appeared in the doorway. "Adam, I can't find Henry. I think he's wandered off. I've been looking everywhere!"

Was that sweat on her face or tears? She was totally out of breath. Adam sprang to his feet. "Oh, for God's sake, he knows better than to leave the yard without an adult." He tied on his running shoes. "He's probably gone toward those rock walls at the property line, looking for mica again. Calm down," he told his wife at the same time leading them downstairs and out to the backyard.

"How long has he been gone?" Adam asked, heading toward the linden trees.

"He didn't come home from the bus stop."

Adam stopped in his tracks. "What? What do you mean, he—"

"He was following Laura on the cow path. He lagged behind. We've been looking for him for, I don't know, maybe an hour?"

"An hour? He could be anywhere by now." Adam turned to Laura, who was fidgeting and staring down at her pink-dotted Barbie sneakers. Clearly, it was part of Laura's responsibility to look after her brother on the walk home.

"Laurie? Did you see Henry go off the path?" he asked.

Antonia's pleading face signaled him to go easy.

Laura shook her head, dug her toe into the grass.

"Weren't you holding his hand?"

"I was. But then . . . he wanted to play follow-the-leader. So I was marching and he was marching, and then, he didn't march any more, but . . . then, I thought he was behind me."

"Did he say anything? Like maybe he wanted to go look for mica?"

"Ummm, he said the little boy Jesus was playing follow-the-leader too."

"Little boy Jesus, again?" He couldn't keep the impatience out of his tone.

"There's nothing wrong with that, Adam. You know how clingy he got when we first moved here. It was a comfort for him that the boy Jesus was with him whenever I was more than an arm's length away."

"Yes, well it seems he's feeling quite bold now about being more than an arm's length away. In fact, he may have wandered to the far side near that pond. Antonia, go back to the house and call the police."

"He couldn't have gone that far. The police? You don't think—"

"Just do it. I'll keep looking. Laura, go with your mother."

Adam followed the paths into the woods. Maybe Henry climbed a tree and couldn't get down. It wouldn't be the first time he'd gotten himself up too high; but that had happened during the autumn in the white birch tree in his own backyard with his parents nearby, sipping hot cider on the patio.

He cupped his hands over his mouth and yelled, "Henry? Henry!"

Adam trekked over the hills—the terrain steep with rock outcroppings and weather-gutted paths—to a valley of great white pines. Rooks floated above the cliffs as the wind snapped at him, making him wish he'd worn a jacket. *I'll find you, buddy. Wherever you are.* "Hennnreeeeee!"

Clusters of evergreens closed in on him. He pushed his way through to where the forest opened up into a field of cypress trees. It was a lofty vault with at least fifty cypresses rising up like thick green pillars. Chirping linnets with red on their breasts flew in. Adam hadn't been this far from their property and figured he was well beyond the State Reservation lines. Pausing to catch a breath, the quiet of the woods settled down on him. A sudden bellow sounded from behind. He turned.

A white-tailed stag in a regalia of antlers stood before him. What a beauty, so strong with bulging muscles and streaks of white flanking his sides.

"Hey there, fella." The animal approached him with soundless hoofs on the ground. "Not afraid, are you?" His antlers, pale against the darkening sky, swept out high in majestic curves. Adam counted twelve points on the head.

Twilight shadows sifted in. The wind stuttered in soft drumbeats around the stag as if he were some lord of the wood. His gleaming brown eyes were stunned fully open, tempting Adam to caress the face.

The stag stamped one hoof. Was that a warning not to approach? If Henry had seen this stag, he would certainly have followed it. Maybe that's what happened. He tried to run after the stag and got lost.

Not moving a muscle, Adam took in shallow breaths, his heart slowing, and in a gesture of submission, he stepped back. From somewhere far off, a liquid humming filled him. From above? Or maybe it was streaming up. Wherever, the rhythm penetrated deep inside his chest—soft hoofs galloping . . . galloping . . . galloping in.

The light seemed to dazzle as a pack of running deer emerged—ten, maybe more, white tails flashing, mighty and fast, they raced across the forest. The stag joined them and all pranced off to the distant mountains. In a blink they vanished, leaving Adam to feel swallowed up by the hills glowing blue with night.

* * *

Sergeant June Reilly from the Concord police department appeared at 24 Eastwick Road within minutes of Antonia's call. Reilly, a redhead with an explosion of freckles over her face, listened patiently. Her smile was reassuring. "We'll find your boy, Mrs. Brooke. What we need are more foot patrols. You say Henry was wearing blue jeans and red-striped pullover?"

"And a blue baseball jacket, navy-blue cap," Antonia said.

"We'll need a recent photo. Does Henry have any distinguishing body marks?"

"A tiny birthmark on his chest. Shaped like a star. Well, that's what we call it."

She scribbled it down into her notepad. "I'd like to check the house, if that's okay. Can we start with Henry's bedroom?"

Antonia led her upstairs. Reilly took her time searching through Henry's toys, clothing, and closet. While she was going through the wastepaper basket, Laura tugged on Antonia's sweater.

"Look, Mommy. Henry's done it again." Laura pointed to the window.

Antonia saw her sewing thimble filled with birdseed and a scattering of seed on the ledge.

"What's that?" Reilly asked.

"Henry's not allowed to feed the birds from his window," Laura said. "Want to know why? One of them flew into the glass and broke it."

Antonia rubbed her forehead, thinking. "Wait, something's wrong here. When I made Henry's bed this morning, I found the thimble and birdseed and I removed it. I distinctly remember I put the thimble back in my sewing basket in the linen closet."

"What time did you make his bed?"

"Around noon, I guess. How could Henry have refilled it when I—?" She looked at Laura.

"I didn't do it, Mommy."

"No, I know you wouldn't."

"Mrs. Brooke, do you think Henry was here between noon and now?"

"How would that be possible? He was in school and then walking home with Laura and then . . ."

Reilly made a note of it. "Certainly is odd. I'll alert the detective."

They searched the rest of the house, the whole time, Antonia trying to remain calm. "I'm sure he's just wandered off. Right? I mean, he couldn't have gone far."

Reilly nodded. "We'll find him, Mrs. Brooke. We have Detective Balducci on the case. He's contacted the N.O.C.—Neighbors On Call—to get a team of foot patrols out there. Meantime, stay here by the phone. If Henry finds his way back, we don't want him coming home to an empty house. I'm going to check out back."

Antonia sat stiffly on the edge of the kitchen chair, watching the clock's second hand. She swallowed the saliva in her mouth, but it kept coming back.

"Can I have a piece of the bread, Mommy?" Laura asked from the doorway. "We didn't have our teatime."

"We didn't?" Absently, she filled the kettle with water, turned on the gas burner, and sliced two pieces of bread. She reached for the raspberry jam from the refrigerator. *I should have picked them up in the car. I should have walked down there and met them. Why didn't I stop writing that damn stupid poem and go get them?*

"Bet Daddy and Henry will be home any minute. And just in time for tea."

She could almost believe Laura. Antonia removed the kettle from the fire, and just as she poured the hot water into the teapot, the phone rang. She got it on first ring.

"Antonia, it's Josie. I just got a call from Frank. The N.O.C. called him to search for Henry. What's happened?"

She swallowed hard. "I think he's lost in the woods."

"I'll close up the shop early. Be right over."

Josie was an angel, the first real friend she'd made in Concord. Josie had helped her with remodeling the bookshop, restocking, and the bookkeeping. Without Josie Wilson, Antonia would have never gotten her business up and running so quickly.

"Mommy? Mom!" Laura pointed across the room.

The gas burner shot up blue flames. Antonia turned it off, shot her eyes to the clock, the twelve black numbers blurring up. *Black-hooked hours.* She shook herself to clear the line from her head.

Henry's missing nearly four hours. The daylight faded into a bruised purple sky.

Chapter Two

WITH A SHAKY HAND, ELIAS HATCH lit candles on his desk under the window in his living room. He sat down and opened the newspaper near the fading daylight, then buttoned up his grey sweater.

"Well, spring is on the move early this year. I can smell it." Elias spoke to himself. "Cold temperatures for tonight. Possibility of rain," he said, pleased with his imitation of the TV weather forecaster's inflections. He pushed the newspaper aside and opened his Bible to the marker at the passage he hadn't finished that morning. With a clearing of his throat, he read the scripture aloud as well as any minister. "The New Jerusalem. 'The foundations of the city walls were adorned with precious stones of every kind, the first of the foundation stones being jasper, the second lapis lazuli, the—'"

Something rapped from above. He paused to listen, then resumed reading.

"'. . . the third chalcedony, the fourth emerald, the—'" Another rap. Squirrels on the roof again? "'. . . the fifth sardonyx, the sixth cornelian, the seventh chrysolite—'"

A louder rap hit again. This time from below. *That damn old furnace.*

Behind him, something rustled like the crackling of dried leaves. He turned his chair to the kitchen doorway, then leapt up at the sight. His arthritic hip made him stumble, and he grabbed the edge of the desk for support. "Dorotheus!"

There she was, wrinkled and bowed, sunken eyes beneath heavy brows, dressed in her thin white gown tied with that nasty rope. She wore her black bonnet with its curly brim cocked to the side.

"What are you doing here in the house?" he practically yelled it.

She gave him a snooty grin, then hobbled over to the coffee table and began pawing in the glass candy dish. "I like to look out your windows. Oh, where are the purple ones? Who's been eating them—was it *her?* What did you call the purples?"

"Dark chocolates."

"We didn't have such things in my day." She held the bowl against her sagging chest, unwrapped the last Hershey's dark chocolate kiss, and let the purple foil drift through the air as she popped the chocolate into her mouth.

The foil landed on the carpet. Elias let out a sigh. "How did you get in here?"

"I come through the passage."

"What passage? Where?"

"I forget. You have any gingerbread today?"She rolled the chocolate around her mouth, smacked her lips. "You know what, Misstaaah Hatch? I know something you don't."

"I'm sure you do."

"It's a secret." She dug her hand into the bowl again.

"Yes, I know you like your secrets, Dorotheus." He turned away, shaking his head, then looked out the window. "Oh no. People are coming up the path." He recognized Adam Brooke but not the taller man with the straight crop of black hair. And a police officer? "Dorotheus, you'd better go. Right now."

She frowned, her dark eyes like an angry monkey's eyes.

"Dorotheus, it's the police."

"Liar."

He grabbed her by her spindly arms and pulled her into the kitchen. "You can't let them see you. You know that." Opening the cellar door, he nudged her. "I'll get more dark chocolates next time."

Dorotheus resisted his gentle shove.

"Now, please. Scat." He walked to the living room doorway. "Go on. Hurry."

Slowly she stepped down. "Make gingerbread next time."

"Yes, gingerbread. Now go." Hatch grabbed his cane and headed for the front door.

* * *

Detective Mike Balducci, with Sergeant June Reilly, and Adam Brooke walked up to the cottage. The detective knocked, called out Hatch's name. He didn't want to startle the old guy but rapped loudly anyway, thinking Hatch might be a bit hard of hearing. He waited a moment before the pine door opened slowly.

"Hey there, Elias Hatch. I'm Detective Balducci. Remember me?"

He took a moment. "You were at that town meeting? Oh, yes, now I recall. Hello, Detective."

Balducci gave his best smile, introduced Sgt. June Reilly and Adam Brooke; they all stepped inside. Balducci immediately cringed at the musty odor mixed with some flowery cover-up scent—dusty lilacs—making it all the worse.

"Is there some trouble, Detective?" Hatch said.

Balducci scanned the room with a quick eye. One shabby green sofa, two mismatched rocking chairs, bookshelves on every wall with the books turned every which way, and a battered desk with piles of notebooks and a microscope. "We're looking for Henry Brooke. He didn't come home from the bus stop this afternoon. Got a team of volunteers combing the woods out back. Have you seen him today?"

"Your little boy." Hatch turned to Adam.

"We're just frantic." Adam said.

"No, I haven't seen him. I've been out most of the afternoon. Just got home." Hatch brushed back a few stray grey hairs from his long ponytail.

Balducci noticed his hand trembling. "You don't mind if we take a look around, do you? Can we walk your property?"

"I suppose. How can I be of help?"

"Do you have any exterior flood lights?" Reilly asked. "We could use more lights soon."

"I'm sorry, just the one on the front porch."

"You live here alone?" Balducci confirmed.

"Since my mother passed on."

"Elias," Adam said, "do you see Henry walking home from school sometimes?"

"I see him with his sister, yes, if I'm outside tending the cemetery. But of course, that was only on those warm autumn days last year. They usually say hello. Such polite children. I've seen Henry tumbling in the leaves. Quite the little athlete."

Balducci heard some faint scratching noises. Not sure exactly where the sound was coming from, he made a few steps into the living room. "You have a visitor? Someone in the kitchen? "

He gave Reilly an eye signal. She immediately did a casual two-step, walk, and turn to scan the doorways of the adjacent bedroom.

"Must be the mice again, Detective. I've had such a time with them. Traps are useless."

Balducci walked into the kitchen. A pile of foil candy wrappings sat next to an empty candy bowl on the countertop.

"It's just mice," Hatch repeated, following him.

"Well, if you leave chocolate out, you'll never get rid of them." Balducci noticed the cellar door slightly ajar.

"Of course you're right—oh, this stupid door." Hatch closed the cellar door gently. "I've got to fix that broken hinge. It's always swinging open, and the musty odor from the basement is dreadful, isn't it?" He kept his hand on the doorknob as it clicked.

Balducci did a head tilt, leaned on his right leg for a strategic pause.

Hatch didn't raise his vision. As the quiet of the house lingered, he kept his eyes fixed on the dusty tiled floor. And, as expected, something scratched again from below. Without a search warrant, Balducci really couldn't go down to the basement. He wanted to; something felt odd here.

"You know," Balducci said with his friendliest smile, "I've had mice in my house too. They were nesting in my basement. I'd be happy to take a—"

"I'm sure you're right, Detective Balducci. You needn't be concerned. I'll take a look for nests tomorrow. Thanks for the tip. Shall I come out to join your volunteers in the search? I'm happy to do what I can."

Balducci noticed Hatch was leaning on a duck-headed cane, hunched, a bit gaunt in the face, and the smallest black eyes he'd ever seen. "Not necessary. We've got plenty of able-bodied men out there. But it would be helpful if you would unlock the cemetery gates. Don't want to leave any territory unturned."

"Unlock the gates? Detective, no one passes through my gates without my permission. Old Willow Cemetery is always secure. I can assure you the boy has not wandered in."

Balducci shrugged, strolled to the front door and turned. "If you're going to deny access, maybe I should get a court order to search the premises?" he bluffed.

Hatch straightened up. "I would never presume to tell you your business, Detective Balducci. A court order won't be necessary." He shifted his gaze out the window. "I'll get the keys. But there can be absolutely no walking over any graves. You'll have to follow the paths. Agreed?"

Outside, they waited for Hatch to join them at the cemetery gate. Balducci noticed Adam restlessly pacing, hands jammed inside the jacket pockets. The guy stood tall with an athletic build—probably played quarterback in college—and handsome as hell with those blue eyes nearly cobalt. The Brooke family name, well known in the Boston area as a sterling investment firm, owned a building on High Street in the heart of Boston's financial district. He recalled seeing the name in the society pages for charity events. Adam Brooke was, no doubt, the little rich kid.

"Listen, Detective." Adam bit his lip. "I gotta ask you something."

"Fire away," Balducci said.

"I'm a little embarrassed to say this, but what do you know about Elias Hatch?"

"Keeps to himself mostly," Balducci said.

"The Hatch families have been caretakers of Old Willow Cemetery since the mid-1800s," Reilly added. "Hatch is probably near eighty years old. Lived here his whole life as far as we know."

"Why? Do you have reason to be suspicious?" Balducci glanced to the cottage to watch for Hatch.

"Maybe. I don't know. Henry talks about the cemetery all the time. The locked gate, the statues, all those birch trees are very attractive to him. He's been explicitly told to stay away from the cemetery, and normally he's not one to challenge the rules."

"You think Hatch knows something about Henry?"

Adam gave a half nod that turned into a shrug. "The day we moved into the house Hatch seemed, I don't know, overly friendly. I didn't think anything about it at the time, but he seemed to pay a lot of attention to Henry."

"In what way?"

"Telling him stories. Dreamy stuff about the talking frogs in the brook. Starlight that can sing," he rolled his eyes. "Hatch seemed . . . a little off. You know what I mean?"

"I'll make a note of it." Balducci lit a Camel cigarette.

"Elias Hatch would never hurt a child," Reilly said. "He's odd but harmless, I think."

Balducci pulled hard on the smoke. "Reilly, give Rogers a call and get a ranger here to search the cemetery with you. Mr. Brooke, you can stay with Reilly and take a look-see in the cemetery if you want. Then I think it would be best if you go on home."

"You don't want me to search any more with the team? Because there's no way I can sit around and wait for you guys to find Henry. You know I can't do that."

Balducci couldn't miss the man's fierce determination. "Take it easy. I know how you feel. I just got a group together to canvass the neighborhood door to door, so for the moment everybody's doing everything they can. Go home and stay with your wife. Antonia, right? She needs you more than we do."

It took a second, but Adam lifted his square jaw in a half nod.

"I'll catch up with you later," Balducci said and headed to the cow path.

As he walked from the school bus stop, tracing Henry Brooke's steps along the cow path, he kept his eyes focused for any clue. The lowering weave of light cast shadows over the clusters of boulders. An oval rock up ahead caught his attention—looked like one of those old-fashioned portrait frames in museums. A flash of his wife's pretty face formed on the smooth stone: tender green eyes, the lips full and content, hair touching her shoulders. These days he saw Maddy's face almost everywhere; in snowy drifts, in wavy rain puddles, and always inside the dappling sunlight that fell across the empty kitchen chair. Her cute upturned nose, even that whimsical smile of hers somehow took form, and he'd enjoy that moment with great satisfaction. Some days he heard her voice. *Voices we hear in solitude,* as Emerson wrote. Only he knew it wasn't really Maddy's voice but more of an inner voice. And here it was again, that voice, as he passed under a beech tree. *All is well.*

At times, that silly phrase would haunt him—he didn't know why.

He continued on the path to the Brooke house. There Balducci settled into the seat cushion on a chair in the kitchen, which was cluttered with European pottery on the top of the cabinets. He made some preliminary notes on his wide yellow pad as he questioned Antonia Brooke about the day's routine. She reported nothing unusual, so he moved on to the main issue on his mind.

"Mrs. Brooke, your husband came home from work earlier today than you expected? What time was that?"

"Daddy came home early to have teatime," Laura said.

Antonia gave Laura's curls a gentle stroke. "He promised the children he'd surprise them. Around four o'clock."

"Any trouble between you two? Domestic situations?"

"Oh, no. We're fine."

"Is it possible Henry might have run away for any reason?"

Laura giggled. "Not Henry!"

Antonia tried to smile. "Henry's a very happy child."

Balducci liked her delicate small shoulders and soft lips, yet those big black eyes seemed to hold a lot of strength. She wore a silver cross right at the hollow of her neck. Maddy had worn crosses too. When they married, he gave her a diamond cross. There was nothing more beautiful or glittering on her neck, and Maddy loved it, said she'd wear it all the time, even to her grave. And she did.

"Any extended family situations? Any relatives who might have picked up Henry without your permission?"

Antonia sighed. "No, nothing like that."

"And your parents, Mrs. Brooke? Where do they live?"

"My mother lives in Italy. We have a farm in Umbria. And my dad, he's in a hospital, long term."

"And Mr. Brooke's parents are retired in Florida."

"Yes. Sam and Maude Brooke."

He flipped to his back-page fact notes. "Your husband's family business, Brooke, Stahl, and Brooke Financial. Can you—"

"Adam left the family company when we married. He's in advertising now."

"Right. Beaumont Communications Worldwide," he read from his notes. "Nice position, CFO." Balducci tapped his pen for a moment giving himself time to move into the line of questioning that was sure to set the woman off. "Have you had any odd phone calls lately? Strangers coming by?"

"No."

"Mrs. Brooke, would anyone have cause to try to blackmail your husband? I mean, the Brooke family name having considerable wealth. Sam Brooke—"

"Oh no. Nothing like that. My God, what are you thinking? Not kidnapping?"

"I'm sorry to be so blunt. Just being thorough. Any bad business dealings you know about? Maybe with your father-in-law?" Balducci had been through these same questions with Adam, but double-checking with the spouse often paid off in new details.

"Nothing that I know of. It's far more likely Henry is just lost out there."

"Probably. Do you get along with your in-laws, Mrs. Brooke?" Balducci wasn't sure where that question came from and the directness surprised him. It was as if someone else was standing by putting words in his mouth.

She looked away, to the weeping willow tree outside the window.

Yep, there it was. Trouble with the in-laws. Balducci waited.

"I almost never see them. They visit the children and Adam every few months, in Boston."

"I see. And what about your siblings?"

"My sister Mona lives with my mother in Umbria."

A photograph hung on the wall: cozy stucco house in a field of sunflowers and what looked like lemon trees in the background. Balducci pointed. "Would that be Umbria?"

She nodded. A tear got loose.

"Mrs. Brooke, I know this is tough. We'll do everything we can to find Henry. I only have a few more questions." He glanced at his notes again. "You didn't go to work today at the bookshop? Home all day?"

"Yes, I did some cleaning out in the front gardens."

He scribbled on his yellow pad.

"You take fast notes, I thought detectives used those skinny little notepads that fit into their pockets—you know, like *Columbo?*" She rattled it all off in one nervous breath. "I'm sorry, what a silly thing to say."

She was cute. "I'm no Peter Falk, as you can see. Yeah, I like to see the details in a straight orderly list too, but it's really the big picture that solves the case for me." He flipped the page. "Can I ask Laura a few questions?"

"Of course."

Laura stared up at him with her father's deep blue eyes.

"I've got just one or two questions," he said to the child. "Do you remember seeing anybody on the cow path when you were walking home?"

"No, sir."

"How about in the woods nearby? Anybody walking around?"

"No."

"Anybody in the street?"

"No."

"Did you see Mr. Hatch when you walked by the cemetery today?"

"Ummm, nope."

He turned to Antonia. "On that cow path, there's a pine grove that opens to the State Reservation. I'm thinking that might be a good place to start with search-and-rescue dogs. I'll need a piece of Henry's clothing to scent the dogs."

"Will his sweater do?"

"Perfect. Thanks, Mrs. Brooke."

"Please, call me Antonia."

Balducci left by the front door and once at the front gardens, he aimed his flashlight. The triangle of light hit the wheelbarrow, the azaleas and dwarf evergreens, a clean patch of soil, a row of footprints. Five toe markings. He examined the heel depth and measured the length and width with his tape measure. Gardening in bare feet? Why would Antonia clean out the garden without shoes? He followed the footprints around to the side of the house where they disappeared into the backyard grass near the weeping willow tree.

* * *

Around seven o'clock Josie Wilson appeared at the Brooke's door with a platter of roasted chicken and biscuits. "Oh Antonia, you must be out of your mind. My God, look at you."

Antonia took the platter and set it on a counter. Josie gave her a hug, and their cheeks brushed each other. "Your face is so cold. It's not raining, is it?"

"Barely. Stay calm. I'm sure they'll find Henry. Frank said they've got over fifty people out there with floodlights and bullhorns. And a trailer is already on Trent Street as central dispatch. I saw Lexington and Manchester police cars all over the place. Where's Adam?"

"He's out there searching with everyone. This is all so crazy. Where can Henry be? Josie, why didn't I pick them up at the bus stop? Why didn't I at least walk down there to meet them? Laura always wants to walk home without me hovering over like a mother hen, so I've been letting them take the cow path by themselves. If I could only start this day over, if—"

"Don't do that to yourself, Antonia." Josie sat down in a kitchen chair, her expression gentle with salt-and-pepper hair around her chubby face and hazel eyes. "That cow path is perfectly safe. This is Concord. You can't find a friendlier, safer town in the whole state. I don't think Concord has ever had a missing child in all its history."

"Suppose they can't find him? My God, what have I done?"

"Mike Balducci is on the case, right? He's the best."

"You know him?"

"For years, when we lived in Lexington, he was our neighbor. Mike supervised the Child Safety Division in Bedford. He'll find Henry. Shall I put on a fresh pot of coffee? You need to eat something."

Josie fumbled around the kitchen. Antonia could see lights flashing at the far end of the backyard. A bullhorn sounded. She took it as a personal call. "Josie, I'm going out there. Will you stay with Laura? Stay by the phone?"

"Of course. But are you sure—?"

"If I sit here and wait another minute, I'll just scream." With her jacket half on, Antonia went straight into Laura's room to tell her Josie was downstairs making her supper. But Laura wasn't in her room, or Henry's, or the master bedroom.

At the bathroom door she knocked. "Are you in there, sweetie?" No answer. She tried the knob and it turned easily. "Laura, I'm coming in." When she didn't get a reply, she opened the door.

Laura sat in the corner, curled up, knees to chin, her tiny face soaked with tears. She tilted her cheeks to slip her teardrops into a long-necked bottle.

"Oh, Laura." Antonia's eyes filled up. The antique tear bottle was Laura's favorite keepsake.

"Mommy, do you want to put your tears inside the bottle too?"

* * *

Huddled in the rain, Antonia stood in a wool jacket at the police trailer on Trent Street. Josie's husband, Frank Wilson, opened the door. He greeted her with a strong hug and so many reassurances, Antonia could hardly stand it. His hand-holding and that big smile under his greying mustache did boost her feelings. That was Frank, like a steady father ready to do anything to make things better.

"Frank, do you know where Adam is? I haven't heard from him for hours."

Frank looked to the police officer standing with two forest rangers. "Officer?"

"Cell phone reception is spotty out there. Latest update reported Mr. Brooke with Cromwell at the ravine," he replied.

"The ravine?" Antonia felt her legs go weak. Of course, there were ravines in the Massachusetts woods, and cliffs, and dark chasms. She shivered.

"Your hands are ice, Antonia. Let me pour you some tea. Sit down," Frank said.

The rangers tossed out their empty coffee cups and stomped out, scraping their clumsy boots across the sandy trailer floor. What good men, to do this on such a cold, rainy night. She gulped the hot tea. The tiny puddles and brown leaves on the floor summoned verses in her mind. *Cold rain . . . curling spiders . . . falling in anxious haste.* "Stop it," she said aloud.

Frank leaned in. "What, honey?"

"Nothing."

An hour crawled by. Frank kept the conversation going with comforting words, but the only thing that would comfort her was to see Adam walk through that door holding Henry's hand. *Adam will find him. Adam's smart and strong, determined, and he'll know exactly where to find Henry. Relax, they're coming home.*

Another hour passed. Frank's buck-up attitude began to wither along with the cups of tepid tea and cell phones ringing in an endless drone. Suddenly police sirens swirled into the parking area like a pack of screeching cats. Frank jumped up and threw open the door.

Red flashing lights spun everywhere. Someone was frantically calling out names on a bullhorn. The sirens were so loud that her ears hurt. *This is it. They've found him!*

Adam came bursting through the doorway. He was drenched, his blond hair dripping. On his chin was a gash the length of a pencil. Panic in his blue eyes set them ablaze with color.

He pulled Antonia to his chest and wrapped his arms around her. No words, just the tightest hug, kisses all over her head. He said something to her, but she couldn't understand his words above the blasting sirens.

"What's happened, Adam? Where's Henry?"

Barely able to get the words out, he stumbled with half sounds, held her face in his hands. "We can't . . . find him."

Antonia swallowed a sob in her throat. "What do you mean, can't find him? He's out there, Adam. He's out there somewhere!"

Something in his eyes, the way he almost couldn't look at her, made her heart race. With a soft cry he placed his mouth against her ear. "They said . . . they want to dredge the pond."

The words went through her like a spear.

Chapter Three

TEMPERATURES DROPPED. A light drizzle dampened Mike Balducci's spirits. He drove his brown sedan down Monument Street, past the Old North Bridge, and through the village square. On Concord Turnpike he parked his car in front of the Waldo Grille, named after Ralph Waldo Emerson of Concord. Balducci took his favorite seat at the end of the bar where a huge carved walnut plank hung on the wall. *Everything in Nature contains all the powers of Nature. Everything is made of one hidden stuff.* Many a night Balducci came up with some of his best thoughts sitting next to this carved wisdom—Emerson and Balducci, unraveling the *hidden stuff* of a case. Progressive reasoning, then deductive reasoning: cause, operation, effect. When necessary, he'd bypass this conscious dynamic and go with a deep and swift instinct. And a few beers didn't hurt either.

"I haven't eaten all day," he told Liv, the steamy brunette bartender he once had in the back office on a blurry St. Patrick's Day. He slipped off his jacket, ran his fingers back against his dark hair still dripping with rain. "Something hot and fast. Only got about ten minutes."

"You got it." She gave him a winning smile and placed a club soda on the bar top.

Her cute scoot into the kitchen didn't miss his eye.

Without meaning to, he overheard a young couple chatting in a booth about the ghost of Emerson in Room 24 at the Colonial Inn—a local tale that attracted a good number of tourists. When he and Maddy had stayed in that same room, the night was completely uneventful: no shadows looming near the fireplace, no whispers at the foot of the bed, no rapping on the walls. Big disappointment for Maddy; she was dying to encounter the famous sage—phantom or figment.

He pulled out his yellow pad of notes: already he'd made at least twenty pages. He wished in that moment he could see through all the details and employ Emerson's famous *transparent eyeball* as his own. What else would direct him to locate the Brooke kid instead of searching random cliffs and ponds and the vast expanse of woods?

Liv put down a platter of fish 'n chips still crackling from the fryer.

His eyes popped. "That's got to be somebody else's order."

"Not anymore."

His cell phone buzzed. Caller ID: Randy Voit. Balducci knew Voit to have the best bloodhound in the squad. This search-and-rescue dog, Dickens, once tracked a cadaver scent in a car trunk on a highway for over fourteen miles. One of Balducci's most difficult cases, solved in three days, and it won him great praise from his department.

"Mike? We got a hit. Dickens is tracking."

He jumped out of his seat. "Where are you?"

"I'm on Eastwick."

"Near the Brooke house?"

"Nope. He's sniffing the sewer grate."

Balducci's stomach lurched. He pushed the platter away, grabbed his jacket, and ran for the door.

Ten minutes later Balducci greeted Randy Voit, a yeasty, balding man in a red flannel shirt and dirty blue jeans covered with dog hairs. Police Chief Dan Hersey and Deputy Paul Owens had just arrived. Police cars blocked off the area.

Dickens, dressed in his red hunting vest, pawed at the curbside sewer grid. Balducci bent down, gave the dog a neck rub. "Hey, Dickens, what'd you find, pal?" The dog returned the affection with a happy yelp.

Balducci hooked his plastic-gloved hand beneath the lip of the sewer lid and pulled out a crumpled hat. "Red Sox. Jesus! Pry open that sewer grid." He couldn't keep the dread out of his voice. Before anyone could even attempt it, Dickens howled, sniffed the cap with delight, sniffed the pavement and grass, and dashed forward, tracking straight toward Old Willow Cemetery. The hound stopped, stuck his nose through the gate iron bars, and pawed with begging yelps.

Voit shouted with a wave to everyone. "Looks like Dickens needs to track more scent, inside the gates."

* * *

Adam stared at the plate of fruit and chicken Josie placed before him. Who could eat at a time like this? Josie was just being Josie. He pushed the dish away with an apologetic glance.

"Two officers were here earlier and looked around the house." Josie sat in the chair opposite him. "And some technicians from the forensic department."

"Forensic?" Adam didn't like the sound of that. He sipped coffee as Antonia came down the stairs.

"Laura's asleep. Thank God. I've run out of scenarios for why Henry's not home yet." Her voice was thin as a wire. "Where *is* he all this time, Adam? I don't know what to do."

"We wait," Adam said. "He's just wandered off. We'll find him tonight. And we'll put him to bed and tomorrow morning will be just like last Saturday morning. Laura will read the funny papers to Henry. You'll make French toast. Everything back to normal."

Her blank face told him that she didn't agree with his declarations. "Right, Adam. Everything will balance out. What is it you always say? Credit and debit, dollars and cents, everything accounted for."

"That's right," he declared in the same tone.

"Be realistic. It's been eight hours! God, what if he's fallen into the—"

"Don't say it!" He immediately regretted the shout. "I'm sorry," he managed and took in a long slow breath. Antonia stood before him, fighting tears. "Annie, sweetheart, let's just focus on what everybody is doing to find him. Look, half the town of Concord is out there. These forest rangers know the woods like their own skin. They've got target maps and landmarks. They send out four at a time to cover each section. The forests are pretty dense, rocky terrain and packs of deer." He paused, recalling the stag in the cypress field. No point in telling her—except maybe she needed something to hold on to. "I saw that stag again. The one with the white streaks and those high antlers."

"Not the same one Henry saw in the backyard?" Josie asked.

"Same one he ran out to see, in his bare feet, in the snow on Christmas morning. Same white streaks."

Antonia sat down. A smile nearly emerged. "Henry's stag? Really? The one he calls White Beauty? You saw it tonight?"

"In full sight."

"In full sight," she let out a sigh of relief. "I just read him the *Miracle of the Stag* again last night."

"Oh, my girls loved that book," Josie said.

"Maybe it's a sign, Adam. Finding Henry's stag in the woods—a little miracle of our own?"

Adam didn't know much about miracles, didn't understand them, didn't believe in them. But Antonia seemed drawn to them with a faith he wished he had.

"We sure could use a miracle tonight, couldn't we, Adam?"

He bit the inside of his cheek.

"Adam?" she repeated.

"Yes," he nodded, "we could use a miracle."

* * *

An hour later, the doorbell rang. Antonia got there first, her heart beating clean through to her throat. Detective Balducci stood on the doorstep.

"May we come in? This is my chief, Dan Hersey."

The chief was short, round, with buzz-cut greying hair and black-rimmed eyeglasses. Antonia shook his hand. Ice cold.

"We've got a lead," Balducci's voice rattled. "Does this belong to Henry?" He held up a plastic bag containing a crumpled blue baseball cap.

"We found it on Eastwick," Chief Hersey said, "near the Bronnell house, inside the corner of the sewer grid."

Antonia grabbed the bag. "Yes, that's the crooked bend we made so it would stay on."

"Henry was in the street?"

"Apparently. There's also a possibility . . . could be a hit-and-run accident," Chief Hersey said. "We can't confirm that yet."

"If it was a hit and run, then where's Henry?" Adam said. "You're not saying the driver hit him and then abducted him?"

Chief Hersey stepped forward. "We've seen cases where a driver hits a kid and panics, doesn't want to be responsible, decides to take the kid to an emergency room, then takes off. We're checking all the ERs in the vicinity."

"Why don't we sit down and I'll tell you everything we have so far," Balducci said.

Antonia sank into the wingback chair, grabbed the chair arms tightly. *Hit and run?* The words pounded inside her head. When Adam sat on the edge of the ottoman, his thigh touched her knee. She pressed harder to feel his body warmth.

"Why do you think it could be a hit and run?" Adam asked the chief.

"It looks like Henry may have been injured. We found some blood inside the cap."

"Oh no." Antonia murmured.

"No reason to panic," Balducci said. "It's a small amount. Small enough to suggest a superficial wound. We'll have the police lab verify with Henry's blood type. Look, I'm sorry, I know this isn't the news you wanted to hear tonight. Can we check a few more details? I need to know, did you hear anything like a car skidding? A horn? Crash of any kind at around 2:30 or so? Antonia?"

She hadn't. She knew she hadn't but thought back to that hour, sitting in the bedroom lounge chair by the back windows, writing in her notebook, playing with the words *faithful violet*. "I didn't hear anything."

"Did you notice any strange cars parked on the street?"

She shook her head.

"Anybody turn around in your driveway? Deliveries?"

"Don't think so."

"Okay. We've got three directions here. One is the State Reservation out back. Two, northeast corridor. If this was a hit and run, Henry could be out of the state by now in some obscure ER in Vermont, New York, even Connecticut or Pennsylvania. We're posting a missing persons report with his photo on the Internet. I've arranged to set up a call center at the Ramada Conference Center."

"And we've contacted the FBI," Chief Hersey said. "The Feds can move this whole thing faster nationally."

"Anything you need, of course," Adam said. "And the third direction?"

"Old Willow Cemetery," Balducci said. "Dickens tracked Henry's scent near the iron fence. I've got a request for a search warrant for—"

"You think Hatch has something to do with this?"

"I don't know. One more thing, Antonia. You mentioned you were gardening earlier in the front flowerbeds. Were you barefoot?"

Antonia blinked slowly for a second. *What did he say? Barefoot?* She rubbed her forehead, her eyes suddenly heavy as if glazing over. The detective's soft brown eyes held her a long moment. He had a fine Roman nose. And that cleft in his chin, remarkable.

"Antonia?" Adam touched her hand.

"Hmm? Oh, I'm sorry. What?"

"Were you gardening today in your bare feet?"

"Oh no. I was wearing my garden sneakers."

Balducci exchanged a look with his chief. "Where are the sneakers now?"

"I tossed them on the back patio. Why is that important?"

"I found barefoot prints in your front garden. Tracked them around back. They were about six inches long. Couldn't get a precise measurement with the rain. Looked like a woman's prints. Small."

"Could even be a child's," Chief Hersey said.

* * *

In the Brooke bedroom, Adam read the night table clock. 3:00 a.m. Maybe being upstairs would be easier than waiting in that damn kitchen or pacing around the cluttered living room. He turned on the television—anything to distract—and flipped to an old Lauren Bacall movie. Black and white, soft voices, easy dialogue.

Antonia kicked off her shoes. They sat together on his side of the bed.

Someone in the woods was talking on a bullhorn. From far away, a police siren died out. A distant buzz fell over the house. Second by second, it grew louder, until the buzz became a loud *chop-chop-chop*.

"What's that?" Antonia asked.

"Helicopters. Equipped with infrared heat sensors."

"What for?"

"Identifies body heat." He watched her wind a loose string from her sweater round and round her thumb. The skin went red, then started turning blue. Abruptly she got up. The bathroom door quietly clicked. Bacall and Bogie's voices slipped beneath the sound of Antonia's furious sobbing.

Sleep didn't come easy. Antonia had dozed off on a stack of pillows, the corners of her mouth hard in a grimace. Adam didn't recall sleeping much but did remember staring at the dark walls and listening to his own pulse beating in his ears for what seemed like eternity. Perhaps he closed his eyes once or twice or maybe he thought he did. He listened to the wind titter, to the house creaks and furnace booms, the muffled tapping of the glass windows and the breathy laughs from the attic's worn-out eaves.

Suddenly Adam jumped from the bed. "Did you hear that?"

"Hear what?" Antonia nearly slipped off the mattress with his jolt.

He stood perfectly still to listen. No house noises, no furnace shaking the metal grates, no wind rattling the roof gutters. He went to the windows and listened again. A voice floated up.

"It's Henry." He practically flew downstairs with Antonia

following close behind. In the kitchen he stopped. "There it is again. Can't you hear it, Annie?"

"I don't hear anything. What! What did you hear?"

He grabbed her hand and they ran out back. Dawn was just giving itself a stretch with pink streaks above the pines in the woods. A long string of giggles spilled from above.

"Oh, my God, Adam, that's Henry! His baby laugh."

Adam's eyes searched the half darkness. "Where is he?" Again the laughter tumbled down. "Henry? Are you here?" The darkened trees, the brightening sky, another giggle. Adam actually broke into a smile. "Henry!"

"Adam, I think it's coming from the willow tree."

The trills of laughter grew louder.

Adam stood in the cold dead grass, chin up, listening again to those silly sounds that belonged only to his boy. "Henry! Answer me." When no reply came, he ran inside the house, grabbed the wide-beam emergency flashlight from under the kitchen sink, came back, and shot the white light clean up the willow tree. He waved it in circles over the criss-crossing branches.

A peal of laughter broke again, as if Henry were tickled by the flashing light.

"Henry," Antonia said, "show me your hand. Wave to me, sweetie. Henry?"

The laughing ceased. Shadows vanished. Dawn broke.

Under the naked willow tree, Antonia and Adam stood in the wet grass, watching, waiting, as a dazzle of sunlight crashed into the empty tree branches.

Minutes later, inside the house—the kitchen freezing—Adam turned up the heat, then glanced to his wife putting the kettle on for coffee. Standing in the middle of the kitchen, still a bit numb, he watched her movements as if she were some strange character in a movie: wife scooping coffee grinds into the paper filter; wife taking out mugs, spoons, milk pitcher; wife grabbing slices of bread for toast. Butter. Jam.

"Please don't do that," he burst out.

"Don't do what?"

"Make coffee like this is any other Saturday morning. Talk to me."

She gave him a roll of her quick black eyes from under slashing brows.

"I mean it, Annie."

"What!" She dropped the spoons on the floor with a clang. "What do you want me to stop doing?"

"What just happened out there?"

"Nothing happened. We're exhausted. We're scared to death and we . . . imagined something."

"We didn't imagine anything. We both heard Henry laughing. You know you did."

"I don't know what I heard."

"That was Henry laughing out there!"

"Was it?" She took a carton of milk from the refrigerator, poured it into the white pitcher. "Maybe I wanted to hear it. Really, I mean, Henry loves that weeping willow tree. Remember the day we moved in here, he ran straight to it and named it Charlie. Maybe we want Henry back so bad, it felt real to us. Imagination can do that, make things feel real. You know, like a hallucination?"

"Christ, Antonia. We both heard it. Same hallucination by two people at the same time?"

"Stop staring at me like I'm crazy or something. You know what I think right now? Maybe this is all some horrible nightmare. Maybe we're going to wake up and find Henry in his bed. Yes, let's do that, let's start Friday, March 20, all over again."

The kettle whistled in the same instant the telephone rang. Antonia got to the phone first. "Yes?"

Adam grabbed the kettle off the fire. "Who is it?" He could tell nothing from her expression as she listened to whoever was calling at six a.m. Her lips compressed to slivers, and there was this annoyed stony glance at him. With a stiff arm, she extended the telephone receiver. "It's your mother."

He made a slow turn back to the stove, finished pouring the hot water into the coffee filter, then took the phone.

* * *

Antonia sat down at the table, not that she wanted to listen (she did), but Adam wasn't saying much. As usual, Maude was doing all the talking, probably making her little jabs about his peasant wife from the farm. Or maybe she was threatening to disinherit Adam for the umpteenth time. She noticed Adam didn't roll his eyes yet; she watched for it.

"The police called you?" Adam said. Then a stream of *yes's* and *no's* and *we hope so's* and a few grunts for good measure. "No, Mother, please, you don't have to come up here. Just stay there for now. We'll let you know the minute we have any information. If we need you, we'll call."

Antonia shook her head at his constant use of the pronoun *we* whenever he spoke with his mother. That woman never got the message no matter how often he said it.

"*We've* got everything under control," he emphasized again. A long pause. Then under his breath, "Yeah, me too."

What was that, *an I-love-you, me too? I love you* from Maude? Doubtful. "Coffee's dripped." Antonia poured two cups. "Was your father on the extension?"

"He's away on a fishing trip, sailing around Nassau."

"Daddy?" Laura clung to the doorframe, chewing her hair, standing with one bare foot resting on top of the other in her Daisy Duck nightgown.

"Hey, there's my Blondie." Adam reached out to stroke her curls.

"Henry's home. Where is he?"

"Not yet, sweetie. Maybe now that the daylight is up, we'll find him." Antonia gave her a pet.

"But I . . . did you look again in Daddy's closet?"

"Laurie, we looked in all the closets. He's not inside the house, honey."

Her blue eyes, swollen with sleep, moved back and forth between her parents. "Are you sure?"

"Yes, sweetie, now go up and put your slippers on. It's cold on the tile floor."

Laurie walked to the stairs with her head down, rubbing her eyes, then stopped and turned at the first step. "Mom?"

"What is it, Laura?"

"I thought I heard Henry laughing."

Chapter Four

EARLY SATURDAY MORNING, as soon as Judge Norman Brady signed the search warrant, Detective Balducci, Chief Hersey, and several police officers were fast on the property of Old Willow Cemetery. Elias Hatch, dressed in a long woolen grey coat, leather gloves, muddy boots, and a frayed brown beret, opened the gates.

"Been raking leaves since sunrise," he told them. "Spring cleanup time."

Randy Voit came up behind them with Dickens on a leash. Other police officers secured the cottage and property as Balducci instructed them. He stuffed the warrant back inside his jacket pocket.

Hatch eyed the dog. "You won't let the dog mess on the grounds, will you, Mr. Voit?"

Voit gave him a smirk.

The liver-colored Dickens, with a circle of white on his chest, gave a droopy-eyed look to Hatch. Nose to the air, the bloodhound headed straight for him.

Hatch veered back. "I don't think he likes me."

Balducci wanted to laugh. "When was the last time you had visitors here, Hatch?"

"We don't get Concord family members any more. In fact, I can't recall visitors for some years now."

Voit rubbed Dickens's ears. "Time to go to work, boy." He fastened the red hunting vest over the dog's back. Voit removed Henry's sweater from a plastic bag, laid it on the ground to cast the scent. Dickens circled the sweater, sniffed, pawed, sniffed again. "Come on, fella, go get'em. Go, Dickens." The hound kept circling and pawing the ground. Then he sat down on his haunches, jowls hanging, ears flopping, paws smeared with dirt.

Hatch took a step toward the group. "Looks like he's not interested."

"You guys want to step outside the gate for a minute. I think he's getting conflicting scents," Voit said.

They obliged, and Voit tried again. This time he moved deeper into the cemetery, sat down with the hound and gave him the ritual pep talk, then recast the scent with Henry's sweater. After much pawing and sniffing, the hound jumped up on his hind legs, came down with his nose to the dirt. Here he rubbed his ears, sniffed and snorted, then began trailing into the garden.

Balducci kept a clear distance behind them. Dickens sniffed the main path as they passed a well-muscled marble cherub. Most of the headstones were the standard oval shape, some very short, others square with Concord family names: Rainsford, Zaroff, Goldsmith. A stone angel was carved with Caselli. The dog trailed in zigzags, sniffing at headstones, crosses, starbursts.

Dickens stopped briefly at a headstone with a winged skull, moved on to the center of the cemetery and sniffed his way to an ivy bed. He pawed the grass and whined like a puppy. Then he let out a series of loud yelps.

"What's he got?" Balducci said, stepping on the ivy.

Hersey came running with Elias Hatch limping close behind.

Voit shook his head with uncertainty. "He's got the scent, all right. The kid's been right here." For the next fifteen minutes, Dickens, nose to ground, led Voit from a leaning elm, to a cluster of silver birches, to the oak at the back gate, and several times to the lilac bush with leaves beginning to bud. He whined there a long time before he trailed to the gate and back.

Voit scratched his head. "Beats the hell out of me. Dickens knows the kid's scent is here. From the way this hound is behaving, I'd say there's no doubt the boy's been in the cemetery and in a lot of different areas. But Dickens can't seem to settle very long on any specific site. All that whining means he's got the scent . . . but not the goods."

"Impossible," Hatch said. "The boy couldn't have gotten inside the gates."

"Dogs don't lie, Mr. Hatch. And Dickens is too good at this work to be making a mistake."

Hatch stroked his beard. "I wouldn't know myself for sure, not having children of my own, but I've seen little ones at the park, and they're very capable little monkeys at climbing high bars. Do you suppose the boy might have managed to climb over the rock wall?"

"Not likely," Balducci said. "Way too high for a five-year-old."

Hatch frowned. "Are you all quite finished here?"

Balducci gave an eye signal to Chief Hersey.

"Have Dickens do the house," the chief told Voit.

Hatch's dark eyes narrowed and his face went white. "You don't suspect me in any of this, do you, Chief Hersey?"

"The kid's been on your property, Hatch. What do you think?"

Balducci turned to Voit. "Hit the basement first."

As they headed into the fieldstone cottage, Balducci spotted Adam walking through the gates.

"What's going on? Do you think my son's been in that house?" Adam kept his brisk pace, eyes fastened on Hatch's cottage.

"Adam, I'm going to ask you to stay back. Can you wait at the house, please?"

Adam headed straight for the cottage.

Balducci grabbed Adam's jacket sleeve. "Hold on a minute."

"Mike, I need to know what's going on."

"I'll tell you what's going on. The chopper was circling most of the night. Pilot didn't want to give up. Kept flying until sunup. We've got a lot of good people out here today on foot patrols. The N.O.C. posted flyers all over town, and they're working on the outskirts right now. FBI is on the case as we speak. All the wheels are turning at full speed to find your son. And," he didn't want to say the words again but he did, "we've got divers at the pond this morning."

Adam blinked hard. "And here? You think Hatch has got Henry?"

"I don't know what Hatch has got. And I don't think your son is in that pond, either, but we're dredging it anyway. Look, Adam, you want to help? Let us do the job we're trained to do. When we're finished here, I'll bring you up to date. Go home. I mean it." Balducci hustled into the cottage.

Dickens worked the six-room cobblestone cottage. First thing, Balducci descended the kitchen stairwell into the cellar. Rank mold permeated the air. At the far end of the basement stood a water heater, furnace, and garden tools against the rock and mortar foundation: ladders, paint cans, rolls of plastic, and a collection of sledgehammers. An officer searched a box of old tiles and used plumbing pipes, examining each for physical evidence, specifically blood or hair. Another officer ran his hands across the stone and mortar wall. "No false fronts that I can see, Mike. Unless this wave in the wall is something."

"What wave?"

"See how it bulges out? Probably from water leakage and ground swell."

"Does it look like it's been tampered with lately?" Mike flashed his light on the wall.

"Nah. It's crumbly as hell, though. Voit cleared the basement with Dickens. No tracks here."

He examined the wall again. If he tore open the foundation and found nothing but dirt, his chief would have his head. And if Dickens didn't find any scent, it's probably clear.

Upstairs in the living room, Balducci scanned Hatch's messy desk by the window. He took note of the magazines with library stickers: *The New Scientist*, *American Journal of Neurology*. He slipped on a pair of plastic gloves and went through the drawers. In a file, he found pages of chemistry symbols, pencil sketches of the human brain, dozens of small drawings—figures of stick men. Some figures had vertical and horizontal lines drawn over them like a grid; one stick man stood in a cage-like oval. "What is this?" he said to Hatch, who was hovering in the doorway like an old crow.

"You wouldn't believe me if I told you, Detective."

"Try me."

He shrugged. "Thought-forms."

"Come again?"

"I play around with a pencil sometimes at night when I can't sleep. Helps to relax me, but I'm not very good at drawing."

"What do these lines mean?"

"Detective, it's much more complicated than I can say."

"I like complicated. What's it mean?"

"Thoughts are invisible vibrations, sourced from the electromagnetic energy of the mind. Everybody knows that. My drawings are floating images of the thought-forms."

"And the stick man?"

"That's the thinker, of course."

"And this one?" Balducci held up a drawing of a stick man inside sagging lines looped into a square.

"You don't recognize it, Detective?"

"Should I?"

"The thought is grief. The sadness of losing a loved one. These thoughts cleave around the body like a cage. Such thoughts haunt." Hatch tilted his head as if to emphasize the point, "Do they not, Detective?"

Balducci stiffened, thought of Maddy, then tossed the file back, slammed the drawer closed. He moved into the living room. Volumes of scientific texts lined the bookshelves. Some German titles. *Making Friends with Death* caught his eye. *American Book of the Dead.* Parapsychology. In the corner hung a plaque inscribed with words he couldn't read. "That's German, isn't it?"

"Yes. That woodcut belonged to my mother. *Und so lang du das nicht hast, Dieses Stirb und Werde, Bist du nur ein trüber Gast, Auf der dunklen Erde.* Johann Wolfgang von Goethe."

"Goethe, huh?" Balducci took the plaque down. Dust flew about. "And what's the translation?"

"'As long as you do not know how to die and come to life again, you are but a sorry traveler on this dark earth.'"

"Dark earth? Guess your mother wasn't a very cheerful type, was she?"

"On the contrary. She died fully conscious of the death process. She was a thanatologist, just like my father, and me."

Balducci raised his eyebrows as if impressed.

A dusty multivolume set of Emerson's writings filled the top bookshelf. Balducci couldn't resist taking one down. This collection was small, only six or seven books, not nearly as extensive as his own collection of Emerson that he had inherited from his father, Mitch. One of the newer publications, *A Dream Too Wild: Emerson Meditations* in a glossy soft cover grabbed his eye. "So, you're an Emerson fan?"

"Aren't we all who live in Concord? My great-grandparents knew Waldo personally. They were devoted transcendentalists at the time."

"Is that so. Hm. Nineteenth-century mysticism comes to Concord," Balducci teased.

"Are you a believer in transcendentalism, Detective?"

"It's a pretty extensive philosophy. In what exactly, do you mean?"

"In the search for reality through spiritual intuition. What else?"

Balducci wasn't about to say yes, although he trusted his intuition every day. And at the moment, his gut was telling him there were red flags all over this guy.

A commotion from above interrupted his thoughts. On the second floor, he found Voit trying to make Dickens go into the small storage room that was filled with boxes and crates. No matter how persistent Voit was with the hound, Dickens reared at the doorway.

"What's the matter with him?" Balducci asked.

"Something's spooked him."

Balducci walked into the storage room and opened one of the boxes. Oil lamps, ripped canvases, dried-up paints and brushes, and a few half-finished landscape paintings. Inside another box were bags of jewelry: pocket watches, pendants and necklaces, pearls, broaches, rings, bejeweled hair combs.

"Have I stumbled on the family jewels, Hatch?" Balducci looked up with one arm still inside the box, "Or have you been robbing the graves?"

"Certainly not! I find them abandoned in the grass."

Jewelry in the grass? Balducci wanted to laugh out loud at that one.

* * *

When Adam got home, he found Antonia in the living room with two FBI agents. A uniformed police officer was questioning some of the neighbors in the kitchen. Another interview was going on in the library. Adam sat down with the agents and went through their routine questions that he thought were overly focused on abduction. The idea that someone would have taken his son off the street because of his father's wealth sent his blood pressure soaring. The phone was ringing off the hook with news reporters, editors from the *Boston Globe,* missing children organizations. *Why is the house crawling with people? Can't they leave us alone?* Adam managed to be polite, encouraging them to leave.

In the kitchen, Antonia paced back and forth, speaking in Italian on the phone. Normally her eyes lit up when she spoke to her mother in Italy. But today her eyes were swollen, red from weeping. She was trying heroically to hold it together and with the whole day still ahead. *And what news will we get today? Please, God, not the pond.*

When she hung up, Adam walked into the dining room. The table was packed with fruit baskets, tins of cookies, and pastries wrapped in colorful paper. "What's all this?" He read a note on one of the fruit baskets. *Our prayers are with you all and for Henry. Love, from the gang at Beaumont.*

Antonia came up to him from behind, slid her hands down his arms, linking her fingers through his. She rested her head against his shoulder. Normally, he loved it when she did stuff like that. But just at that moment, he stiffened.

"Lew Beaumont called while you were out. He wants to help."

"What can he do?" Adam loosened his fingers, moved to the window, looked out at the brown patchy lawn. "He's in Chicago making that deal with Gillette. The trip I was supposed to go on. Thank God, I didn't."

"Lew asked if we thought about offering reward money."

His eyes shifted to the side hedges.

"Adam?"

He turned. On the table was a gift basket of wine. "Christ, I don't know, Antonia. Does reward money really work? I guess we should think about it." He read the card: Joe's Wine Connection. "How's your mother? Did you talk to your sister?"

"Mama was hysterical. And Mona wants to get on the first plane to Boston. I told her not to come."

He glanced up briefly.

"Mama needs her. She depends on Mona for everything these days."

"Does your father know?"

"No. This news could trigger another episode. He still sings lullabies to *Bambino Enrico.* Forgets that Henry isn't a baby anymore."

He looked to the foyer steps. "Where's Laura?"

"Josie took her to the bookshop."

"What's she going to do there all day?"

"She likes to dust the books. I thought it was a good idea. So much going on here. Did you see Mike when you went out?"

He lifted an apple from a fruit basket. "They have divers searching the pond."

"Don't tell me about that."

"They're searching Hatch's property. With the search-and-rescue dog."

"I hate the idea of that dog," she said. "It's like they're looking for a corpse instead of a lost child. The longer this goes on, the worse the possibilities? Isn't that the way it goes?"

He tossed the apple back into the basket. "I don't know. I can hardly think any more."

"The *Globe* wants an exclusive interview. Called three times."

"Fuck the *Boston Globe.*"

"Honestly. Keep it together, will you?"

"I don't want the *Boston Globe* reporting about our life." He massaged the kink in his neck.

"June Reilly said it might be helpful to do a TV interview. If someone out there knows something, it might prompt a person to speak up. Adam?"

"What?" He noticed a wallpaper seam peeling near the window sill.

"Adam, why don't you just say what you're thinking?"

"Say what?"

"That I should have walked to the bus stop to meet them. Or that I should have driven to the school to pick them up."

He pressed the wallpaper seam back into place with his thumb.

"Isn't that what you're thinking? Adam? That I shouldn't have let them walk home alone? I thought we agreed that Laura and Henry needed to learn to be responsible. Independent, you said. That whole trust thing."

"But I also said you should follow them a few times." He drew his vision to the china cabinet.

"I did. The first time, the second, the third. I hid in the damn bushes so they wouldn't see me. They walked the cow path perfectly, holding hands."

"Well, good."

"Adam?"

"What?"

"Why can't you look at me?"

He turned and raised his eyes to her. "Antonia, please," and walked out.

Across the foyer, in the small library, he sat at his desk by the window. The tight cluster of birch trees that Henry loved to climb wore a sunny patch. His eyes roamed the swing set and the linden trees, sweeping inside to the fireplace mantel where he focused on a row of baby photos.

In the center stood Antonia's white alabaster tear bottle—a gift from Antonia's mother. The Scarlattas believed that this tear-catching bottle symbolized God's blessings and would heal all their sorrows.

Had he the energy, he might have walked over to the mantel, picked up the bottle, and with one thrust—

He covered his mouth, caught a small scream in his hand.

* * *

The afternoon dragged on. The heavy silence in the house became unnerving; even the phone didn't ring. When it finally did, Adam grabbed it.

Antonia's footsteps banged down the staircase. "Who is it?

"Mike," he told her and hung up. "They've got Hatch at the police station. There's evidence Henry's been inside the cemetery. I'm going to the stationhouse. I'll get Laura later."

On his way out of Eastwick Road, he noticed several police cars parked at the corner, and in town dozens of flyers with Henry's picture posted on telephone poles and in storefront windows. In the police parking lot, he had to push past reporters, denying a photographer a picture before he actually got inside the door. The stationhouse buzzed with radio static and ringing telephones.

Sergeant June Reilly waved him over to her desk. "How you holding up, Adam? What can we do for you?"

"Mike said you're questioning Elias Hatch." He took a seat next to the sergeant's desk that had a picture of what was clearly June's little boy.

"We did, and we've just released him. This minute, in fact."

"Why?"

"We have no evidence to make a charge against him. Henry may have been inside Old Willow Cemetery, but that's not cause to charge Hatch with any wrongdoing."

"Did Hatch make a statement?"

"He says he didn't see Henry on Friday. Claims he was at the library all afternoon. And that does check out. Hatch puts himself home around four-thirty. That part is a little shaky since we have a witness at the library that remembers him being there around noon, but not after two o'clock. Truth is, Hatch might have been reading in the reference room as he says. Or maybe not."

"Is Mike here? Can I speak with him?"

"He just left. Adam, go home. There's nothing you can do. Mike's got everything under control."

Adam drove to the bookshop with his mind as congested as the traffic that snarled before him. If only he could line everything up. Put it all on a ledger sheet of plus and minus and the sum total. The cow path, the cemetery, the street, the pond. No, not that scummy pond!

At the bookshop, Laura napped on the sofa. She woke up in a daze when he carried her out to the Wrangler Sports Jeep.

"Did they find Henry?" She peeked open an eye.

Put it in the plus column. "Soon we'll find him." Once inside the house, Laura ran to the kitchen. When she didn't find her mother there, she burst into tears.

"Where's Mommy?"

"She's gone to St. Therese's." Adam read the note Antonia had left on the refrigerator door. Tomorrow would be Sunday, and Antonia was a Eucharistic minister at Sunday mass. She likely went to tell Father Jim Blaze she couldn't assist—and to seek his comforts.

Antonia had volunteered at St. Therese's when they first moved to Concord. Her school days of studying with the nuns in high school and reciting Bible passages had ingrained a faithful discipline to the church community. Laura especially liked receiving the Eucharist from her mother. Adam admitted he enjoyed the same moment of sanctity with his wife. And Henry, not of age yet to receive, would walk up, holding Adam's hand, watching with the most innocent desire. This Sunday they would not have such pleasures.

"Hey there." He crouched down with his daughter. "She'll be home any minute."

Laura fell sobbing into her father's arms. Leaning against the fridge door, he soothed her, at the same time wanting to crash himself. Of course he didn't, but a tear slipped down his face. Laura lifted her head and kissed the tear off her dad's chin. *Nothing, absolutely nothing goes deeper than a child's love.*

Chapter Five

UNDER THE NIGHT'S BLACK AND BLUE SHADOWS, Father Jim Blaze from St. Therese of the Roses Church rang Elias Hatch's doorbell at Old Willow Cemetery. The wind rose harshly. He shivered, glad he'd worn his cable-knit sweater under his wool coat. With a sniffle he waited for the familiar shuffle of feet.

"Hello? Elias? It's Father Jim."

A damp gust chilled his ears; his shaggy brown hair didn't offer much warmth. He flapped up the coat collar. Spring might be here by the calendar, but somebody forgot to tell Mother Nature. Finally, he heard the stump of Elias's cane on the floorboards. The door opened a crack.

"Father Jim? What brings you here so late?"

"I tried to call. Is your phone out of order again?"

"Oh that. Service will be restored soon. Tomorrow." Elias widened the door an inch more. "Sorry to have inconvenienced you."

"Elias, service will only be restored when you pay the bill. Do you need some help with that again? I'm happy to—"

He waved his hand as if swatting a fly. "I don't need a telephone most days."

"Everyone needs a phone. Are you all right, Elias?"

"Why, shouldn't I be all right?"

Father Jim inhaled a deep breath for patience and wedged closer to the door opening. "I hear you've had the police here today. And you've been down to the station house." Elias got the hint and opened the door. He stepped in.

"Nothing to be concerned about. Just routine questions."

"Well, good. I brought the book you asked for."

"On St. Helena? Wonderful." Elias took the book with a smile.

"Elias, tell me what happened when the police were here today."

"You know Henry Brooke is missing."

"All of Concord knows. And today Antonia Brooke came to see me. The woman is in pieces. We talked a while and your name came up in the conversation."

"Don't tell me she thinks I've done something to her boy."

"No. I didn't mean to suggest she did. But she did tell me that the police have evidence that Henry has been inside the cemetery. Inside the gates? Elias, what—?"

"I've no explanation for how he could have gotten in," he shouted.

Father Jim kept his patience. "I have to ask, what of Dorotheus?"

"What about her?"

"Is she still wandering about?" He used an especially gentle tone.

"Crazy old bat that she is," Elias said with amused contempt. "You know, she's afraid of people most of the time and stays away, but lately she's gotten quite bold. She's been wandering much farther than ever before."

"Elias, have you been observing her like I told you?"

"Whenever I can. She's usually not around during the day."

"Have you been able to get a handle on her routines?"

"Her routines?" Hatch blinked dramatically. "At dawn, I see her sending off flurries of kisses to the roots and vines inside the ironworks. There, is that the report you want?"

"Elias, don't make fun. This is serious."

"Everything is serious. Honestly, I don't know what she's doing. I can tell you this. She's taken to carrying ashes in her pockets now. Sprinkles them in a little trail."

"Where does she get ashes?"

"Haven't a clue. At night, I've seen her giving little speeches to the owls. That witchy voice of hers! And today I found her inside the house again. I send her away but she's so restless and clinging, I can hardly stand it. Father Jim, if you don't mind, I'm rather tired. It's late. I'd ask you in but I . . ."

"Of course. I just wanted to make sure all was secure. Sorry to intrude, Elias. Good night."

Blaze got inside his car, started the engine, and drove out, stopping short before the end of the long driveway. He turned the car engine off, killed the lights. It was a while before all the lights went out inside the cottage but once they did, he got out of the car and closed the door with a quiet click. He made his way around Hatch's cottage, between the great weeping willows, and up to the iron fence at the cemetery.

Half a moon shed white light. A great horned owl flew overhead, picking up the light on its spotty feathers as it swooped into the blackthorn tree. Most blackthorn trees grew no higher than thirteen feet, but this one was easily fifteen and had tightly hooked thorns. Elias had spoken of this tree often. A shadow beneath the blackthorn shifted. The priest made his way closer to the southern end to get a clearer view. That shadow shifted again. The top appeared curved, then grew larger, transforming into a figure of sorts: a blurry figure rocking, then swaying.

That owl wooed mournful notes with the murky figure moving to its rhythm, back-back, way back and forward . . . back-back, way back and forward. In that odd jerking, the figure expanded, releasing a misty silhouette. Small and slender, this silhouette moved away from the figure, then away from the blackthorn. Blaze squinted to see more clearly, but all he could make out was a shape of a rounded triangle pointing down. In a second, it reshaped into a gauzy sphere with a smaller sphere on top. Small cloudy limbs stretched out, plump little arms and legs. Short, sparking, and white as milk. A child?

Blaze made a mad dash back to the cottage, stumbling over rocks and roots, before he finally reached Hatch's door.

"Elias, open up! Come quickly."

It was forever before the old man's feet shuffled across the floor. The latch jiggled, and he peeked out. "What is it?"

"Get the cemetery keys. I think I saw Dorotheus. And . . . just get the keys. Do you have a flashlight? Hurry."

Elias fumbled for his keys in the kitchen drawer and hustled out with Blaze leading the way. They soon reached the gate where

Elias struggled to insert the gate key.

"What's the combination to the padlocks?" Blaze said. "I'll do it."

Elias looked up with a frown.

"For the love of God, you can trust me! What is it?"

He gave Blaze the numbers and in minutes the priest was through the gate and running to the south side of the cemetery. Elias followed a distance behind. Blaze flashed the light through the dark garden for any movement or small figure as he ran the paths.

Beneath the blackthorn tree, Dorotheus sat on the quarry rock, finger-combing her long grey hair beneath that lopsided bonnet. He rushed over to her, grabbed her up by the shoulders. Her face was flushed pink, her body feverish.

"Where is he? That boy you were holding."

Dorotheus trembled under his grip. "No boy here. No boy."

Elias came limping over the path, breathing hard. "Father Jim! Please, let her alone."

"But I saw . . . something."

"Did you? What, exactly?"

Moonlight streamed over the tangled vines wrapping the headstones like threadbare blankets. Through the thicket of hooked branches, that horned owl perched inside the blackthorn tree. It began wooing incessantly, its feathers puffy with the cold wind.

"I thought I saw . . . a child."

Owl-light flashed. The bird's binocular eyes forward-facing in a brilliant yellow, watched over Dorotheus rocking back-back, way back and forward . . . back-back, way back and forward.

Elias Hatch turned and walked away. "You saw nothing. Only Dorotheus."

* * *

On Sunday morning, Laura played on the playground at St. Therese of the Roses Church. From Father Jim Blaze's office window, Antonia kept her eyes on her daughter sitting alone on the swing, her legs splayed as she twisted the swing chains up so she could spin out. With her back to the priest, Antonia half-listened. His advice to trust the will of God washed over her like acid rain. At one point, she couldn't endure his words another second and turned on the priest, lashing out without thinking.

"This is more than Henry just wandering away from his own backyard. They're dredging the pond! This might even be a hit and run. This horror, this madness is God's will?" She sucked in a breath to compose herself. "I stopped by today to tell you I've decided not to continue in the Eucharistic ministry."

"You told me this yesterday. I understand that you need a break from—"

"This isn't temporary."

His mouth dropped.

"Father Jim, find someone else for Thursday and Sunday masses, permanently."

"Antonia, we so value your—"

"Don't try to talk me out of it." She turned away, skimming his desk piled with Bibles and hymnals and little glass angels. *I have to get out of here.* "Father Jim, I don't want to think about God now. I've made my decision."

"I understand, of course. May I . . . just let me tell you that I've organized a novena to St. Helena of the Cross for Henry."

"St. Helena. Oh, please! You think novenas to a saint will find Henry?" It came out as mocking, which she really didn't intend. Father Jim revered St. Helena as the most perfect of saints. Her picture sat on the top of his file cabinet, the stately robed woman with a face so angelic, it rivaled the Virgin Mary's face.

"Helena's intercessions are bountiful. More than I can tell you."

She glanced out the window to check on Laura. The swing hung with an empty seat. "Laura!" She bolted from the office and found her daughter standing outside near the open office window.

Blaze came running after her as she hustled Laura into the car.

"Antonia, I know you're angry with God, and it's okay. We pray every day to Helena at noon, if you change your mind and want to join us. Antonia?"

She sped away, biting her tongue, shutting out the image of the angelic St. Helena.

Prelude to a Saint

The Holy Land A.D. 326

Sunlight fell. Withered as the grass around her, Helena wandered slowly beyond the hills of Jerusalem. Walking in barefooted peace, she inhaled a sweep of wind. In this breath, she found a bold sweetness—not the delicacy of the orphaned lily petals nearby, or the sharpness of the reckless roses on the stone walls. This was the mighty fragrance of the evergreen. And yet not a single pine or cedar stood in sight across the vast plain.

She tested a mark into the rocky soil with her foot. One long grey braid hung down her back like a thick rope swaying back and forth as she scraped her heel north to south, east to west. Above, she spotted a circle of doves. Suddenly, the brisk taste of pine, bittersweet and woody, filled her mouth. Tossing her staff away, she let the Lord give her firm footing.

"Here," she instructed her companions. "Dig here."

They toiled for ten days in the dry hot valley, digging through rock and sand, around curling white snakes swarming among thorns. And when they brought up the wood and nails, Helena's heart leapt into her throat. Not by any archaeological instinct but by her determined heart, she had discovered the true cross of the Christ.

Chapter Six

Adam Brooke had just stepped out of the shower when he heard the doorbell ring. He toweled himself off, thinking Antonia would get it. Was there news of Henry? Someone who'd seen him? Something had to break soon. How did parents go on, hour after hour, not knowing about their child? With a glance in the mirror, he knew he looked bad: eyes swollen from lack of sleep, a sagging jaw, a scruffy two-day beard. The doorbell rang again, this time furiously without pause. He zipped up his jeans and pulled on a red cotton-knit sweater. In his bare feet he pounded down the steps, yanked open the door, expecting Sergeant Reilly or Mike. Instead, he saw a trim woman with perfectly groomed silver hair and pearls over a tailored blue suit.

"Mother?"

"Adam, I just had to come," she said. "Your father arrives tonight."

She stepped in, brushed her cheek to his cheek. Their shoulders stayed neatly apart in the standard Brooke style. They didn't kiss. In fact, Adam couldn't remember when he'd actually felt his mother's lips on his cheek or gotten a real hug.

"I can't believe you're here."

"Why shouldn't I be here? Henry's my grandson. And I'm just sick with worry over this."

Hearing her voice tremble, Adam had the wild idea for a second that she might burst out crying. He couldn't recall ever seeing his mother cry. He looked at her again. No, the brown eyes were hard and clear, shoulders straight, blush and mascara perfectly neat.

"Why didn't you call us?"

"I don't know why I didn't call. I just got on a plane and here I am. Where's Laura?" Out of her lizard-skin handbag she withdrew a small package wrapped in pink bows.

He escorted her into the kitchen, which was a mess of breakfast leftovers, newspapers, and a basket overflowing with laundry. The bathrooms were unspeakable. "Let's see, um, you want some coffee?"

"I've had plenty on the plane." She made a quick look around, raised a brow, then sat down in a kitchen chair, straightened her skirt and folded her hands on the table. "You must tell me everything that's being done to find Henry. I want every detail. Do you know that the police questioned me as if we had abducted him! What did you tell them?"

Adam turned to the stove and poured himself a cup of coffee he really didn't want. "They're questioning everyone. They even questioned Antonia's family in Umbria."

"Well, I'm not surprised. After all, there is the fact of Antonia's father. I mean, the man's been in a mental institution."

She stated this a bit too quickly for Adam. "He suffers from schizophrenia, Mother. He's on medication and doing well."

"He's considered dangerous, isn't he?"

"Only to himself. Let me put on another pot of coffee." He searched for the filters in the cabinet.

"Where is Laura? And Antonia?"

"I'll get them." Adam went to the stairs and gave a shout. When he got no answer, he ran upstairs and scanned the bedrooms. Quickly he put on socks and sneakers and went back down to the kitchen. "I don't know where they are at the moment. Maybe outside." He opened the back door and saw that her car wasn't in the driveway.

"Pretty view." Maude poked her nose near the window. "That weeping willow tree is frightfully close to the house. What if it falls on the roof? You should have it cut down."

"That tree is solid as a rock. Besides, we're building a tree house in it for Henry." He detected her classic disapproving huff, observed her eyes performing a visual checklist on the furnishings and size of the rooms.

"Awfully tiny. Those floorboards need repair. Well, you seemed to be managing considering you work for an advertising agency."

She inspected the dusty floors, kitchen sink filled with dishes, cardboard boxes of flyers, disarray of gift baskets and flowers in the dining room. He sat down at the table, knowing there would be a zinger coming any second.

She sniffed. "I suppose you can't afford a maid?"

"What for?"

With a *tsk,* she flapped her eyes at him. "What about Henry? How did this happen? Where was Antonia that Henry was able to wander off into the woods?"

Adam took in a breath, his blood surging. "Stop it right there. Don't you dare come here accusing Antonia. I won't have you in my home, doing your blame routine."

Wide-eyed, Maude held herself erect in his harsh gaze. She looked almost hurt by his words. He didn't care.

"Adam, I'm just sick over this." Her voice went limp, just a little.

"Mother, can you just please not criticize for once?"

"I didn't mean to imply—"

"I know exactly what you meant. So, you've come here today to do what?"

"To help, of course." She made a dramatic plea with her hands. "I know this is a horror for you both. All right. Tell me. What's being done?"

Adam brought her up to date and she listened to him without interrupting or dictating her opinion, much to his surprise. When the doorbell rang again, he dashed for the front door and found Josie holding a bag of jelly doughnuts.

"You're an angel. And your timing is miraculous." Behind Josie, in the driveway, Antonia and Laura had just pulled in and were getting out of the car. Laura came running up the walk.

"Hi, Daddy. We went to church. Know what? Mommy's mad at God. She's not going to be a Eucharistic minister anymore. Is it okay to be mad at God?"

"As long as you don't stay mad too long," he said, watching Antonia come speeding up the path, eyes down, face flushed.

"Stop," Adam grabbed Antonia's arm. "Listen. Don't scream.

My mother's here."

She didn't scream but her exasperated huff might have blown down the front door.

"Good morning, Antonia," Maude said tonelessly from her seat at the kitchen table when Antonia walked in. Maude tilted her head to her daughter-in-law. "How are you doing, dear? What can I do to help?"

Antonia made her polite greetings, as she always did with his mother, never failing to use her gentle endurance and kindness. He gave her hand a squeeze.

"Hello, Maude." Josie came in. "Adam has told us so much about you and Sam."

"Grandma? Hi, Grandma." Laura scooted around her father.

"There you are, little girl. Look how you've grown up." Maude gave her a quick kiss on the cheek.

"The police are going to find Henry today," Laura announced.

"I'm sure they will, honey."

"What's this?" She lifted the pink package from the table.

"A little something from me and Papa. And something for Henry, too, when he gets home." Maude took out a navy-blue wrapped box from her handbag. "Now, Laura, I want you to save this for your brother. Will you put it in a safe place for him?"

"I will." Laura tore open her own gift. With a dramatic gasp, she fingered the two silver hair barrettes glittering with purple stones. "Ohhh, I love them. Mommy, look, they're purple diamonds. My favorite color, how did you know, Grandma?"

"Well, purple is my favorite color too."

Purple? Adam couldn't remember seeing his mother dressed in anything but navy, beige, grey, or black.

"Can I wear them right now, Mommy?"

"Of course you can," Maude said. "Let me put them in for you."

"Take out the plastic red ones."

Maude removed the red barrettes from Laura's hair. "Oh, your blond curls are just like your daddy's when he was little."

"Now he's got some grey hairs, huh, Daddy? Right near your eyes."

Adam watched his mother fuss with his daughter's hair, soaking in what seemed an unusual but soothing moment.

Maude clipped in the barrettes with a fan of her well-manicured hands. "There." She ruffled the curls. "You look absolutely stunning, my pet. Go look in the mirror."

"Thank you, thank you. I have a mirror upstairs in my room, Grandma. Do you want to see my room? It's purple. You'll love it. Purple grapes, everywhere." She pulled on her grandmother's arm. "Come see."

"Of course I want to see. You show me the way, honey," and she gave Antonia a sidelong glance as she passed out of the kitchen.

"Would you prefer that I leave?" Josie said quietly.

"Don't you dare," Adam said.

"How long is she staying, Adam?" Antonia asked. "And *where* is she staying?"

"I don't know, but my father arrives tonight. They probably got a room in Boston. I didn't know you were going to church. You might have told me."

"Laura said she wanted to go, so we rushed out. Did you go to the trailer on Trent Street to check in?"

"Not yet."

"Good, then I'll go. I'd like to do something productive instead of sitting around here waiting. Josie, can you come with me?"

* * *

As they drove out, Josie driving, Antonia held a jelly doughnut in her hand, not sure she really wanted it. With her stomach in knots, this overly sweet thing might just make her feel all the worse. "Can you believe that woman shows up here after Adam specifically told her not to come?"

"I just love her hair," Josie poked Antonia's rib.

"That silver job? Woody Woodpecker-styled pomp, not a hair out of place. Yeah, that's Maude Brooke."

"And that triple strand of pearls? Wow. Stunning."

"Cartier. Adam says she wears them constantly. I think she

probably sleeps in them. And did you ever see such perfectly straight white teeth on a woman her age? Could her manicure be any redder?"

"That's it, girl. Let it all out."

She bit fiercely into the jelly doughnut.

At the trailer dispatch center, Deidre, the ranger on duty, showed them the logbook with a list of the foot patrols combing the woods and a map of the county with red and blue markers over various points. Reading and Burlington were unmarked. Glad to have an actual task, Antonia agreed that she and Adam would do those two towns that afternoon.

When Josie drove Antonia back, they passed Old Willow Cemetery. "Josie, stop the car."

"Why?"

"Look how high those walls are. Henry could never have climbed in by himself."

"Antonia, do you want to go in and have a look around? Most Hatch could say is no. Come on, let's try." Josie drove around to the stone cottage. Their persistent knocks and calls went unanswered, even though Hatch's faded 1950's Studebaker was in the driveway.

Back in the car, Antonia couldn't keep her eyes off the high fence. "He keeps that place like a fortress. It's excessive. Josie, what did Elias do for a living before he retired?"

"Taught physics at a small college, I think."

"Adam said Hatch had triple padlocks on the cemetery gates."

"Because of all the vandalism they've had. There were spooky stories going around that one of the statues wept tears. Weeping Woman of Old Willow, they called her. Kids used to dare each other to climb in and see it. My own girls scaled the rock wall with their friends on a Halloween night. I grounded them for two weeks. Thank God those teen years are over and they're off at college."

"So that's why there was a patrol car parked at the gate on Halloween?"

"Yeah. A year ago, a gang of fraternity pledges smashed open the gate locks and actually dug up a headstone." Josie shook her head. "They said Elias was just wild. The board called a town meeting and that's when the cops increased security."

"Well, what graveyard doesn't have some ghoulish stories?"

"Tears from a stone statue aren't exactly earth-shattering, I mean, really, the Weeping Woman of Old Willow? Who cares?"

When Antonia walked into the house, she saw Maude and Laura sitting together on the sofa in the living room with the television on. Cozy. Adam stood in the kitchen on the phone. She stopped mid-foyer. "Anything?"

He gave her a no sign. "I'm going to talk to Antonia about it, and I'll check with the detective. Thanks, Lew." He hung up. "Lew Beaumont. Wanted to talk about offering a reward to speed things up."

"It certainly will speed things up," Maude said from behind Antonia.

The three stood uncomfortably close in the doorway of the kitchen. Antonia moved to the stove. "I've got a terrible chill. Need something hot. Anybody want tea?" She grabbed the kettle and filled it with water.

"Thank you, no, dear. You must be exhausted. How are you doing?"

God, if she asks me that one more time, I'll scream. "Managing." She tossed a teabag into a cup. From behind, she felt little hands circle her waist and she returned the embrace. Laura hung on tightly.

"Can I go shopping for a new dress with Grandma?" Laura asked.

"Shopping?"

"Antonia," Maude said, "I came here to do what I could to help, and I thought it might be a good idea if I took Laura to Boston with me for the afternoon. We can pick up Papa at the airport." She had her hand on Laura's head. "His flight arrives at seven-thirty, and Laura tells me she loves to watch the planes fly in. Would that be all right?" She looked directly at her son for this last part.

"I don't know, Mother. I really don't want Laura out of my sight right now."

"Can I, Daddy? Please?"

"She'll be with me, safe every minute. I won't let her out of *my* sight. And I've got a car to pick us up door to door. You remember Harry, the driver from Patriot Limo service? He's waiting for my call. I had planned to go to the airport to meet your father anyway. We'll just go in a little earlier, buy Laura a new dress. Laura can watch the planes take off, and we can have dinner at that nice restaurant in Boston. What's the harm in that?"

"Daddy, can I?"

"I guess so. Antonia, okay?"

"Oh, Mommy, please, don't say no. Just this once?"

So now I have to be the bad guy? Just as Antonia opened her mouth to speak—

"Good, then, we're all agreed." Maude petted Laura's curls. "You've got such a good daddy."

"Just this once, Laura," Adam said. "And only if you promise to hold Grandma's hand. No running off."

"I promise, I promise."

"Now, my pet, let's get you out of those nasty brown corduroy pants and find a nice dress to wear today for your papa."

"I have dresses in my closet, Grandma. But first . . ." She looked to her mother. "I have to feed the birds for Henry. He always did it on Sundays."

"Just one cup of seed," Antonia said. "And don't leave the yard, sweetie."

"One cup. Henry will be glad I didn't let his Sunday birds go hungry."

"What a sweet child," Maude said and headed upstairs to select a dress.

Minutes later the kettle blew, and Antonia poured hot water into a mug. She sat at the table, steeping the teabag, swirling it around, feeling Adam's eyes on her. If he expected her to speak, he was out of luck. All she wanted was to sit and be quiet for just five minutes and gather her thoughts. He must have sensed this because he sat with her for a full minute without a word. Then he got up, grabbed the milk from the fridge and poured for her, his hand steady on hers.

"You know, Annie, my mother just wants to help. She gets on my nerves too. Laura will be fine."

"I know. I just don't like how she railroaded me into it."

"She's a master at it. Take my advice, work around it."

Maude's heels clicked down the stairs. She came into the kitchen carrying one of Laura's dresses. "This is the best I could find in that silly little closet of hers. Her room is an absolute slum."

"Mother, please."

"My apologies," Maude said it in a little tune. "Well, where is she?"

"Outside, feeding the birds."

* * *

Standing on Henry's stool, Laura poured a cup of seed into the clear plastic tube that hung on the tree. With a handful of cookies, she sat on the low rock wall to watch the chickadees and wrens descend for their meal. A chickadee swooped to the feeder and then flew off to a tree at the far end. At the edge of the back lawn, she spotted the girl with the long braids by the linden trees.

The girl appeared to be hiding behind the wide trunk, but Laura had her in plain sight. Those light brown braids were wonderfully thick, tied with white looping ribbons that hung down to the hem of her white and blue dress.

"Hello!" Laura called.

The girl ran back a few steps, then looked over her shoulder. Laura jumped off the rock wall and trotted after her to the linden trees.

"Hey, don't run away. What's your name? Mine's Laura."

The girl stood perfectly still as Laura approached.

"You don't have to be afraid of me. I have cookies. Want one?" Laura dug her hand into the bag and brought up two oatmeal and raisin cookies. "They're the chewy kind, not crispy."

The girl took the cookies and a quick bite.

"I love your braids! How does your mom get them so smooth like that? Can I touch them?"

The girl shook her head. "Shhh, don't tell anyone you saw me, promise?"

"I promise."

"I'm not supposed to be here."

"Why not? You can come to my house any time."

"It's a pretty house." She looked up to the windows. "Which room is yours?"

"The one on the . . ." Laura stopped to figure out which side. "The left. Yeah. Henry's room is at the other end, near the chimney, on the right."

"What color is his room?"

"He has wallpaper with sailboats. It's all blue water and white. Mine's purple grapes. You want to come in and see?"

"I can't. I have to go before someone sees me. Remember, you promised not to tell." The girl fled into the forest, braids flying behind her, the white streamers disappearing.

"Laura? Laura!"

"I'm right here, Dad," she yelled, running toward the house. "Your face is all red. What's the matter?"

"I didn't see you back there in those trees. Come inside."

"Dad?"

"What?"

"Did you ever break a promise?"

"No."

"But when you make a promise and don't know why you made it, can you break it?"

"Just come inside. Your grandmother wants to leave soon."

"But can you? Break it?

"A promise is a promise. You promised to hold your grandmother's hand. And don't keep her waiting."

Chapter Seven

ANTONIA DREW UP HER STRENGTH for the three hours of jumping in and out of the Jeep over miles of local roads to distribute the flyers to Reading and Burlington. It was exhausting, but she found herself invigorated too, her mind racing, her pulse zooming, her body screaming to just rest. When they got home and collapsed into the sofa, ten phone messages were waiting for them on the answering machine. None had any significant news except the last one from Detective Mike Balducci. "We have a suspect. I'm at Sudbury police station. Call me."

As soon as they arrived at Sudbury police station, Antonia breathed a quieter breath and felt grateful Mike was at the front desk to greet them. He had such reassuring eyes and that easy smile hinted good news. *It is good news, isn't it?*

"What'd you do, eighty miles an hour all the way from Concord?" Mike crushed out his cigarette.

"I don't know, I never looked at the speedometer," Adam blurted out. "Who is this suspect, Mike?"

"I just finished questioning Margie Quinn. Got another officer giving it a second round. She's sixteen years old, lives with her father and stepmother. She was on Eastwick Road on Friday afternoon, at the Bronnell house. She gave Katie Bronnell a ride home from school, which puts her on your street about 2:35."

"The Bronnell's are the third house on the street," Antonia said.

"Their driveway is only a few feet from where we found Henry's cap in the sewer grid. I'll bring you in, see if you recognize her."

Down the hall, he opened a green metal door into a dark room the size of a large closet but with a one-way glass window. The girl sat at a table. She kept wiping tears off her face and glancing away from the officer who sat opposite her. Behind her was a bulldog of a man with red cheeks and beefy arms folded over his leather-jacket chest.

"Is that her father?" Antonia asked. "What's she saying?"

"I can't let you listen in. Either one of you ever see her before?"

"Never," Adam said easily.

Antonia examined the girl's long pointy nose, thin reddish hair, silver bracelets on both wrists, and royal blue nail polish. "I don't know her. She looks like a scrawny, terrified bird. "

"Henry ever mention anyone named Margie Quinn?"

"No," Adam said. "Can I speak with her?"

"I wouldn't. No official charges have been filed, yet. You're both sure you've never seen her around? Does Henry know Katie Bronnell?"

"We hardly know the Bronnells," Antonia said. "Henry doesn't know either of them."

He opened the door. "Then we're done here."

Adam put his hand across the doorway. "I want to listen, Mike."

"Bad idea, Adam, take my word for it."

"I don't care. I've got to hear this."

He paused, covered his eyes with one hand, then pointed to the speaker switch and left the room.

Antonia flipped it on.

The officer in the room pushed a box of tissues toward the girl. "And then what happened when you backed out of the Bronnell's driveway?" the officer continued.

"I thought I felt a bump?" Margie said. "Like I hit the curb? I'm not sure, cause the radio was on?" She lifted her voice at the end of each sentence. "And then I stopped the car? I looked in my rearview mirror?"

"Are you asking me or telling me, Margie?" the officer said.

"She's telling you, for Christ's sake," her father yelled.

"That's just the way she talks sometimes, don't you, honey?" From the stepmother, in the back of the room.

"Yeah, yeah, that's how she talks," the officer said.

Antonia saw Mike enter and sit down at the table; he sat on the edge of his chair.

The officer continued, "How fast were you going when you backed out, Margie?"

"I don't know."

"We have it from the Bronnell girl that you stepped on it pretty heavy. When you looked in your rearview mirror, what did you see?"

Margie raised her watery eyes to the ceiling. "I don't—can't—remember. All I remember is I opened the door and looked out and . . . and that's when I saw his . . ." She burst into tears and covered her face with both hands.

"You saw what, Margie?"

"You know what she saw," Quinn said. "Why the hell are you making her—"

"Mr. Quinn, I'll say this once. Don't interrupt again or I'm going to make you wait outside."

"She's just a kid. You can't question her without a parent being present. I know my rights."

"I can exclude you, Mr. Quinn, and I will. Final warning. Now tell me again, Margie, for the record, what did you see when you looked behind the car?"

She wiped her eyes. "I saw . . . his red sneaker."

Adam grabbed the top frame of the window frame with both hands.

"Did you get out of the car?"

"I don't know, umm, I think . . . no, I didn't get out. I drove away."

"You left him there?"

She nodded.

"Speak into the microphone."

"I'm sorry, I didn't mean to . . . hit him."

Antonia stifled a sob.

"And then what happened?

"I started down the street, and at that curve I looked in my rearview mirror and I saw him . . . lying in the street. I thought he fell or something." She blew her nose and took a sip of water. "And that's when I saw the person."

"This person," Mike said. "Tell us again exactly what you saw."

The officer stood up and walked out of view.

"I couldn't see. I was crying. My eyes were all blurry, but somebody was there. So I figured the boy was okay."

"Was it a man or a woman?"

"I don't know."

"Did you see what color clothes the person was wearing?"

She shook her head.

"Was this person short? Tall? Heavy? Thin?"

"I don't know! Just somebody huddled down over him. It was only a second that I looked, and then I drove out."

"Did you tell anyone about it?"

"No."

"Why not?"

"I didn't want . . . to get in trouble."

The chair screeched across the floor as Mike stood up and leaned over her. "That little boy you hit is missing for three days. You're in big trouble, Margie."

"I'm thinking," the officer said, "there's no *person* at all. I'm thinking you put Henry in the car and drove him somewhere. Isn't that what you really did, Margie?"

"You listen to me." Her father wagged his stubby finger at the officer. "She didn't take that boy. I know my kid, and she didn't take that boy."

"Margie's a good girl," the stepmother said. "She had an accident, that's all. She got scared."

"I swear I didn't take him. I left him there and I went home!"

"Not good enough, Margie," Mike said and walked out. When he came into the viewing room, he flipped the speaker off and escorted them to another room where he poured cups of coffee.

Adam declined the coffee. "How did you find out about this girl?"

"The stepmother called the station. She wanted to know if we located Henry Brooke. And then she started asking way too many questions. The pieces fell into place, one, two, three. So, right now we've got a team searching the Quinn premises."

"Where do you think she took Henry?" Antonia asked.

"Not a clue at the moment but the stepmother probably knows more than she's telling."

"Let me speak with them, Mike," Adam said.

"Forget it, Adam. If Margie put Henry inside her car and brought him somewhere, we'll find the evidence. The parents could be witnesses or accomplices, and I've got to keep control over my investigation. I want you both to stay out of it. I just wanted to know if you could ID her."

Adam shoved his hands into his pockets. "And now what?"

"Go home."

"But she knows where Henry is!" Antonia wanted to grab Mike and shake him.

"Go home. I'll call you the second I get something."

* * *

Adam drove back to Concord with his hands tight on the steering wheel, taking each turn a little recklessly. Antonia said nothing, kept her knees locked and eyes forward as they zoomed by peripheral houses and trees. When they pulled into their driveway, Sam Brooke came out the front door. Father and son greeted each other with their usual handshake.

"I'm so sorry, Antonia," Sam hugged her. "We'll find him. I know we will."

She looked deep into his baggy blue eyes. He had a head full of wavy grey hair and a straight scoop of nose, much like Adam's nose—and Henry's. She nearly fell to pieces right there on the lawn.

Inside the house they sat at the dining room table. Maude had put away the boxes of food and arranged the flowers on the end tables in the living room, which brightened the room considerably. Adam took his chair at the head of the oak table, and his father sat at the side as they talked, glasses of iced scotch, the bottle of Johnnie Walker between them. Adam gave him an update on the area searches and on Margie Quinn.

"I just want to check on Laura," Antonia said and headed

upstairs. She found Laura asleep, snug inside her covers, and left a kiss on her nose. A silk dress hung on the closet door hook. She admired the delicate print of purple and pink tulips and pearly lace collar. Even the hem was trimmed with lace and the long sash at the back hung in a dramatic bow. In a shopping bag was a shoebox: black patent leather shoes and a child's purse with a gold chain. Antonia read the price tag hanging on the dress: $175.00. *Salty dollars, shells of an old house.* She shook the words from her head as if they were dust.

When she went back into the dining room, Maude had put out some sandwiches and fruit from the gift baskets.

"Adam said you haven't had a meal all day." She pushed the plate toward Antonia. "You look terrible. Eat something."

Adam was already biting into roast beef on a roll. He seemed to down another scotch as quickly as he polished off the sandwich.

"I'll have one too." She put out her glass.

"There's a list of phone messages in the kitchen, Adam," Maude said. "Lew Beaumont called again. Tell him, Sam."

"Lew and I talked a while. And I agree with him that offering a reward is a smart idea. You want to do it, don't you?"

Antonia watched Adam take a long slug of the scotch, swallow hard, then another.

"Adam," Maude said.

"What do you think, Adam?" His father's voice sharpened. "One hundred thousand dollars is a powerful incentive for someone to come forward."

"Is that what you suggested to Lew? A hundred thousand?" Adam swirled his glass.

"Yes, as a matter of fact."

"And this one hundred thousand is . . . from where?"

"What does that matter? Do you want to offer a reward to get Henry back or not?"

"As if this whole thing were that simple. Whose money is it?"

Sam tapped his thumb slowly on his glass, leaned back in his chair, cocked his head. "It's yours."

"Mine? I don't have a hundred thousand dollars, and Lew

doesn't have that kind of cash to hand over to me. He was talking about setting up an account for twenty-five thousand through a lawyer. And I'm not sure a reward will do much good, anyway. The chief on the case said that offering a reward in these cases is dicey. It brings in a lot of prank callers and dead-end leads. Maybe he's right, maybe not. But I do know that I don't want them wasting their time going in the wrong direction. The detectives are onto something with this Margie Quinn. Let's see what happens tomorrow."

Sam took out his wallet and removed a blue deposit slip. "Here." He slid it to his son's hand. "A hundred thousand dollars. It's yours. You're authorized to withdraw it at any time. You want to use it for a reward? Fine. You don't? That's your choice."

Adam looked at the deposit slip, then to his father who stood up and slipped his arms into his blazer.

"Let's go, Maude. Call Harry for a pick-up. We'll just make it to the airport if we leave now."

Maude retrieved her cell phone from her handbag and dialed.

"I don't know what to say." Adam stood up, which put him eye level with his father. "I don't want to take your money, Dad."

Antonia heard the defeat in her husband's voice and stood up with him.

Sam shook his head with disappointment. "Don't you remember what I—"

"I know. You don't have to say it, a thousand times is enough, Dad. *A deal is a deal.*"

"Yeah, I've said that a lot through the years. Hell, you were seven years old, Adam, selling pretzel rods to your playmates for twenty cents each when they cost you a nickel."

"I was grossly overcharging my own friends. That's bad money."

"A deal *is* a deal, Adam. Your friends agreed to pay it. Second grade and you're making successful deals on the playground. I was so proud when that school principal told me about it." Sam capped the scotch bottle slowly. He lifted his eyes. "Adam, there's no such thing as bad money. Money is how we keep score. It's liberty, a control lever."

"The almighty dollar."

"Yes, it *is* almighty. And it's a goddamn servant. Adam, money is a goddamn servant!"

The two men locked eyes. Sam's blue eyes blinked first.

"What else can I give you, Adam? Money is what I have. Do you want to do everything you can to get Henry back? Then take it."

* * *

From the front door, Adam watched Maude and Sam walk down the path to the waiting limo. He wanted them to go as much as he desired them to stay. It was a confusion he had struggled with most of his life. He shook off the gloom. In a second, the limo's red lights faded down Eastwick Road, and he went back to the table and sat down, eyes fixed on the deposit slip.

"Adam?"

Almost afraid to see her face, he looked up. "I know what you're thinking, Annie."

"We take the money. That's it. Look, I know Sam thinks his money can *buy* Henry back. This is business for him, right? Just like you say. Sam Brooke is the best dealmaker in America. He throws money at everything. So what, Adam, so what."

He couldn't answer. He let the momentary silence settle in, held the glass of scotch with both hands.

"You know what else, Adam?"

Her voice nearly startled him.

"I've never thought of money as being a servant. Of course, Sam's right about that one, isn't he?"

His lungs didn't have much air right at that moment, so he took in a long breath. "Annie, you know what's attached to this money. One hell of a purse string. I'll be choking on it the rest of my life. My mother would see to it. This is why I left the firm. This is why I don't give a damn about his threats to disinherit me. I hate his money."

"Adam, your father threatened to disinherit you because you flew off to Umbria to marry me. I'm not society. I'm not what they wanted for you. But you married me anyway. Wasn't that defiance enough?"

He downed the last of the scotch. "I'm going up to take a shower." His last glance was not to his wife but to that damn deposit slip on the table.

Half an hour later he heard Antonia stirring in Henry's room. He peeked in. She was running her hands over Henry's bedsheets, his books, the brown stuffed bear he used to keep in his crib. In the closet she straightened his outgrown Keds. But he wanted to shut his eyes when she sniffed Henry's white terrycloth bathrobe, crushing it to her face.

When Antonia climbed into bed she automatically slipped her arms around him, placed a kiss on his shoulder. No one had higher passion than Antonia, and he rolled on top of her, kissed her face, her neck, moved down to her breasts. He wanted to be smothered by them, wanted her to spread her legs and feel that long shuddering glide, in that deep surrender she faithfully gave him.

"Adam, I can't." She tried to push him off.

He locked his hands over hers, forcing her legs apart.

"Stop."

He went after her as if starved.

"Get off me. Stop it."

"Come on, Annie, you want it."

"No, I don't." She beat her fisted hands against his back. "Get off!"

He rolled off, swollen and throbbing.

"How *could* you!"

"I don't know, I'm . . ." He reached for her.

Her eyes flashed as she pushed him away. "Don't touch me."

"You're overreacting, calm down."

"No, you calm down. What's the matter with you?"

"I didn't mean it. I'm sorry."

"Yes, you did. You want to hurt me. Why don't you just say it? Henry's lost because of me. He could be hurt. He could be dead. And it's my fault."

He sat on the edge of the bed, with his back to her. "Please, Antonia, I don't want to hurt you. I—"

"You do." She jumped up, pounded to his side of the bed. "You want to screw me, make me the victim of your actions." She paced back and forth. "I know you blame me. I blame myself. But I can't undo that day. I don't know why this horrible thing happened. I wasn't being a bad mother, Adam. I'm not a bad mother!"

The words splintered through the air.

He pressed back his own tears. "I never said you were. I don't think—"

"You do! It's in your eyes. On your face. In your voice."

He stared at the floorboards, at his tossed sneakers near the dresser, her bra hanging off the armchair, Henry's red fire engine beneath the end table.

"Get out. Get out and leave me alone!" She shrilled at him. The vibration of her voice went clean through him.

* * *

Sleepless on the sofa in the library, with a snarling rain hitting the roof, Adam endured hours of reckless thoughts. He turned on the lights, tried to read the newspaper, but couldn't keep his mind on the words and smashed it into a ball. Then he shot it across the room directly into the hoop of the wastepaper basket.

He meandered around the house, sat at the kitchen table, watched the sunrise on the weeping willow tree. Sunbeams streamed through the windows. He felt it on his face and soaked in clean pools of light. A cardinal flashed through the willow tree. He watched it zoom up to the treetop—the spot where Henry wanted his tree house.

Adam had already begun the search for tree house plans. He had a folder stuffed with blueprints in his desk drawer. Henry loved to go into the drawer and examine the blueprints with a magnifying glass, not understanding a thing but wanting to know everything. *It's going to be great, you know that, don't you, Dad?* Henry liked to say that a lot. It was a phrase he had picked up from his sister. And it always gave Adam an amazing feeling—the little boy reassuring the dad.

At seven a.m. and still shaky, Adam dialed Lew Beaumont at his home. "Hi, Lew." He tried to clear the gravel in his voice. "Didn't get you out of bed, did I?

"Nah. Been on my run already. What's up?"

"I've decided . . . Antonia and I have decided to go ahead with the reward money. Can you call your lawyer to set up the fund? I'll tell Mike Balducci."

"Yeah. We said twenty-five thousand?"

"A hundred thousand. The old man came through. You know Sam Brooke, money's what he does best."

Just as he hung up, Antonia came into the kitchen, tying her robe, looking panicky.

"Who was that? What's wrong?"

"Nothing's wrong. I just made something right." He studied her for a moment. God, she looked awful. Where was that beautiful happy woman that greeted him with so many kisses every morning? "I told him to set up the reward account." He waited for her response, which was deadpan. "What, did you really think I would refuse a hundred thousand dollars if I thought it had even the slimmest chance of finding Henry?"

She collapsed into the chair, her hair hanging in her face. "I don't know what I thought."

"Well, that makes two of us."

* * *

The reward announcement for any information leading to the discovery of Henry Brooke of Concord, Massachusetts, went out over television, radio, newspapers, and the Internet. Calls flooded in for days. The investigators scrambled to follow every lead from Boston to Los Angeles. A report of a child fitting Henry's description at Lake Lugano, Switzerland, startled Adam at first. Another caller claimed to have seen the child in a London suburb. The FBI assured the Brookes that these were typical false leads. What Adam couldn't understand was why it was taking so long to find any concrete information from the investigation into Margie

Quinn's story. For days the only word he received from Mike was, "We're working on the Quinns. Sit tight."

Unfortunately for Adam, patience was a piece of bitter fruit. By the end of the week, he hadn't heard from Mike or anyone on the team. Late on Sunday night, when the phone rang, Adam practically tackled Antonia to reach the receiver.

"Mike, what's happening? We've left messages everywhere for you."

Antonia ran to the hallway phone.

"I'm sorry. We've been in so many directions, but I don't have anything new to tell you, except we suspended Margie Quinn's license and charged her with a hit and run." Static cut in and out of his cell phone. "And you'll be happy to know that the pond is clear. Divers went home."

Adam let out a sigh of relief. "And what happened with the Quinns?"

"We had Dickens track the entire house and property. Not a trail of Henry anywhere. Not in the house, not in the yard, and not in any of their cars."

"And?"

"Looks like Margie Quinn was telling the truth. She didn't take Henry. Somebody abducted your boy off the street. And in a matter of minutes, and it looks like this person may have done it without a vehicle."

"Well, that narrows it down, doesn't it? I mean, the only place we know Henry's been besides his own backyard is in that damn cemetery. You know Elias Hatch is involved in this. Can't you arrest him?"

"On what exactly, Adam? I don't have a nickel's worth of evidence on Hatch. It's late. Get some sleep, you guys. Goodnight."

"Goddamn!" Adam yelled as Antonia walked back into the bedroom.

"My God, Adam, Margie did see someone in the street with Henry."

"You bet she did. Hatch! And that bloodhound picked up Henry's trail all over that cemetery. That's it, Annie, Hatch has got him."

"But they searched the cottage and the cemetery grounds. If Hatch has got him, where is he?"

Adam stared out the window in the direction of Old Willow Cemetery. Then he dashed to the closet, pulled on his blue jeans, and yanked a sweater over his head.

"What are you doing?"

"I'm going over there. I'm going to catch Hatch unprepared and find out where Henry is." He drew on socks and boots.

"Adam, please, don't do this. Mike's doing everything—"

"I don't give a damn what Mike's doing. It's over a week now! Stay here with Laura." He grabbed a flashlight out of the dresser drawer, tested it, then snatched his jacket from the hanger.

"What are you going to say to him?"

"Not a damn thing. Hatch is going to do all the talking." He dug out a metal box from the top shelf of the closet, spun the cylinder combination lock, opened the lid, and pulled out a black metal gun.

"Adam!"

Quickly he opened his dresser drawer and loaded the revolver.

"Where did you get that? Adam! You can't go over there with a gun."

"Leave this to me." He shoved it in his jeans, pounded down the stairs and out the door.

Chapter Eight

DEEP INTO THE DARK NIGHT, a hovering rack of clouds descended. Packs of deer scattered, their hooves drumming off into the jagged line of trees. Adam trailed the rainy mists along the cow path in his hooded red jacket. A brooding owl hooted in the distance. He slowed his pace through the pine grove and listened to that owl screech again. What an eerie sound. The rain surrendered, leaving fog to rest domed and drowsy on the trees. Arched hemlocks hung with wet cobwebs. Vapors drifted in.

Behind him, he heard a crack. Eyes wide, he turned to the parting mist. Ashen faces floated up from the earth. He blinked—no, just fallen willow twigs forming foggy images over flat rocks. Adam took in a deep breath, blew it out slowly. Once more something screeched. A quick call. He shook off a chill. *Relax, for God's sake. It's just that owl.*

He aimed the cone of light to the left. In the distance he saw Hatch's crumbling cottage. His boots squeaking, he kept a steady pace until he reached the strip of clearing that Elias Hatch called his backyard. The beam of light diminished into a dull stream under the mist that smelled like soil and sweet moss.

The cemetery's iron fence dripped with reflecting raindrops. Adam passed the beam across the wrought iron bars, streaming it to the top. Moving closer, he seemed to lose the iron bars from sight. A second later, he saw why. The double gates of Old Willow Cemetery were wide open. On the ground, three padlocks lay abandoned in the grass. Hatch left the gates open? Was someone inside? Who's there?

Walking through the entrance, a beating of wings followed him.

That owl again. Or a bat. Something swiped at his head. A hard wooly claw brushed his cheek. He flailed his arms. It flew off into the lashes of the trees. Inside the cemetery, he waved the white light over rows of curved headstones. He passed a statue of an eagle, a marble saint holding a cross, a series of cement squares. Something scurried ahead. A swish? Or somebody saying *hush.* In the distance, a blurry white object stretched across the ground like a patch of snow.

Blinking to clear his vision, Adam stepped slowly. As soon as he got within a few feet of a stone slab, he saw the white object was a long white gown. At the top, a black curly bonnet perched. Leaning in, he aimed the light into the bonnet.

Face full of wrinkles. Eyelids shut tight. Lips stretched thin as if stitched. He veered back at the sight. Spindly legs stuck straight out like beanpoles from the gauzy gown. Boney toes. He looked again. They twitched furiously.

Suddenly his feet went out from under him—as if someone had pulled the rug out—and he toppled to the ground. The flashlight flipped out of his hand, pitching its light askew into the cemetery.

The old woman rose up. With the wind flapping her white gown, she ran off.

"Hey! Wait! Stop!" By the time Adam scrambled to his feet and retrieved the flashlight, the woman had melted into the dark mist.

He swept his flashlight in an arc through the dreamlike fog. Blue vapors folded in. Something hissed. He spun around. A huge brown rabbit scooted off to a cluster of trees where an odd blue light pulsed.

The light shimmered. Whorls of mist circled his feet. Voices came. Children? Women? Soft whispers lifted into the air.

"Hellooooo."

A blue helix of light tumbled before him like a football. Then a second spiral came at him. He toed the sparkling oval and watched it zoom over a mounded grave. Another blue spiral appeared and Adam kicked it up, sending it spinning like blue diamonds into the darkness.

"*One . . . two . . . three . . .*" a voice whispered.

Adam yanked off his hood.

Rows of shimmering footballs spun before him. Three more swirled from above, tumbling over each other. He followed them on the path through the headstones.

"*Four . . . five . . . six,*" the whisperer spoke again.

Adam stopped, withdrew his weapon. "Seven . . . eight . . . nine."

"*Ten . . . eleven . . .. twelve.*"

"Thirteen . . . fourteen . . . fifteen."

"*Sixteen . . . seventeen . . . eighteen.*"

This was a child's voice. But from where? Above? No, it was flowing from behind, or maybe in the distance ahead. He spun, eyes searching, holding the gun down at his side. "Nineteen . . . twenty . . . twenty-one."

"*Twenty-two.*"

"Twenty-three. Henry? Henry, is that you?"

"*Twenty-four! Touchdown!*"

"Henry! It's Dad. Henry!"

"*Twenty-four. Twenty-four.*"

"Where are you? Keep talking, pal. Henry?"

Up ahead a cedar leaned. A ghostly pine swayed. Blue points of light spread. The fog grew darker. It expanded into a hard grey substance full of folds and curves. Adam wanted to touch it, feel the rock or whatever it was and reached out just as it came crashing down on the side of his head.

* * *

At the house, Antonia kept watch out the front window and flew outside in her robe just as Mike Balducci turned his car into the Brooke driveway.

He rolled down his window. "Got your message, but my cell just died. What's so urgent?"

"Adam's gone to see Elias Hatch. And Mike, he's got a gun."

"Jesus!"

An hour later, after pacing the floor and trying to remain calm, Antonia swung open the front door to find Mike bracing Adam up.

Blood dripped down her husband's face, and he was white as chalk. "What happened?"

Mike guided Adam into the house. "He refused an ambulance. But he needs a doctor."

"It's nothing. Just a bruise." Adam fell into the armchair in the living room, holding a bloody wad of tissues to his head.

"I'll get some ice." She flew into the kitchen and was back with a compress. "Let me see how bad it is."

"Could be a lot worse," Mike said. "Could be a gunshot wound, for Christ's sake."

"Are you dizzy, Adam? Do you feel nauseous?"

"No."

"What happened, Mike? Look at him!"

"I found him inside the cemetery. Passed out. Weapon in his hand."

"The safety latch was on." Adam winced as he moved his head.

"Well, that just makes everything all friendly now, doesn't it?"

"I was only using it as protection."

"That's crap. You went there to threaten Hatch. You got a license for that, Rambo?"

"Of course I have a license."

"This is a serious cut, Adam." She blotted the wound, wishing she had stopped him from going there, wishing she had gone with him. "Did you fall?"

"No, I didn't fall. Something hit me. Probably Hatch. He used a rock or something."

"Well, Hatch denies it," Mike said.

"Christ, Mike, Hatch denies everything."

"Hatch claims he didn't even know you were on the property. He intends to press charges for trespassing."

"Big deal. Why were the gates open? Did you ask Hatch?"

"He thinks you did it."

"Oh, Adam," she said, hearing the regret in her tone. "Why did you go into the cemetery at all? What were you thinking?"

"Yeah, Rambo, breaking and entering is a handy charge too. You like that one better?"

"I didn't break into the cemetery. The gates were unlocked and wide open." Adam described the blue swirling lights, the voices, the counting game with Henry.

Antonia could hardly believe it. She exchanged a look of shock with Mike.

"I swear it was Henry, Annie, counting with me to twenty-four. It was Henry!"

She didn't know what to say. She wanted to believe him but none of it made sense.

"Henry's voice, huh? Did you see him?" Mike said.

"It was too dark, too foggy to see anything."

"You're sure it was Henry's voice? You might have—"

"I know my own kid's voice."

"And that's all Henry did? Count numbers?"

"To twenty-four. Just like the football plays we call out on the lawn. You know, Annie, in a series of three's." He leaned forward. "I'm bleeding all over the place here."

Antonia handed him a clean towel. "How can you be so certain it was Henry, Adam. I mean, if it was Henry, did he know you were there?"

"I think he did, yes. His voice was absolutely clear. Just like when we heard him laughing in the willow tree that morning."

Mike shot his eyes at Antonia. "What's this?"

She closed her eyes and sighed. "It's nothing, Mike."

Adam grabbed the towel from her hand. "Nothing? Stop trivializing it."

"Trivializing what? Adam?"

"We heard Henry's voice in the willow tree. The morning after he went missing. He was laughing. Antonia, don't deny it. You know you heard it."

"What are you talking about? Explain." Mike held an unlit cigarette.

"I don't have an explanation. All I know is we heard Henry's laughter in the willow tree. No mistakes. It was Henry."

"But you didn't see him?"

"No, we didn't see him!" Adam practically spit the words out.

"Just like I didn't see him tonight either."

Antonia saw Mike page to a clean sheet on his yellow pad and scribble furiously. "Is this accurate, Antonia?"

She pushed herself back on the ottoman. "I did hear Henry that morning in the willow tree but then after, I wasn't sure. I mean we were exhausted and upset and—"

"Laura heard it too." Adam cut in. "We all heard it! But we couldn't put our hands on him."

Antonia gave a nod. "I don't know how to explain it, Mike."

"Okay, so let me get this straight. You claim you both heard Henry in the backyard. And now, Adam, you claim you heard Henry inside the cemetery."

"Write it down in your yellow pad, would you?" Adam yelled. "Because I know you don't want to believe me. Are your men still searching the cemetery?"

"Of course they are. Yeah, I believe you. I'm ready to believe anything at this point. I wish you'd have told me this before. Anything else I should know, Adam, as long as we're playing catch-up?"

"There is one other thing. I saw someone in the cemetery tonight. A woman."

Mike raised a brow, fingering his unlit cigarette. "What woman?"

"She was lying on the ground, wearing some kind of nightgown and an old black hat."

"And?"

"And she ran off. But she was there, legs stretched out and wiggling her toes. I remember that."

Mike dropped his cigarette. "Toes? She was barefoot?"

"Holy Christ, she was," Adam said, his jaw dropping.

"Holy Christ, she was," Mike repeated. "I'll alert the team."

Chapter Nine

THE NEXT MORNING, BALDUCCI rang the Brooke's front doorbell. What a night he'd had searching Old Willow and the cottage again. But now things became terribly messy: Chief Dan Hersey, putting on the pressure, insisted on joining him for this meeting with the Brookes. Balducci successfully talked him out of it.

"Good morning," Balducci said when Antonia opened the door. He flashed a smile. Would that cheer her up a little? Most people smiled back on reaction. Not this time. Her well-scrubbed face, puffy eyes, and mouth looked permanently sad. Best to move on to business and get it over with. Maybe take a moment for personal interest first. "How many stitches did the ER do on Adam last night?"

"Four. They said he'll be fine. He's out, driving Laura to school."

"That's good. Keep the routines normal."

"That's what everybody says. So we're just following the rules here. You look like you need some coffee. Come in."

In the kitchen she poured him a mug. He stalled, sipping the coffee, watching her sip hers. "Antonia, I do have one piece of good news this morning. Hatch has decided not to press charges against Adam for trespassing."

"Well, goody for him."

He stirred more milk into his coffee and spotted the *When Your Child Is Missing: A Family Survival Guide* booklet on the table. The National Center for Missing and Exploited Children had likely sent a representative. "Is the guide helpful?"

"I guess as much as it can be. The reps are very supportive. They called us within twenty-four hours. Good people. Adam's been working with them more than I have actually."

He nodded, dreading what he had to say next. "Antonia, at this point, as part of this investigation, and this is becoming standard procedure in these kinds of cases, so don't feel offended, would you be willing to take a polygraph test?"

"A lie-detector test?"

"You and Adam. We'll keep it quiet so the press won't get all over it."

"You can't honestly think we had something to do with this."

"Me? No, I don't. This is not my idea. The department needs to rule out some things and we—"

"Those tests aren't even accurate, are they?"

"Generally, they can be. How do you think Adam will feel about it?"

"Not happy, I can tell you that."

"I know he must be feeling pretty raw today. I went back to Old Willow last night and again this morning. We did discover a few bare footprints in the cemetery. I got a couple of toe markings."

"Do the footprints match the ones you found in the front garden?"

"If I had to bet on it, I'd say they did not match. The prints in Old Willow were a bit larger, but the ground was muddy so . . ."

"So, you can't be sure. Why am I not surprised?" Antonia tilted her head toward the kitchen door. "I hear the car. It's Adam."

When he walked in, Adam's greeting to Balducci wasn't much more than a hard glance.

Antonia said, "Mike wants us to take a polygraph test."

This was not the approach Balducci had planned on using. He noted Adam's gaunt, unshaven face, the hollow eyes, and the stitches on the top of his forehead looked brutal.

Adam tossed his car keys on the countertop. "Well, Detective Balducci, aren't you just fucking clever? Amazing detective work you're doing here. My son gets hit by a car, practically in front of our house. The driver is some flaky teenager. Henry's missing for over a week now and you've got his tracks all over Hatch's cemetery. I get bashed in the head, and you think we're guilty? What the hell is wrong with you?"

Hating having to say it, Balducci did his job. "The FBI is pressing us for a polygraph test on both of you. I sure don't think you guys are guilty, but the Feds are running the national end of this investigation, and we have to cooperate. It's a matter of ruling you two out. Be at headquarters today at 1:30. Both of you. Agreed?"

* * *

Not really agreeable, the Brookes arrived at headquarters. Adam passed his test easily and walked out of the room confident as steel. Antonia's test recorded extreme anxiety on all counts. Even when the technician asked her name and address, she felt her whole body tremble. They deemed her results inconclusive and tossed the test into the file.

"That was pleasant!" Antonia remarked when they sped onto Walden Street. "My head is splitting. We need to get Laura at Josie's. Cut over to Cambridge."

"I know we need to get Laura. You don't have to tell me."

"Fine." She tried to calm down. "And why haven't you told me about the gun, Adam?"

"Because I knew you'd get crazy about it."

"You should have told me."

"You're right. I'm telling you now. Antonia, I keep a gun in our closet. It's a .38-caliber revolver. Smith and Wesson, six-shot, double-action. And it's got a light squeeze on the trigger so if you ever had to use it, you could."

"Double-action? As if I would even know what that means."

"It means, it cocks the hammer and—"

"Why do you need a gun, anyway?"

"Why does anyone need a gun? For protection. For God's sake, Antonia, you're my wife, we have two children. How could I not keep a weapon in the house?"

"Where did you learn to shoot?"

"At a shooting range, where else? So what, Antonia? So what?"

"I'll tell you so what. I don't want a gun in my house."

"I keep it in a locked box, and the bullets in the back of my dresser drawer. Are we settled on this now?"

She wanted to scream.

Adam's foot hit the gas pedal and she lurched back. He weaved crazily in and out of the traffic on Cambridge Turnpike. Antonia didn't even care at the moment; the speed felt good. Everything whizzed by, familiar scenery all blurring and vanishing from sight. Suddenly flashing lights swirled behind them. The short bleep of the police car siren drew Adam's eyes to the rearview mirror.

"Oh, Christ." Adam slammed on the brakes, pulled over to the side of the road. Adam opened the window, drummed his fingers on the steering wheel, waiting for the officer to do his walk over.

The trooper leaned toward the window. "Adam Brooke?"

Adam blinked with surprise. "Yeah? I know I was speeding."

"I didn't pull you over for speeding, Mr. Brooke, although you certainly were over the limit. Headquarters radioed the patrols in the area. There's been a sighting of your boy."

Antonia almost jumped out of her seat. "Where?"

"At the library on Main Street, but that's all the information I have. Check your cell phone. I'll escort you into town."

Something released inside Antonia's chest. She could actually breathe again. "They found him, Adam. Thank God! Hurry."

Twenty minutes later, they pulled up to the Concord Library on Main Street. In seconds they were running up the library steps through the crush of police. Chief Dan Hersey greeted them. As Adam approached, Hersey put up both hands like a stop sign.

"We're searching the building right now. Every exit has been sealed. If Henry is here, we'll find him."

"What do you mean, if?" Antonia cried out.

"Was he with anyone? Who saw him?" from Adam.

"A woman by the name of Lucy Wusang claims she saw Henry in the Children's Room. Balducci is questioning her now."

Antonia followed Hersey into the Children's Room, nearly running up ahead of him. Henry loved this library and in her mind's eye she pictured her boy sitting on the colorful carpet of the map of the world, the boot of Italy his favorite spot.

Mike Balducci sat with a tiny Asian woman in her sixties with streaky grey and black hair tied back with a floppy yellow bow.

"Are you the parents?" Lucy Wusang asked. "You poor people must be out of your minds. I saw your boy, right here."

"Did you speak to him?" Adam said.

"Are you sure it was Henry?" Antonia asked.

The woman furrowed her brow. "I'm so sorry. I've been telling the detective here that no one was around, and I didn't want to approach your little boy or scare him, so I went to the circulation desk to get help. Just across the hallway there. By the time I got back . . . I was only gone a single minute. I went back and he wasn't in the chair any more. I looked around. We all did. He must have walked out."

"Walked out by himself?" Antonia asked.

"I didn't see anybody else. Yolanda was away from her desk at the time."

"*Hola,* Antonia," Yolanda said in her Spanish accent. "I'm so sorry I wasn't here. I feel just awful, but I was in the staff room. I never saw Henry. You know I would have called immediately."

A rookie cop came up to Chief Hersey and spoke softly in his ear. Hersey balled up his fists. "Nobody leaves the building. Everybody here remains in the reading room for the time being. Have you a list of names yet?"

"Yes, sir, nineteen people here at the time. Six employees."

"Did any of them see Henry Brooke?"

"Negative."

"Get the director to get us a printout of all the cardholder transactions for today."

"Yes, sir."

Balducci stood up. "Lucy, you mentioned Henry was looking at a book?"

"Yes, he seemed very absorbed in it."

"Where's this book? Did you put anything away, Yolanda?"

"No. I came back and all of this was happening."

"Henry might have put it away himself," Antonia said. "He liked taking the books out and returning them to the shelf."

Yolanda went to the computer at the desk. "I can print out a recent list of the books he's borrowed. Would that help?"

"Lucy, how did Henry look? Was he hurt?" she said, almost afraid of the answer.

"Oh no, he seemed fine, dear, just sitting there, quietly reading." She reached over and squeezed her hand affectionately. "Your boy looked happy. I don't see how he could have walked out the main entrance without my seeing him. I was standing right in the doorway."

"Mike," Hersey said, "there's only one entrance into this room. Aside from that fire door."

Balducci walked to the far end of the room, released the emergency exit lever and pushed open the metal door.

No siren.

Yolanda released a gasp. "That siren is always turned on. I'll call Mr. Keck in maintenance."

Balducci closed and opened it again. "Get the fire chief out here."

The printer spit out a page and Balducci grabbed it. Yolanda led everyone to a low row of bookshelves. A dark blue book sat sideways on top of the others, poking out of line. Balducci removed it.

"That's *Nightdances.*" Antonia said, taking the book. "Oh my God. Henry *was* here. This is one of his favorites. It's out-of-print so we take it out regularly."

Antonia sat down, her hope restored. *He is here!*

The search continued throughout the building. An hour passed. Antonia watched Adam pace awkwardly by the windows.

An officer came by. "The library is secure, Detective. Outside crews are still searching the grounds, parking lot, and streets."

The streets? Antonia cringed. *I don't think I can stand this another minute.*

A dog dressed in a hunting vest appeared in the doorway.

"Is that Dickens?" Adam asked.

Randy Voit introduced himself. He went right to work and scented the dog with Henry's sweater. Antonia watched in awe as Dickens laid his nose down, sniffed, and immediately darted out, yelping. He headed over to the carpet map, then the chair where Lucy had seen Henry.

"He's got it," Voit said. "The kid's been right here in this chair. Let's get a trail." Voit loosened his slack on the leash.

"Hang on," Adam said and wrapped his arms around her waist. His body felt incredibly warm. "We're almost there, Annie. At least we know he's okay. That's a whole lot more than we knew yesterday."

Dickens sniffed a trail from the chair to the windows, to the carpet map, to the main entrance doors. And there the hound halted.

Voit frowned. "I'll work him outside for a while."

Another hour passed. Chief Hersey rushed in. "Voit's not getting anything outside. Looks like the only track Dickens has is right here in the Children's Room. We're going to release the people from the main reading room."

People filed out through the main lobby. A teenager wearing a Red Sox T-shirt gave Adam a thumbs up. Antonia wondered about Henry at that age: going to baseball games, graduating from high school, living in a college dorm, getting married. Her daydream vanished when she spotted the last person to leave the reading room. The old man wore a black beret over his long grey hair and walked slowly with a duck-headed cane.

"Elias."

He averted his eyes and exited the building.

* * *

At police headquarters, Balducci wanted to smash something. For the second time, Elias Hatch walked out of the stationhouse. Three hours of questioning the cemetery keeper had produced not a single lead. Elias Hatch spent many afternoons at the library. Had he seen Henry there today? No. Had he entered the Children's Room? No. The conversation went from nowhere to nowhere. Balducci wanted to reach across the table and choke him.

Dan Hersey gave Balducci a pat on the back. "Take it easy. Start fresh tomorrow."

"Where the hell is this kid, Dan? The boy was sitting right there in the library. And there's Hatch, same place, same time, within an arm's reach of Henry." He enjoyed a momentary vision of hurling his ugly metal desk lamp right out the window. Instead, he sat down with a thud into his chair

"Keep focused on Hatch. Something will turn up," Dan added with a shrug.

"Give me a motive, Dan. Why would Hatch want the boy?"

"Maybe it's not a motive in the classic sense."

"Hatch is so guarded, so damned elusive. I want to do another search. I want to tear that cottage apart."

"We did that. And, besides, Dickens didn't get a single trail inside the cottage. And that hound has got the boy's scent, we know that."

"There's something else. There's another lead here somewhere."

"Which is what?"

"Whatever Hatch is hiding." Balducci tossed a crumpled-up paper into the wastebasket. "This case is like writing with a black pen on black paper. I can't see it, but it's right there in front of me. I know it is. What am I missing, Dan?"

Dan gave a snort. "The evidence. You're missing the evidence."

Every day Balducci went over the details. He'd never had a case with so many dead ends. What especially haunted his sleepless nights was Adam's insistence that he'd heard Henry's voice counting to twenty-four in the cemetery. And Henry laughing in the backyard tree. Was Adam cracking under the stress? Was this little family projecting the boy's voice purely from desire? Or was this a clue to something else?

He tapped his pen on the desk, letting the rhythm soothe him. If enough of the *arc of truth* is established by fact, intellect, and reason, then intuition would have to complete *the circle* in order to accomplish the task—Emerson's *circular character* of human action. *Every end is a beginning.*

The following day, Balducci let his intuition take the dead ends to task. Working backwards from the most recent event, in the library Children's Room, he walked between the bookshelves, sat near the chair Henry had sat, let the daylight and the sounds penetrate. When he tested the fire door, the alarm startled everyone, even though Yolanda had announced the test over the PA system. Had someone disabled the alarm that day? Log sheets showed the door alarm had a spotty history of malfunction. Maybe it just malfunctioned again.

On Eastwick Road, curbside, near that sewer grate where they found Henry's cap, he focused on that spot for a long time. No new insights surfaced.

In the Brooke's backyard, that weeping willow tree was sprouting leaves now. Balducci stood beneath it, looking up, imagining a child's laughter. What was that old Anderson fable, *Under the Willow Tree*? He remembered the story from when he was a boy. Something about a willow-father and a gingerbread maiden. *Stay focused. Don't get distracted.* But this momentary distraction confirmed that if memories surfaced so easily, his instincts were heightening. Intuitive energy flows from subconscious to conscious. A familiar tingling penetrated his skin; the arc of the circle was tightening. He walked the yard to the linden trees where the lowering sun made the pieces of sky collect into strings. *Let go and let nature guide me.*

Walking the cow path, he spotted a bunch of wild hares. Manic squirrels chased each other up and down trees. From the woods beyond, he caught a sound. Rustling? No, it was more like raindrops tapping pond water. Yet no rain fell. Near the pine grove, a thatch of holly bushes ruffled with a sudden breeze that drenched him in a fragrance: fresh, clean, an edge of sweetness. A familiar scent. Peonies? Maddy loved peonies. She couldn't live in a house without flowers, and peonies were frequent visitors. But peonies didn't bloom until June. This wasn't peonies. This was sweeter.

The aroma grew stronger, and he followed the scent deeper into the pine grove. The evergreens seemed to float with slow shafts of light—pale sea green, a dusty evanescence rolling through the branches. And then as quickly as he blinked, the radiance vanished with the sun's dip.

Balducci made a complete circle, searching the evergreens and the distant elms. And there was that watery tapping again, louder now and more distinct.

With a few steps forward, each one silent and cautious, he let the pine needles touch his shoulders. Eyes wide, alert, he focused his conscious thought on each tree as he passed. There was a path here, narrow and winding. He followed it until he reached a small clearing. Twilight descended. He turned to view the grove of evergreens. The massive pines struck him. But it wasn't so much the trees but the spaces between the evergreens. Something odd. A dark form.

A shadow of a tall robed woman faded from his sight.

He plunged into the thicket of evergreens, scanning the branches, running from tree to tree, eyes fixed to locate the robed woman.

He stopped. Darkness surrounding, all sounds vanishing.

Is this an illusion? Or is the fact of the illusion the lead?

He thought again.

What is speaking here?

Book Two

Green April

The motive of science was the extension of man
on all sides, into nature till his hands
should touch the stars,
his eyes see through the earth,
his ears understand the language of the beast
and bird and the sense of the wind . . .
heaven and earth should talk with him.

Ralph Waldo Emerson,
The Conduct of Life, Beauty, 1876

Interlude

Ancient Rome A.D. 327

Sunlight rose. Darkness thinned. Helena awoke with a familiar trembling. Each day, the light faded a little more from her eyes. Strength drained away like water. All her bones felt racked. Her lips, dry and cracked, parted to take in a breath. Waiting for the Shepherd of Death to end her days, she found tears to be her daily bread.

With her crabbed hand, she crossed herself. Prayer was the gift. Her weary heart quickened with a stabbing pain in her chest, but she opened her salutation of the day. "Lord, your law is in my heart. Grant me your tender care today."

From afar, she could hear a single voice singing splendid alleluias. She often heard these little praises drift in at dawn. But this morning the soprano grew into a chorus as if from silvered throats. Quickly she found her way to her writing desk at the window, vision blurred, one foot dragging across the stone floor.

Struggling to see, she wrote down each word of the hymn in her journal made of loose sheets of parchment. . . . *a spangled heaven lies . . . swimming polished skies.*

Helena lifted her eyes from the page. Inside the white sunlight, she saw twelve angels frosted like frozen glass. They sang a streaming rhapsody. Had she the strength, she might have waltzed around the room with arms swaying. Instead, she sat back and let the sonata take her away.

Then suddenly, by the wave of a gentle hand from above, her eyes burst, her ears thundered, her body gave a great heave. "Ah, at last, so this is death?" She asked the Christ to take her. "Rescue me," she prayed.

No rescue came. The universe opened up with bright cold stars. With beating tambourines spiraling in her head, Helena observed the celestial earth before her. The angels sang their hymn with flutes of light, sailing strings, and horns muscular with brio.

A dozen crystal spheres floated down over the blue and green planet like a shower watering the earth. The angels dropped their spheres into the rich wet soil, hid them under the clearest rivers, buried them in the darkest of caves or beneath the rocky mountains.

The morning sun splashed through the window, washing Helena's face with light. The woman lifted her goose quill, dipped it into the inkpot, and with a feverish passion wrote down her vision of the twelve crystal angels.

Chapter Ten

As the days passed, the Brooke household turned fishbone bare. Routines resumed. Adam drove to work in Boston. Laura got off to school in her usual way. Antonia slipped back under the bedcovers. Most days she spent reading poetry for hours, darting from verse to verse as if she were a heat-maddened fly on the page.

She opened the bookshop late nearly every day. On Main Street, at the Brooke Bookshop, Antonia had designed a Van Gogh tea room to attract customers to settle in and read. Colorful prints of the artist's most famous paintings of sunflowers, blue irises, and wheat fields hung from the vaulted ceiling at the front of the shop. Dutch-blue club chairs and a cupboard filled with ceramic tea cups and boxes of flavored teas became a popular spot for many in town.

Ordinarily her regular customers would stream in to browse and chat. But today, the torrents of rain would keep many at home. With a hundred things to do in the back office—cartons to unpack, books to log in and price and shelve, emails to answer—Antonia let it all fall from her mind to watch the rain-pocked sidewalks. The water swirled over the curb and she let her eyes follow the dizzying spins. She poured herself a cup of wild blackberry tea and curled up to watch the traffic crawl through the village. Rain pummeled the roof as if it were beating into her brain.

The tea turned cold and bitter and she tossed it out. Finally, at two o'clock, Josie arrived and Antonia left to pick up Laura at school.

* * *

For Adam, work was a daily trial. He went numb at meetings, stalled the agendas, failed to complete his projects. On Friday, with the rain unrelenting, his thoughts unable to endure the phones and chatter another second, he walked out of the office without a word to anyone—just wanted to disappear. The commute to Concord went faster than usual; he hardly remembered even driving the highway. When he walked through the front door, the house felt damp and too quiet: dishes piled in the sink, toast crumbs on the table, trash overflowing.

Rain knocked on the windows. Big mean drops slid down the glass, which made the willow tree look like it was truly weeping. Antonia would be home any second with Laura. He waited in the empty chill.

When Laura came in, she threw herself with abandon at him. Antonia, her face and hair misted with rain, slapped wet bags of groceries on the kitchen counter and began unpacking them.

"Didn't expect you home so early." She tossed veggies and milk into the fridge.

He put the sugar, salt, and coffee in the pantry, which was remarkably bare. It was about time she restocked it. "Can't keep my mind on anything." He reached for a kiss. She turned to unload another bag.

"Can you empty that trash, Adam? I forgot this morning."

He stood in the center of the kitchen, shirtsleeves rolled up, watching her stack cans and boxes on the shelf. She folded the bags hurriedly, then moved to the desk alcove and turned on the computer.

"I thought you might be baking bread today," he said.

Her eyes remained fixed on the screen. "I'm out of flour."

"Oh." He noticed half a bag at the back of the pantry. "Out of flour. Yeah, I get it," he mumbled and emptied the trash. Upstairs, as he passed Laura's room he poked his head in and scanned the crumpled sweaters and shoes strewn on the floor. "Laura, when are you going to clean up your room?"

"Tomorrow," she said, head down at her desk piled with scraps of newspapers and a dish of something that had dried into weird lumps.

"How about today?" He grabbed a handful of hangers. "Here, start by putting your clothes away. What are all those newspapers cut up like that for?"

She scooped up some clothes from the floor and dumped them into a giant mound on the bed. "Funny papers for Henry's scrapbook. When he comes home, I can read him the ones he's missed."

Leafing through the scrapbook pages, Adam saw that she had indeed pasted every day's *Peanuts* strip.

"This is an awfully big job," she said, kicking a decapitated Barbie's head away with her toe.

"I'll hang the clothes. You pick up all those crayons and markers, and what's this dish? Since when do you eat in your bedroom?"

"I didn't do it. Grandma gave me ice cream in bed when she was here."

"This dish has been here for how many weeks?"

She grimaced, then giggled behind her hands. "Didn't she give you ice cream in bed when you were a little boy?"

"Never." He hung up the sweaters on the closet bar and accidentally knocked a shoebox from the shelf. Little bits of colored paper came spilling out.

Laura ran over. "Ohhh. I'll get them. You just keep hanging up the sweaters. And the socks go in the top drawer. And my tights in the bottom."

"Man, you're bossy." He hid a smile as she frantically swept the pieces back into the box with her hand. "What is all that?"

"Nothing." She quickly placed the top on. "It's a junk box. Mommy said I can have a junk box."

"What's in it?"

"What do you think? Junk!"

"Can I see it?

Her eyes widened. "Umm, it's secret junk. Mommy said it's okay."

"Did she?" Adam took the box from her hands. "Why is there an H written on the box? Shouldn't there be an L if it's your secret box?"

"Oh, Daddy, I'm not supposed to tell. You keep secrets, right?"

"Is this Henry's secret box?" He opened the box and examined the pieces of crayon-colored paper. "Who tore this up?"

Laura looked away.

"Laura, answer me."

"Oh, okay. I did."

"Why? What was it?"

"Just a picture I drew for Henry and tore it up."

"A picture of what?"

"It's Henry's secret. I promised I wouldn't tell."

"Fine. Finish cleaning up and don't come down until it's done." He brought the box into the kitchen and dumped the pieces on the table.

"Your daughter is cleaning her room. Have you seen this box?" He spread out the ripped pieces of paper, turning each one colored side up.

Antonia pulled her eyes away from the computer screen. "Henry's secret box? What about it?"

"Laura had it in her room. She drew a picture for him, then tore it up."

Adam began putting the pieces together. Antonia joined him in matching the long patches of blue. She paired up bunches of yellow wavy hair around a smiling face. He found gold triangles and placed them around each eye.

"Hm," Antonia said. "The eyes are little star bursts. And look at these fingers. Laura's so good at drawing detail. What a lovely long blue cape."

They placed the last few pieces into the picture.

"You weren't supposed to do that," Laura said from the kitchen doorway.

"Who is this?" Antonia asked.

"A lady," Laura said.

"What lady? From where?"

"Don't know."

"Where did you meet her?"

"I didn't. Henry told me what she looked like. He asked me to draw it. I think the lady is make-believe."

"Like his dog Lucky that he feeds under the table?" Adam asked.

"Uh-huh." Laura folded her arms across her chest. "And that stupid dog can't eat Cheerios."

Adam was fully aware how Henry guarded his imaginary playmates. And how Laura liked to tease him that they were not real and couldn't eat Cheerios. At such a statement, Henry went wild, punching his sister, the argument ending with Henry screaming and kicking, and Laura in tears.

"Laura, where did Henry meet this lady?" Adam asked.

"I don't know. The lady made Henry promise not to tell."

Antonia gasped. "None of his make-believe people ever said that."

"Laura, if you know something about this lady, you need to tell us."

"Why?"

"Because this lady . . . she might know where Henry is. What did Henry tell you about her?"

"I promised I wouldn't tell."

Adam put his head back, summoned patience.

"Sometimes," Antonia said, "it's okay to break a promise, because sometimes it's more important to tell the truth. You want to help the police find Henry, right?"

"Uh-huh. But, Mom, the lady is make-believe."

"Maybe she's not," Adam said. "The police can find out. We need you to help us, Laura."

She observed her father for a moment.

"Laura, Henry would want you to tell us because he wants to come home."

"Do you know the lady's name?" Antonia asked.

"Henry said she didn't have a name."

"No name? What did Henry call her?"

"Cat. But that wasn't her real name."

"Laura," Adam said, "Why did you rip up the picture?"

"Because . . . because the lady was going to do magic."

"What kind of magic?"

"Henry said, rip up her picture, and the lady will put it back together. No glue. No tape."

"Was she going to come into the house to do the magic?"

"Don't know."

"Did Henry say where she lives?"

She rolled her eyes. "In the silly trees."

Adam sighed.

"I told you, Dad, the lady is make-believe."

"Which trees? Where?" Antonia asked.

"Don't know."

Adam got on the phone with Mike Balducci; within minutes the detective walked through the door to see this picture of the lady who lives in the trees. They taped the pieces of the drawing together and Adam gave it to Balducci in a grey envelope. As he headed out the door, Laura ran after Mike.

"You can't take that. Daddy, don't let him take the picture away."

"Laura, stop." Adam pulled her back as she began screaming. "Stop it. He has to take the picture to the police station. I'm sorry, Mike." He had Laura in a bear hug, keeping her wrists under his hands, but it didn't stop her kicking.

"I promised Henry! Give it to me."

Balducci turned to Adam. "I've got everything I need in my notes. Here, take it. I'll put out an APB on her description and get the wheels turning."

Five minutes later, Adam found Laura in her room, cutting up the picture again. She put the pieces back inside Henry's shoebox and climbed on the stool to return it to the shelf.

"A promise is a promise. You said so."

* * *

Sunday morning broke with more cruel rain. Adam slept with the covers over his head. He felt a tap on his shoulders and peeked open an eye.

"What is this?" Laura called out. "You're still in bed?" She fumbled with the sash of her purple-tulip printed dress, all crooked on her shoulders, her cork-screwy hair all over the place. "It's Easter Sunday. Aren't we going to mass?"

Adam cringed. Of course Laura expected the family to be at mass on Easter. Antonia hadn't been going to Sunday mass, so no one went. Even Laura accepted that her mom didn't feel well these days, so it was okay to skip mass for a while.

Antonia surfaced from beneath the pillows as if drowned in her sleep.

"Mommy, aren't we going to Easter mass?"

She sat up like a shot. "What?"

"You said Easter Sunday was your favorite."

Adam saw tears welling in Laura's eyes.

"What about the Easter story?" Laura said.

Antonia said nothing.

"You mean the gospel?" Adam corrected her.

"Yeah. Mom! You know the part with Mary and the angels. You love that part. Don't you want to hear that story again? Why aren't we going?"

"We're going." Adam slipped out of bed. "We just overslept, honey, that's all." He headed for the bathroom, then stopped when he saw Antonia fall back into bed.

"Daddy will take you, sweetie." She rolled over.

Laura shook her mother. "You can't stay mad at God forever. Oh please, Mommy, come on, you don't want to miss it, do you?"

At St. Therese of the Roses Church, parishioners packed the pews: little girls in straw bonnets, young boys in pinching neckties, babies whimpering. When they all stood to hear the gospel, Laura tugged at her mother, then reached for Adam's hand. He squeezed it. She was absolutely glowing through every word that Father Blaze read—much to Adam's impatience— slower than usual.

Adam sat stiffly in the pew, half listening to Blaze's homily about Christ's pattern for resurrection for all who choose it. The "fruit of the grave," he kept repeating. Having no formal religion, Adam had converted to Catholicism only because Antonia was so steeped in it from childhood and some of her enthusiasm literally rubbed off on him. The white of the lilies on the altar faded away as he drifted to images of his wedding day inside the Umbrian village church, kneeling next to this woman flowing in miles of white veils. They had vowed to each other, not *until death do us part,* but, *to be together from eternity to eternity*—because for Antonia, the forevermore was that dreamy mysterious other side belonging to both God and man. She would talk about it, write poems about eternal life, sometimes shed a tear about it. Adam had no idea how to grasp the timelessness of no beginning and no end. But he often envied her fidelity in trying to understand it.

He looked over to his wife, her solemn face, hands splayed on her lap, eyes staring blankly ahead. When the congregation walked up the aisle to receive communion, Adam and Laura rose to join them. Antonia remained alone in the pew.

* * *

After mass, when Adam drove the car into the driveway, Antonia saw a single potted Easter lily left on their front step. She placed it near the kitchen window and read the note.

> My Dearest Antonia:
> My prayers are with you for a Blessed Easter.
> Anytime you need, call me day or night.
> Your friend in Christ, Father Jim

Inside the envelope was a holy card of St. Helena of the Cross, a glossy print of a stately woman holding a full-size wooden cross. Antonia went to her Bible, opened to a random page, placed the holy card inside, and began preparing their holiday meal. During dinner, she noticed that Adam ate little of her roasted lamb with lemon and olives. He pushed the crisp potatoes around his plate. Later he fell asleep in the armchair with a book unopened on his lap. Even Laura took little pleasure in her Easter basket. One by one, she put the chocolate eggs and marshmallow chickens into Henry's basket that sat expectantly by the window.

At least the rain stopped and sun broke the clouds. Laura came into the kitchen.

"Mom? I'm going to sit on the front steps. Okay?"

"Kind of wet out there." She paused from loading dishes into the dishwasher.

"Looks dry to me."

* * *

Laura scooped up a few chocolate eggs and dashed outside to sit on the front step. In

the side hedges, the greenery shook. With a quick look back to the opened front door—her mom still busy in the kitchen—she walked to the hedges.

"Hi," she said to the girl with the long braids. The girl's face lit up and she motioned for Laura to enter between the hedges. They snuggled together behind the greenery wall. "This is a great place to hide. What's your name? Mine's Laura."

"Emily."

"I have a friend at school named Emily. She pronounces it Emileee. How old are you? I'm eight."

"Eleven. You didn't feed the birds today, Laura. You should feed them when the sun comes up. That's when they are most hungry."

"Okay. Do you like our hedges? Henry likes to hide here too."

"I love secret hiding places," Emily whispered. "I have lots."

"I have a great place to hide in the back of my closet. It's called the eaves. The ceiling comes down really low. You can hide in my eaves any time you want." Laura gave her a handful of candy.

"What are these?"

"Chocolate Easter eggs. Where do you live, Emily? I'll come to your house sometime."

"You can't. I stay in the passage." She unwrapped a chocolate and popped it into her mouth.

"What's the passage?"

Emily shrugged.

"Is it like my house? Does it have a roof and big rooms?

"No."

"Where is it?"

"I can't tell you."

"Can you show me the passage?"

"I better not."

Laura moved in closer to Emily's face and whispered, "Is it a secret hiding place?"

Emily let out a giggle.

"I'm the best at keeping secrets. Henry has secrets and I keep them all the time. If you show me the passage, I promise never ever to tell, not in a million years."

"Not now. I have to go." Emily slipped out of the hedges.

"When will you come back? I'll show you the eaves in my room."

"When you feed the birds." Emily crept down low by the house windows, then trotted off to the linden trees.

Chapter Eleven

MORNING ROOKS CROAKED in the leafy elms. *Cage the minute.* Antonia scribbled the phrase into her notebook, then tossed the notebook aside. Why bother? She couldn't write more than three words these days. She glanced at the clock—just after nine. The warm sun drew her outside to the bench on the flagstone patio. She closed her eyes, sun on her cheeks, and imagined Henry running across the back lawn. There he was, those button-eyes, his brown curls bouncing in the breeze, a playful grin as he came closer. She indulged in the sudden pleasure of his warm body, those plump arms hugging her. She could actually smell the sugary scent of him.

A rustling noise gave her a start; she opened her eyes. At the side hedges, a stag emerged. Henry's stag. She stifled a gasp. Such unwavering grace. *Cage the minute,* indeed. She rose silently from the bench. He retreated a step, stared back at her almost comically, those antlers like a lopsided crown.

The stag pranced over the grassy mound, stopped, and let out a deep throaty call. He trotted out. Antonia dashed after him beyond the linden trees and oaks and over rock walls. Breathlessly, she navigated the terrain, her sneakers slipping on the moist ground. Thankfully he stopped to nibble some greenery where she could catch her breath.

He quickly darted out again, this time leading her deeper into the forest. How many times had she chased after Henry like this? The minute he learned to run, the child raced everywhere nearly as fast as any deer.

Unfamiliar with where she was exactly, it took her a few minutes to realize that she was on the far side of the Hatch property. In the distance, she spotted the backside of his cobblestone house. The stag paused, then galloped away.

Rows of split logs filled the lean-to style shed, twenty feet or so away. She decided to take a closer look and stepped inside: brick floor, a scatter of rusty tools, and a perfectly straight row of purple-foiled Hershey's chocolate kisses on a ledge. She almost laughed.

"Good morning."

Antonia spun around.

Elias Hatch walked toward her, his grey hair spread out over his shoulders in dry lifeless strings.

"Oh, Elias. You startled me." How best to explain her snooping on his property? "I was out walking this morning and I . . . lost my way. I couldn't resist following that gorgeous stag. Lord, I was relieved to see your house." She gave a little laugh.

"Oh, you mean White Beauty? He likes to feed on the holly bushes here."

"White Beauty?"

"That's what we call him. Deer are territorial, you know. He's here all the time."

Antonia nodded, trying to hide her surprise. Henry had called the stag White Beauty on Christmas day. And who did Elias mean by *we?*

"I don't allow any trespassers. Of course you know that. You know your way back?" he said with a frown.

"I do now. Sorry, Elias, I didn't realize where the property lines were. What a wonderful shed you have here." She decided to feign interest. "Adam and I have been talking about buying a cord of wood for next winter and building a shed for it. Yours looks quite sturdy. Did you build it yourself? Quite a good job."

"I did. Decades ago."

She gently patted the post of the shed while an uncomfortable pause hung between them. "You know, I recall Henry called that stag White Beauty. You must have told him the name?"

His blank stare was unsettling. Almost as if he didn't hear her. "Elias, you know what? I'd really like to take a walk through your cemetery. Would you be so kind as to let me?"

"What for? The police have searched it several times. Detective Balducci too. Adam's been through it with Sergeant Riley."

"That's exactly the point, isn't it? Everyone but me."

"My dear Antonia, believe me when I tell you, I do wish with all my heart that they find Henry. But I can assure you, he is not inside Old Willow."

"I don't want your assurances." She marched up to him and stood close enough to smell his musty flannel shirt. "Everyone has been inside your cemetery, including my boy. I'm Henry's mother. Don't exclude me, Elias."

Something softened in his expression. The black piercing eyes didn't bore into her just then. "It's not my intention to exclude you, Antonia. It just seems pointless."

"Not to me. What if it were your mother looking for you? Would you want your mother denied the opportunity to see for herself?"

A thoughtful smile emerged. "Is that what you want?"

"I want to see for myself where my son has been. You can understand that, can't you?"

Now he gave a small laugh. "I suppose my mother would stop at nothing, just as you won't. I can almost hear her urging me to say yes. All right then. You are a delight, Antonia. You shall have the nickel tour."

At the cottage, Antonia stepped in while Elias fetched his keys in the kitchen. Dust motes flew everywhere. She noticed a medieval-styled skeletal model of the earth sitting on his coffee table.

"My father has a metal armillary sphere like this in his study on our farm." She touched the metal with her pinky, just like her father had taught her. "When I was little, the north and south poles fascinated me, the lines of force running between them."

Elias fumbled in the kitchen drawer for the keys. "Ahhh, yes, the earth's magnetosphere. That piece belonged to my grandmother Sophie. Does your father still live in Umbria? What's his name?"

"He's in Rome. Paolo Scarlatta."

"He must be very proud of you. Here you are a successful bookshop owner in America, married, with such a lovely family."

Was he proud? Her father had been too ill to walk her down

the church aisle on her wedding day. *Daisies in my brain* was how he described his illness.

"Here we are." Elias jangled the keys. "Just give me a minute to get my sweater."

Antonia waited outside on the porch near a homemade pinecone urn filled to the brim with sparkling stones. She was half tempted to scoop up a handful. *Henry would love to dive his little hands into this urn. Maybe he did.*

Elias came out and unlocked the cemetery iron gates. They walked in side by side. "You've come just in time to see the lilacs blooming. We have quite a large arbor."

"Who do you mean, *we?*"

Elias grinned with a shy roll of his eyes. "I'm a silly old man, Antonia. I've lived alone most of my life. But when I'm here with all the magnificent trees and friendly birds, I never feel quite so solitary. My parents are buried right over there," he pointed, "and my grandparents and great-grandparents. Ah, there are my lilacs up ahead."

Thick bunches in purples, lavenders, and whites created a lacy skyline. A flock of birds floated down among the blossoms like tinkling chimes.

"Are those bluebirds?"

"A rare breed. They come every spring when the lilacs bloom."

The weeping willow trees hovered over the perimeter of the rock walls. "What a spectacular border. Great design, whoever planted them."

"No one planted the willows. That's the genius of nature, to create its own design."

They walked on quietly as Antonia read some of the names on the headstones.

"Anybody famous buried here, Elias?"

"Oh, no. This isn't like Sleepy Hollow on Bedford Street. Let's take that path to the left. I have a bed of early red tulips that are fully bloomed. So, how is your poetry coming along?"

"I'm sorry?" Antonia wondered what he could know of her poetry.

"Didn't you tell me you wrote poetry? On the day we met, back in August?"

Antonia was certain she hadn't told him about her poetry. Most of their exchanges were confined to the weather and such. "I don't think I mentioned it."

"Maybe it was Adam. Yes, we were chatting on the day you moved in. He mentioned that you spend a lot of quiet time, much of it writing poetry. He called you his Emily Dickinson."

"Adam might have compared me to Dickinson."

"My favorite is Walt Whitman. How long have you been writing, Antonia?"

"Since I was a child. I'm always running lines over in my head. I'm a little obsessed by it, I suppose."

"Adam said you recite poetry like an angel. He seemed quite proud."

"He enjoys it when I toss him a line or two. Anything more dense than that overwhelms him."

"Might you throw me a line or two? Maybe something from Emily Dickinson?"

The dogwoods' pink and white flowers filled her vision. Below them sat banks of white baby's breath. The lines came up easily. "'Each that we lose takes part of us; a crescent still abides, which like the moon, some turbid night, is summoned by the tides.'"

"Lovely. You were thinking of your little boy, just then?"

She stopped, faced him squarely. "How could you possibly know what I was thinking?"

"It's just a matter of perception. I like to think of thoughts as a weave over the body. If one focuses on that weave, on the vibration there, one can get a direct sense of the thought."

"Is that so? What am I thinking right now?" She felt his gaze on her like a dark shadow.

"You want to know about Henry . . . if he's ever taken a fistful of mica stones from my porch urn."

She blinked. "Has he?"

"Not to my knowledge."

They continued walking past a row of Irish crosses and through an archway of stone doves.

"Shall we rest here?" Elias sat down on the stone bench. He seemed completely out of breath.

Antonia admired the clusters of birch trees. Not far off was a grey marble statue towering above all the others. "So, this must be the famous Weeping Woman of Old Willow?"

Leafy red maple trees arched over the statue of the hooded woman. Behind her were three little round headstones barely above the earth. So tiny.

"Her children," Elias said.

"What?"

"You were looking at the babies' headstones? The boy died of scarlet fever, the other two . . . I don't remember now."

Antonia tried to read the carved letters beneath the moss that covered the top of the base of the statue.

"The sculptor was Mary Ann Delafield DuBois," Elias said. "She did portraits, too, at the time. I think she did a fine job with this piece. Studied in Paris, they said."

"They?"

"My grandparents. They had commissioned a good deal of the sculptures here. My grandmother Sophie did some sculpting herself."

"I love the rough crystals on the base." Antonia walked around the statue, examining the heavy folds of the cape that draped to the toes. The hood hung in folds around the face. And the hands were expertly carved with delicate fingernails, tiny humped knuckles, lovely veins. She pushed the ivy vines back to see the inscription.

"What's the name on her stone? I can't read it."

"Javouhey. Died 1889."

"*E-n-p-e-u.*" With her fingernail, she scraped enough of the moss to see the remaining letters, then stood back and read the epitaph. "*En peu d'heure Dieu labeure.* 'God works in moments.'"

"You know French."

"I'm quite rusty by now. My mother was a translator. She spoke four languages, completely self-taught. Javouhey, huh?" Antonia stepped on the base of the statue, searching for the eyes under the hood. Beneath the carved folds were partial formations of a slender nose, full parted lips, and eyes cast down with heavy lids. "The Weeping Woman of Old Willow. Have you ever seen her weep, Elias?"

"Of course not. It's a stone."

She examined the eyelids closely, which looked oddly puffy and just a bit wet.

To get the full view, she stepped back, hands on her hips. "So! What's your story, Mrs. Javouhey? Let me see your tears. Why do you weep?"

"Like you, I cry for my lost child."

Antonia turned to the voice behind her.

A tall woman draped in a long blue cape made three steps forward with feline grace. Blond wisps of hair swept out like clusters of feathers from the blue hood. She flashed great tear-trembling eyes fringed with heavy lashes, the irises star-flecked with copper colors. Her complexion looked so delicate, like parchment paper.

A sudden sweetness filled the air. Antonia inhaled it, almost to the point of feeling dizzy. "I know you. You're Cat? Henry's Cat?"

"Catherine Javouhey. Yes, that's what Henry calls me." She turned to Elias sitting on the bench. "Good morning, my dear Misstaahh Hatch. I'm quite pleased to see you again."

Elias raised his eyes, slightly dazed by her.

"Oh, don't look so glum. What is the trouble today? Shall I call up the flowers for you again?"

Instantly green stalks sprouted in the grass at the headstones, and then more popped up randomly over the grassy patches until they dotted most of the cemetery. Tiny white bells appeared out of each stalk. Antonia blinked, unsure she could believe what she was seeing.

The woman bent down, plucked a few flowers, then brushed the white velvety bells against Antonia's cheek.

"The dead are just as tender." Catherine took Antonia's hands and placed the flowers inside her palms.

Cat's touch jolted Antonia. The fleshy hands felt like hot milk spilled across her palms.

"These white bells look exactly like baby teeth, don't you think? What a pity that flowers cannot speak. You know, Antonia, Henry does not like to see you so sad. Rest your eyes on this lily of the valley and know that he is just as perfect."

Without a look back, Catherine walked down the hill.

"Wait! You know where Henry is?"

The woman stopped. "Henry is safe. Hasn't Mr. Hatch told you? You must tell her, my friend, about our dear Henry. The time is ripe to let the fruit fall."

"Tell me what? Where is my son!"

The wind ran fingers through Catherine's long blond hair as the hood dropped. "There is nothing to fear. I've come to tell you, Henry is safe with me. Please know, we did not let the child go cold in his own dead salt."

Catherine turned and glided down the curving hill.

Antonia charged after her. She ran the hill and paths, past the ivy bed and elms and maples, and there she stopped. The flock of bluebirds soared outward in the air above the lilacs.

"Catherine!" She couldn't have just disappeared. This was no ghost. She was flesh and bone. She was warm. "Catherine! I know you're here. Where is Henry? Please!"

A sudden breeze made chilly wreaths around Antonia's legs and riffled the feathers of the starlings that had gathered at her feet. Far away she could hear the rhythmic slapping of oars on water.

Chapter Twelve

BALDUCCI GOT THE CALL. In minutes he alerted his chief, put everybody in motion, gave his instructions, and zoomed out of headquarters. His car couldn't go fast enough to Old Willow Cemetery. Half a dozen uniformed cops got there with him and spread out to search the property. With both feet planted firmly on the grave site of the Catherine Javouhey, Balducci read the inscription and name on the headstone. He heard Antonia's voice call him as she came running over.

"We got it all on video," Balducci told her quickly, seeing the panic on her face. "Our surveillance camera covered about forty percent of the cemetery. My technician alerted us only a few minutes before you called me."

"Great! Your guys will find her, right? She couldn't have gone far."

"You said she identified herself as Catherine Javouhey, the name on the grave?"

"She did. Mike, I looked everywhere for her. I don't know where she disappeared to."

"We'll find her. Guess she thinks she's clever using the name of a woman who died in 1889. I've got APBs everywhere. She's not going far."

"You've got enough roadblocks to choke the whole town," Adam said breathlessly as he came up the path. "I broke through two of them speeding to get here."

"Don't think so, Rambo. I instructed them to wave you through."

"Can we see the video, Mike?" Antonia asked.

Balducci pressed play and showed them the viewer screen. After a few seconds, Antonia grabbed the camera. "Something's odd. I don't see the lilies of the valley here. I don't see that on your video."

"What lilies?"

"See these white flowers in the grass here?" She pointed. "Catherine made the lilies bloom right here. But your video didn't catch that."

Balducci picked a stem off one of the graves, took a whiff. Sweet. Familiar. He pulled up another one, this time bringing up the roots. He looked into the viewer and ran the video again. The camera angle didn't focus low on the ground. "*She* made them bloom? Say again?"

"I know it sounds weird. Hatch must have seen it too. She *called up the flowers,* is how she put it."

"*Called up the flowers?*" Adam said. "What does that mean?" Balducci shook his head. "Let's just put that event aside for the moment. I'll check it later. Right now I need to focus on where you were when you lost sight of her."

Antonia walked to the hill. "Right here and I don't know how she managed to leave the cemetery so quickly."

Balducci surveyed the grounds. "Maybe she didn't leave the cemetery." He walked a few paces to get perspective, then played the video again. "I've got her in full view on the hill where you say." He reversed the film and ran it again, this time in slow motion. "There she is in the center of the frame. There she is walking . . . down that hill . . . walking . . ." He stopped the tape on the next frame. "Gone." He ran it once more. "Damn! This perspective is too small. Hey, Louise? You got that map of Old Willow on you?"

After a few minutes of examining the map, Balducci found a glitch. "Well, here's something. That ivy patch over there is identified as grave site number twenty-four, if I'm reading this layout correctly. How come there's no headstone, if it's a designated grave site?" He paced off a few feet. "Yep, that hill, where I can't see her on the screen, is number twenty-four in that ivy patch."

"Twenty-four?" Adam said. "Twenty-four was what Henry counted to—"

"Yeah, yeah, Adam, I know. You like that number, don't you?"

It wasn't much, he admitted, but it was all he had: a conflict.

Long shot, sure, but maybe there was something here to follow. Seeking the shadow—that's what this case was all about. Balducci poked a tree branch in random places across the ivy. "Looks too steep to be a grave." *What the hell is beneath that ivy?*

"What do you think it is?" Adam asked. "Mike?"

Christ, what a pain in the ass he is.

"It's not a grave, is it? Mike?"

"I don't know what it is. Louise? Call for a crew." He turned to Adam. "Maybe you folks should wait at the house. No point in you hanging around."

"You going to dig it up, Mike? What is it?"

"It's probably nothing. Why don't you guys go home. I'll call if—"

"If it's nothing, why are you going to dig it up?"

Balducci ignored him and reverted to the map with the sharply printed twenty-four. Not another single grave in Old Willow was numbered on the map or on a gravestone. He scanned the surface of the cemetery as far as he could see and didn't see any other ivy patches. Ivy patches prevent erosion on hills. Maybe that's all it was. Most of the ivy looked tight and healthy in the soil. Except for one corner that had roots exposed and shredded leaves like an animal had clawed it up. Or someone with a sloppy hand rake. Was something freshly buried under there? *Twenty-four. Goddamn twenty-four.* His stomach lurched.

He riveted his eyes on Adam. "Take your wife home."

Adam pretty much froze in his stare. He looked back at the ivy, then at Balducci again, then grabbed Antonia's hand. "Come on." She jerked away.

"I'm not leaving."

"For Christ's sake, Annie, he's going to dig up site twenty-four, Henry's twenty-four. Let's go. I'm taking you home."

She walked over to a stone bench and sat down, clasped her hands tightly on her lap. "Catherine said she had Henry safe with her. Catherine was here in this cemetery. I'm staying. You can stay with me, or you can go home and wait and wonder what's going on."

Balducci saw Adam exhale a surrendering breath. If that were his wife, he'd have hauled Maddy out, kicking and screaming, but out she would go.

"We'll wait over here, Mike," Adam said and sat down.

A crew arrived within minutes, carrying shovels and sledgehammers. They tore up the ivy, the vines with worms and bugs in mossy clumps. The men sweated through their clothes. Evidence Officer Pam Peterson arrived and snapped a few pictures. Soon enough, the shovels hit against something solid. Flinging shovelful after shovelful, they exposed wooden planks. The banging was deafening as they pried open what appeared to be double doors. Instantly, foul air emerged. They turned away, coughing.

"Take a break. Let it air out," Balducci said.

Chief Hersey arrived, his boots making fast tracks over the graves. "What have you got here? Is it a tunnel, maybe?" He glanced at the dark smelly opening. "Oh, man. Who you taking with you down that shithole?"

"I'll take Miguel," Balducci said.

With his handkerchief to his nose and waving his high-powered flashlight, the detective led Officer Miguel Aquellas down the steps. He made sure each footing held on the loose quarry stones.

"You think there are bats down here, Mike?" Miguel asked from behind his handkerchief.

"Nope. Light scares them off. Ever done this kind of investigating before, Miguel?"

"No, sir. Only been on the force two years."

"Not exactly in the manual, huh?" Balducci landed on a brick and dirt floor. "Looks like some kind of root cellar."

They flooded the interior with their flashlights. Both men had to crouch under the low ceiling that had been reinforced with wooden beams dripping with spider webs. Fuzzy bugs crawled on the rock ledges. A series of holes had been dug out on two of the walls.

Balducci spotted a barrel in the corner and a makeshift table covered with what appeared to be a layer of dirt and mold. He ran his gloved hand across the table, then moved on to the lidless barrel. Mushroom-like barnacles caked the rim. He aimed his cone of light down to the bottom.

"Miguel?" he could feel the man literally breathing down his neck.

"Yeah?"

"Want to step back, inspect the left wall there? I'll do the right side."

"Yes, sir."

Balducci examined each hole, some caved in, others shallow. He aimed the light into one small cave. "Miguel, get Peterson down here."

Miguel gave a yell to Peterson and looked over Mike's shoulder. "Man, that's the biggest ball of cobwebs I ever saw. What are those two black holes inside it?" He flooded the cave with white light. "Holy shit, man, that thing's got eyes. It's lookin' at us."

Pam Peterson came down the steps wearing a mouth and nose mask tied on around her blond hair. She pulled it off.

"Not so bad, huh?"

"Not once you get used to it," Mike said. "Take a look."

The evidence officer peeked inside the dirt cave, jabbed the cobwebs with a small instrument, then snapped a photo.

"I can't tell what it is until I get it out of there." With plastic-gloved hands she reached into the hole and gently wrapped her fingers around it. "Damn, it's solid. Got the bag opened for me, Miguel?" She withdrew the object. Sniffed. "Looks like solid mold on rock." She placed it inside the bag and then into the evidence box with a thud. When she lifted her hands, she wiggled her fingers. "Feels weird. My fingers are tingling. You want a preliminary lab report? Soil samples too?"

"Soon as you can, please. Call me."

Balducci, Miguel, and Peterson emerged from the root cellar.

Hersey came running. "Anything?"

"Nothing I can identify immediately," Peterson said.

Balducci saw Adam approach. The detective quickly leaned over to whisper to Hersey. "I need you to follow up with Brady. Where's Hatch?"

"He's saying his prayers. Just what we thought. At St. Therese's." He peeked into the evidence box just as Peterson was closing it.

"What's in that box?" Adam asked.

"Nothing," Balducci said. "We're done here."

"You're going to arrest Hatch, right? Mike?"

"Go home. I'll call you later." Balducci waved him off and hurried out of the cemetery.

* * *

Antonia dashed out to catch Mike. "Damn, where's he going? Mike!"

Adam snagged her arm. "Wait. I've a better idea. Listen."

Antonia turned and lifted her eyes to the sky. A flock of blue jays in their bright acid-blue feathers cruised into the cemetery like a fleet of jet bombers. They zoomed over the torn-up ivy, circled the root cellar, and in a stunning formation neatly patrolled the headstones. One by one they landed, silent as their shadows, perched on the grass with pointed noses in the air, perfectly still as statues. "Those blue jays, Adam. What are they doing?"

"I don't know. Weird."

"Are they protecting something?"

"Who knows? Never mind them. Get in the car. We're going to St. Therese's."

"What? Why?"

"Because that's where Hatch is. Mike's going to arrest him, and I'm not going to miss this. Are you up to it?"

"Yes, but . . . Adam?"

"What?"

She hesitated to even say it. "I can smell Henry all over you."

Chapter Thirteen

BALDUCCI HAD EVERY AVAILABLE COP searching for the alleged Catherine Javouhey. But one thing was certain, he was going after Elias Hatch himself.

Sergeant Riley, and Adam and Antonia stood behind him on the front steps of the small colonial-style house that served as the rectory of St. Therese of the Roses. Balducci wasn't pleased to see the Brookes pull up at the rectory, but after thinking it over, he reluctantly agreed to let them tag along—not exactly according to procedure. Having the parents of a victim present had often proved effective (rattling the suspect just enough to get the truth) and with this case, he needed every advantage.

Two solid panels of sleek green lawn stretched out in front of the rectory. Mighty sparse landscaping; Balducci noted only three overgrown boxwoods and not a flower or another shrub on the entire property. One giant oak offered shade on a wooden prayer bench with worn-away dirt patches. He glanced to the street with hopes he'd see Chief Dan Hersey's car.

Father Jim Blaze answered the door dressed in jeans and western boots. Was that a twinge of panic on his face? Three police cars in front, two police officers at the church driveway, and two more heading to the back property would unnerve anybody.

"What is this about?" Blaze asked.

"May we come in?" Balducci flashed his ID.

The priest stepped aside, opening the door just wide enough for each to enter single file.

Inside, the parlor was jammed with two beige-striped sofas against crisp white walls, odd wooden chairs scattered about, and bookshelves stuffed with—what else?—lives of the saints.

Balducci moved his eyes across the room, stopping on the royal-blue carpet. It had a just-vacuumed look, all smooth with long roller marks. He noticed everyone making footprints into the room. The high-gloss cherrywood door near the front windows caught his attention. Closet? No, more likely a doorway to the kitchen or office. He set his tape recorder on the coffee table, which had a set of glass angels that looked like some leftover Christmas decoration.

"You here alone, Blaze?"

Blaze attempted a polite smile, greeted Adam and Antonia. "I know, Detective, you're looking for Elias Hatch. I can't pretend to you that he's not here." He sat on the sofa and gestured for the others to sit. "Is it really necessary to have the entire church grounds under police guard?"

"Yes, it is. Where is he? Upstairs?"

"Elias has taken refuge here at the rectory. He doesn't wish to speak with the law at the moment."

"Refuge," Balducci said. "Isn't that cozy. I'm not leaving until I speak with him. And if I have to have my officers go upstairs and haul his ass out of hiding, I will."

"Here at St. Therese's we have the authority to offer aid for anyone in need. And Elias is welcome to stay." Blaze brushed strands of brown hair off his forehead.

"Do you realize you could be charged with aiding and abetting a criminal?"

"Elias Hatch is no criminal. He's broken no laws. Detective, perhaps I can be of help. Exactly what do you want from Elias?"

Balducci glanced at his wristwatch. He was counting on Dan to show up soon. This case was going to break open right now, and the chief was going to make it happen.

"Tell me, Blaze, how long have you known Elias Hatch?"

"A few years now."

"Take his confession, do you?"

Blaze's bland expression switched to a frown. He looked thoroughly pissed off. "I take all members' confessions."

"I don't care about all members. Do you hear confession from

Elias Hatch?"

"The seal of the confessional is inviolable. And you know it."

"Yes, I do know it." Balducci strolled to the window near the oak door. The tapestry drapes were open just a sliver.

"What is it they say? 'Every sweet has its sour; every evil its good.'" He spoke softly, moving the curtain aside. No Dan yet. With a smooth slow turn, he yanked the cherrywood door open.

And there was Elias, a bit unsteady from the abrupt exposure. Dressed in black pants and a white shirt that looked too big on him, he had groomed his hair into a tail down his back. He sheepishly stepped into the room. "Well, did you hear my approach at the door, Detective?"

"No, Hatch, you left your footprints running out of here on the carpet."

"You're a regular Sherlock, aren't you? Hello, Sergeant Reilly. Adam. Antonia," he said as if they all arrived for cocktails.

"Take a seat, Hatch."

Elias took his place in the armchair, neatly crossing his ankles.

The front door of the rectory swung open, and three agents entered. Balducci kept his vision on the front hallway. Dan didn't follow them in.

"Father Blaze," one of the officers said, "we have a search warrant for the premises." He handed a document to Balducci. Two agents hit the staircase while the other began searching the first floor.

Blaze rose slowly. "Detective Balducci, I don't . . ."

"What is it, Blaze? You want to see Judge Brady's signature on the warrant?"

He sat down. "Detective, exactly what are your agents searching for?"

"The woman who claims to be Catherine Javouhey. This imposter has admitted to taking Henry Brooke, to knowing Elias Hatch, and look at Hatch here, all nice and comfy, dressed like he's going out to dinner. Blaze, have you offered the woman refuge too?"

"No one is here except Elias and me."

"I don't know what this is all about, Detective," Elias said.

"You remember, Elias," Antonia spoke up, "the woman who met

us in the cemetery this morning. Your friend, Catherine."

"Oh, my dear, what *did* happen this morning? I saw you become so distraught. No doubt the strain of this past month has taken its toll." He turned to Adam. "She flew out of the cemetery in tears. I had no idea why."

"She flew out of the cemetery to find Catherine," Adam said. "And you know where this woman is, don't you?"

Balducci gave Adam a look to back off. He retrieved the video camera from his bag and ran the scenes. "Take a good look, Hatch."

Blaze jumped up to view it.

Hatch watched for a minute, then looked away.

"There you are," Balducci pointed. "There's Antonia. There's Catherine in a long coat. So where is this woman now?"

"I've no idea." Hatch's eyes skirted the room, the window, the ceiling, and settled on the priest at least twice.

"Hatch, right now, I have enough evidence to arrest you for suspicion of conspiracy with this woman in the kidnapping of Henry Brooke."

This raised the old man's eyes up. "Conspiracy?"

"That alone will get you ten years in the state penitentiary." Balducci listened to a car motor outside. Must be Dan. He let a few beats pass, then went over to Hatch, leaned in close to his face. "And I'll get you on the kidnapping charge. I'm this close." Balducci pinched an inch with his fingers.

"Detective, you've got this all wrong," Elias said, panic in his voice.

"Really? Good, then set me straight. Tell me about your friend in the dark blue coat."

Hatch had his eyes on the video screen. He raised them in an admission of defeat "It's periwinkle blue. And it's a cape."

"That's good, Hatch. Keep going."

"I don't know how to convince you, all of you, that I'm innocent of any wrongdoing concerning Henry Brooke."

"Elias," Antonia said, "is Henry really safe? Was Catherine telling me the truth?"

"If Catherine said Henry is safe with her, then I suppose he is. Maybe you should take some comfort—"

"My son," Adam burst, "isn't safe unless he's home with us. Do you understand, Hatch? She's taken our boy, and you've known about it all along. It was Catherine who snatched him off the street, wasn't it? And you helped her do it."

"Adam," Balducci said with reproach in his tone. His cell phone buzzed. "Excuse me a second, I have to take this call."

He walked into the foyer. Must be Dan. Was there some delay?

"Mike, it's Jake at the lab. Pam said you wanted a report ASAP on the specimen from Old Willow."

"Yeah, what'd you find?"

"I've got most of it cleaned up and soaking in benzyl alcohol." Jake laughed. "Man, you gotta see this. It's a skull! What is this, Halloween?"

"Just give me the details."

"At first I thought it was clear glass, but I think it might be made of crystal. Pam's got some background research going. But listen, since I can't microscope it or fingerprint-match it, it was caked in mold and dirt, what do you want me to do with this thing?"

"Lock it in the evidence room. What did Pam get?"

"Hold on, I'll conference her in."

Pam came on. "Hi, Mike. Here's what I've got. Skulls are historically known as the Lord of the Dead. Necromancers use them in rituals to raise the dead. Black magic. One report says they use fresh bones of the dead in ritual sacrifices. If it's crystal, as Jake suspects, then I need to research another subcategory. Shall I move on that?"

"Yeah, thanks, Pam." Quickly he dialed Dan. Voice mail answered. With a snap, he folded his cell phone and went back into the parlor. He had to keep Hatch talking until Dan got there. This was not going to slip through is fingers. Not this time. "Hatch," he said, clearing his throat, "do you perform rituals with a skull?"

Hatch's eyes went wide with shock. He couldn't even draw a breath.

"Do you and this woman Catherine worship the dead?"

"Never," he swallowed the word, looking to Blaze. "Father Jim?"

Blaze, visibly stunned by the accusation, withdrew prayer beads from his pocket and began whispering.

"You know what we dug up on your property today, don't you, Hatch?"

"Dug up?"

"That's right. Under that ivy patch. You've got a skull buried in your root cellar."

Blaze rose slowly from his chair. "Detective, I can assure you that Elias does not worship the dead or participate—."

"Sit down, Blaze," the detective said, keeping his eyes on Hatch. "Necromancy. Crystal skulls. Lord of the Dead. You know what I'm talking about."

Hatch shook his head, lips trembling, hands shaking.

Antonia murmured, "Dear God," and slid down into a chair.

"See here, Detective," Hatch struggled to steady his voice. "I didn't know . . . I . . . no, you can't think that I'm a necromancer! I am not responsible for what's buried in the root cellar. I didn't even know where the root cellar was located. I thought it caved in decades ago." He took out a handkerchief and wiped his brow.

"Detective, having a skull buried in Old Willow is hardly a crime," Blaze offered.

"I'll decide what's a crime here."

"What about Henry?" Adam said. "You don't think they . . ."

"Stop right there, Adam." Balducci focused on Hatch. *Yeah, he's scared. Look at those beady eyes darting, his chest heaving. Even that stringy grey hair looks whiter.* "Hatch, is there anything you want to add here? Anything you want to tell us about Henry Brooke or this woman using the name of Catherine Javouhey? Because it's looking very bad for you right now."

Hatch attempted to speak and then clamped his lips.

"Are you practicing some kind of skull magic with Catherine? The black arts? Is that what's been going on here?"

Hatch was doing his best to be stoic. Balducci let the silence in the room work on him a few moments. "Hatch, you've got exactly one minute to explain what you know about this woman, or I'm hauling you in on charges of conspiracy."

"Listen here, I know almost nothing about Catherine. Most of it was told to me by my grandmother Sophie, and some by my mother, Hannah."

Balducci pushed the tape recorder closer. "What's this woman's real name? I want the truth."

He shifted his eyes to the priest, then back to Balducci. "The truth is, the woman in the cemetery today *is* Catherine Javouhey. She's . . . how shall I say this? She's the same woman who died in 1889 and was buried under that statue."

Balducci shook his head. "Oh, for Christ's sake! That's your explanation, is it?"

Hatch lifted his chin and found some strength. "I swear it."

"Well, that woman Catherine Javouhey in 1889 is dead, and this woman we saw today is alive. You want to explain that?"

Hatch clasped his hands together, looked Balducci straight in the eye. "It might interest you to know, Detective, that there are some things in this world that transcend explanation. We don't know *everything* about those who die, do we?"

"I want the truth about the woman in your cemetery this morning."

"The truth is, Detective, no one knows these things. Do you think you know *the dead?*"

Balducci shifted his weight. Say the word dead to him and all he could think was Maddy: the images of her in that steel hospital bed, her white coffin riding in the funeral car. *Stop.* Right now he had to remain clear, objective, persistent. "What I think isn't the point."

"Isn't it? That is precisely the point. Maybe some things in this life do not die, but only retire a little from sight and afterwards return again. These are not my words, not my thoughts. We have Emerson to thank for that nugget of wisdom. Detective, if you really want to locate Catherine and the boy, you'd be wise to learn Catherine's history. Is not history biography?"

Just maybe if I give this guy enough rope . . . "What history is that?"

"Catherine and her husband relocated from Paris to Concord in 1880. Christopher Javouhey was a Unitarian minister. Just like Emerson. They were colleagues. Did you know, Detective, that the Javouheys became transcendentalists? Just as my family were transcendentalists."

"Where are you going with this, Hatch?"

"Into the metaphysical world, Detective. *Meta ta physika,* 'after the things of nature.' The reality that exists beyond our immediate senses, beyond our rational explanations. In 1889, Catherine died and was buried in Old Willow Cemetery, alongside her three children. Some time later, Catherine became known as the Weeping Woman of Old Willow because her tears were seen streaming down the statue."

"Who made up that spooky tale?"

"My grandmother Sophie said there were many witnesses who saw tears break forth from the stone. In fact, Henry Sidgwick, president of the British Society of Psychical Research, came to Concord in 1900 to investigate it. His examination showed the tears to be human and leaking from the eyes of the statue. Sidgwick declared it a supernatural phenomenon and published his report with the Metaphysical Society of London. His documentation is still considered viable today."

Balducci had visions of strangling the old man. Where the hell was Dan? "Here it is, Hatch. We have evidence that Henry Brooke has been inside your cemetery. Evidence of a woman in the cemetery who claims she knows you, and admits she has Henry. And now we have convincing suspicions that you may be fooling with skull magic."

Hatch shook off his chill and focused directly at Antonia. "My dear Antonia," he said in an earnest voice, "if the woman in the cemetery this morning told you that she is Catherine Javouhey and that she has Henry safe with her, then I would believe her."

"Oh Elias, this is madness! How can I believe her or you or any of this business."

"Because Henry's disappearance has nothing to do with me, and everything to do with Catherine and . . . and the skull. Because Catherine lives. She is not dead. Because—"

"You're a crazy old man," Adam practically lunged at him, "and no one here is going to fall for your ridiculous story and that stupid skull!"

"That skull belongs to Catherine. She buried it in Old Willow over a century ago. That skull restored her—"

Bang! The front door shot open. Dan Hersey came pounding in. He slammed a warrant on the table. "Elias Hatch, you're under arrest for suspicion and conspiracy of the kidnapping of Henry Brooke. You have the right to remain silent. Anything you say can and will be used against you in a court of law. You have the right to an attorney. If you cannot afford an attorney, one will be appointed for you." He pulled out handcuffs.

Father Blaze was on his feet. "Surely that isn't necessary."

"Cuffs are always necessary."

"Elias Hatch doesn't deserve any special privileges. He's in our custody now," Hersey said.

Balducci knew the warrant charging Hatch wouldn't hold for more than 48 hours unless they came up with some hard evidence. He gave a grateful nod to his chief. "Just in time."

Dan snapped the cuffs on Hatch's wrists. "That'll do. Let's go."

"Wait! Chief Hersey, I'm innocent. It's Catherine you want. I have nothing to do with this."

"You can sing that story in lockup," Balducci said. "You and your skull."

"Tell them, Father Jim. Tell them that the Lord of the Dead is really the *Lord of Life.*"

Blaze kept to his prayer vigil, beads held tightly in his hand.

"Tell them I did nothing. It was Catherine. She lives!"

Dan propelled him forward toward the door.

"Yeah, Blaze, tell us about Catherine. I thought Jesus was the only one who could raise the dead," Balducci added.

Blaze put his prayer beads into his pocket. "Detective, in Christ's language of Aramaic, *death* translates, *not here, present elsewhere.*"

Balducci huffed. "You're a piece of work, you know that, Blaze?" With his pulse racing, his head throbbing, all he could think was *'Everything is made of one hidden stuff,'* and *I'm going to find the fucker.*

The afternoon sun streamed out as Dan and Sergeant Reilly led Hatch down the walkway to the waiting police car. Balducci followed with Blaze and the Brookes behind him.

"Look," Antonia called out.

They all turned. In the panels of smooth green grass, sprouts of white lilies of the valley appeared. Hundreds of them spread across the church lawn in neat little bunches. Balducci yanked up a handful. The sweet aroma hit him. He recalled now where he knew that fragrance—in the pine grove, that elusive shadow between the evergreens.

What is speaking here?

He shot his eyes to Hatch standing at the open door of the police car.

The old guy gave a slow blink. "Metaphysics, Detective. Catherine's teasing you."

* * *

The search of the rectory, church, and grounds produced no hard evidence of Catherine Javouhey but did bring to light the relationship of Elias Hatch and the ambitious Father James Blaze. Balducci secured a number of medical invoices and letters that verified how closely the good priest was taking care of the cemetery keeper who had been struggling with voices and visions of the dead for a number of years.

In his search, Balducci scanned the office bookshelves, filled mostly with volumes on the Vatican, some in Italian. Guess most priests knew Italian or Latin; Blaze had spent two years studying at the Vatican. On his desk sat a volume of Teilhard de Chardin's *The Divine Milieu* with a partially written homily stuck inside the front cover. *Science and Religion, Two Hands at Prayer. If you're looking for truth, look to the creation of this world, not to the magisterium of the church. The world is God.* Balducci tossed it aside. "He's bolder than most. I'll give him that." He picked up a hardcover tome, *Book of Enoch,* tabbed with stickies.

"Mike?" Deputy Chief Paul Owens walked into the priest's office.

Balducci had his eyes on Blaze's drawings of the planet earth and what looked like weather patterns between the north and south poles.

"Dan called."

"Yeah?"

"They just rushed the lab tech, Jake Kras, to Emerson Hospital."

"What?"

"That skull you dug up in Old Willow? It's radiating some kind of heat. Knocked the kid out cold."

Chapter Fourteen

THE LOCAL TELEVISION NEWS broadcast the arrest of Concord resident Elias Hatch for suspicion and conspiracy of kidnapping five-year-old Henry Brooke. The reporter spoke from curbside at St. Therese of the Roses Church Rectory, where the arrest took place.

Adam shut off the television. Suspicions played in his mind exactly how much Jim Blaze really knew about all this and why Elias ran for cover to the rectory. In the kitchen Antonia was making a bread salad for dinner. He poured himself a glass of red wine and one for her. He noticed she seemed oddly calm as she chopped a mess of green olives.

Just the two of them at the table—Laura having dinner at Josie's—they ate the salad in an uncomfortable silence until he couldn't stand it another minute. "What are you thinking, Annie? I can see it all over your face."

"See what on my face?"

"Your thoughts. Only I can't figure what they are."

She pushed her plate away. "I'm thinking that Henry is safe. Catherine told me Henry is safe with her. And, I believe her."

He poured himself a second glass of wine. "You think we should take the word of a woman who's impersonating a dead woman?"

"Catherine seemed very genuine to me. I don't know why, but I feel that she just might be telling me the truth that our son is safe."

"Really? Antonia, at the very least this woman is a fraud, emotionally unstable if not completely wacky, and she's got our son."

"Explain the sudden burst of lilies in the lawn at the rectory, and in the cemetery. You saw them."

He huffed. "I don't know. Maybe there is such a thing as skull magic. And maybe Hatch knows the tricks. He was there both times, wasn't he?"

The doorbell rang. When Antonia opened the door, she stepped back in surprise. "Father Jim?"

"I'm sorry to just show up like this. I hope it isn't a bad time."

Adam noticed the priest clutched a leather Bible. He was dressed in black with the white clerical collar and wearing a crucifix on a chain around his neck. "You look very official, Blaze. What brings you here?"

"I came to offer my help. To put your mind at ease. This skull business. Elias does not try to raise the dead. He is not a necromancer. I want you both to know that."

"You're here to defend Hatch? Why? Maybe it doesn't look so good for St. Therese's to have a parishioner arrested on church property for kidnapping. Have you seen the news tonight?"

"Father Jim," Antonia said, "all we want is to find our son. Come in."

Antonia led him to the kitchen table to sit. Adam remained standing, hands in his pockets, feet firmly planted, hovering over him.

"Do you have any information from Elias about Henry, Father Jim?

"I'm sorry, I don't."

"What about the woman?" Adam asked. "What do you know about Catherine?"

"Nothing. I'm sorry. But let me say this. Please know that God and the angels are here, all around you."

"Where is that?" Antonia slapped out the words. "What kind of a God gives me a child and now that he's been taken, abandons me?"

"Henry is God's child too." Blaze took an object from his pocket that was wrapped in white tissue paper and offered it from the palm of his hand. "This is for you, Antonia."

She tore the paper off. Slightly bigger than a thimble, it was a clear greenish-blue glass fashioned into the shape of a tiny angel.

"Father Jim, this is your blue crystal angel. I've seen it in your office."

"Yes, now it's yours. A friend of mine, Sister Rita, made it many years ago."

"I can't accept this, Father Jim."

"I insist. Keep it in your home as a reminder of God's protection for you and your family."

"Why do we need protection?" Adam asked. "You think this glass angel is going to protect us? Against what?"

"God protects us. The Father often uses earthly materials to extend His graces. The angel is an efficacious sign for God's grace to be present. Angels bring messages of comfort."

Adam scooped up the angel. Pearls covered the wings. Antonia would love it; pearls were her weakness. "Where's this from?"

"It's made from the purest aquamarine crystal from the mines of South America. Sister Rita dug up the gemstone herself. The history is a lovely story. After the creation, when heaven's holy water fell through the frigid air, the angels petrified it so it became frozen into solid ice inside the caves of earth. We call these gemstones holy ice."

"I've never heard of holy ice. Is it some parable in the Bible?" Antonia asked.

"The actual term is not scriptural in this Bible. But the term *chrysolite* is mentioned repeatedly in the Old and New Testaments. You've read the terms *Urim* and *Thummim* in Exodus, right? And *chyrsolite* is in the *Book of Enoch.*"

"Book of Enoch?" Adam didn't hide his mocking tone. "Who's Enoch? Look, Blaze, I don't care about any of this. It's all a distraction. If you can't help us locate Henry, or this woman who calls herself Catherine, then just go."

Father Blaze rose from the chair. "I'm sorry to have intruded." He walked to the foyer, then turned.

Adam had his eyes fastened on him.

"To answer your question, Adam. Enoch was great-grandfather to Noah."

The door closed softly behind him.

Antonia placed the blue angel on the windowsill next to the vase with the lily of the valley Catherine had given her. "You don't like Father Jim, do you?" She lifted the vase of lilies. "Smell this."

"No thanks, I can smell them from here. It's clear you like him."

"Father Jim feels terrible about all this. He makes a novena every day at noon to St. Helena of the Cross for Henry."

"Yeah, who is she?"

"Helena founded the true cross of Christ, excavated it in Jerusalem. The wood was said to have cured people."

"Another miracle, I suppose?"

"And what's wrong with miracles? I shudder to think of living in this world without miracles and being left entirely to ourselves . . . or skull magic and tricks."

"Nothing," he said to calm her. "I'm sorry. It's just that miracles violate the laws of nature. That's all I'm saying."

"Good. Perhaps we should redefine the laws of nature then."

He placed a kiss on her head. "Perhaps we should. Oh, look at the time. I'll go get Laura at Josie's."

"Josie's going to drive her home after they watch a movie."

"What time is that?"

"I don't know. Nine or ten, I guess."

"On a school night?"

"Oh, Adam, please. Let her get out and relax. She loves staying at Josie's."

Suddenly a voice echoed from upstairs. "*Mommmmmeeeeeeeee.*"

They both looked up to the ceiling.

"*Mommmmmeeeeeeeee.*"

"That's Henry."

Adam was up the stairs, ahead of Antonia by several feet. He pushed open

Henry's bedroom door just as a powerful wind slammed it shut. With his shoulders, he pushed again and again, but the door kept slamming shut. Using all his strength, he inched it open about a foot. He fought off a spiral of wind, leaves, and grass. Twigs flew everywhere.

"Daaaaaddeeeeeee!"

Adam kicked the door while Antonia pushed. A gust of wind sent them back. The thick air made Antonia hunch down coughing.

They both hit the door again and sent it banging against the wall.

With both arms up to protect his eyes, Adam crossed the threshold. "Henry? Where are you? Henry!"

The wind spun, shaking the walls, cracking the ceiling. Inside, Adam leaned against the wall for support. Suddenly the wind broke into small funnels—six, seven, eight or more— spinning leaves over the floor. Through the dark windows, under the exterior house lights over the back lawn, Adam thought he saw something white flap near the linden trees.

Suddenly the wind died. A deep hush fell over the bedroom.

"Henry?" Antonia said. "Are you here, sweetie?"

A scattering of leaves sailed down like tiny birds across the bed and carpet, drifting over the lampshade, throwing shadows on the walls.

"He's here. I can smell him, Adam. He's right here!" Antonia dropped to the floor, crawling in the blanket of leaves. "Where are you? Henry?" She grabbed a bunch of brown leaves, brought them to her face and inhaled. "Oh, yes. Henry, please, come home, sweetie, come home."

As she scooped more leaves into her arms, Adam saw the leaves turn white and crumble into ashes. They dusted her face and hands. When she saw the ashes, she broke into tears.

Adam felt something touch his hand. Small warm fingers slipped into his right palm and squeezed. He squeezed back slowly, ready to see his little boy, ready to look into those spectacular brown eyes. He glanced down. White dust sifted through his fingers.

Sinking to his knees, he cried out, driven to his own tears.

Chapter Fifteen

AT POLICE HEADQUARTERS, after taking what was an absurd statement from Elias Hatch—his claiming that the *Lord of Life* had regenerated Catherine Javouhey, a devoted transcendentalist from the 1800s, and that she had taken Henry Brooke by her own admission—Balducci locked Hatch up without a look back.

Balducci found his chief in a foul mood and talked him into having a quick beer at the Waldo Grille. They sat in a quiet booth in the corner.

Dan drew his eyes away from the bar's TV screen. "Julie has got dinner waiting for me. The boys are back from basketball camp. I can't stay too long. Wives get pissed when you miss dinner all the time, you know?"

"No, I wouldn't know. Maddy never got pissed."

Dan winced. "I'm a jerk. What a thoughtless thing to say. I'm sorry."

"Forget it. Maddy's gone three years. *I* need to stop being a jerk. I saw an ad the other day about treating ovarian cancer, and I actually had the thought to call Maddy at work and give her the phone number."

"I guess these things take time, Mike."

"I guess. Give me the update on Jake Kras? I'm just sick over this."

"Still unconscious. Some kind of cardiac arrhythmia, they said. Poor kid, only twenty-five years old. That stupid Hatch and his skull, the *Lord of Life*. What kind of a term is that? Did you hear Hatch claim that term came from Ralph Waldo Emerson? I didn't know Hatch was a transcendentalist. What the hell, they aren't active anymore, are they?"

"Of course not."

Dan looked relieved. "Transcendentalists didn't try to raise the dead through a glass skull, did they?"

"No. They were about nature, science, art. Inherent intuition was a big deal. The Javouheys and the Hatch family must have been some bizarre offshoot."

"And what cause did you have to go digging up that grave site, anyway?"

"The number twenty-four. I trusted Adam's instinct. That and the fact that I can't explain how that woman goes off the video screen at that exact location."

"I hate this case. Where's that damn skull now?"

"Dropped it off with the guard at the Baldwin Research Center. Jake wasn't certain it was quartz crystal or glass crystal. I'm having them take a look at it."

"Was it still radiating heat? Because the damn thing was throwing off waves of heat when they found Jake on the floor. Lab must have been near a hundred degrees."

"Not that I saw. Actually, Dan, it was cold when I handled it. A hundred degrees? That can't be right."

"I don't know, but it was hot as hell in that lab and it's always at sixty-five degrees down there. What do you know about this skull?"

"Not much. Dr. Phillippa Allan at Baldwin is going to examine it first thing in the morning. She used to teach at MIT with Maddy."

"You know her?"

"I met her briefly at Maddy's wake. Don't even remember what she looks like." He took a long slug of his beer. "Dan, I wanted to talk to you about something I'm moving ahead on. And you're not going to like this, but . . . I've asked Judge Brady to sign a court order to exhume the coffin of Catherine Javouhey."

That must have shot Dan's blood pressure up, because he flushed full red.

"Mike, don't you go exhuming coffins without probable cause. I don't care what your instincts are, borrowed or otherwise."

"It's a stretch, I know. Brady will go for it—he owes me. And

I'm not removing the body or sending the remains away for analysis. I'm taking a look, that's all, and the coffin goes right back under."

"And what are you expecting to find? Not Henry Brooke, I hope."

"I expect to find the woman's remains."

"What a fucking morbid business, opening a coffin."

"Yeah, well." He took another gulp of beer. "Did you know that Emerson opened Ellen's coffin?"

"What for? Who the hell's Ellen?"

"Emerson's first wife. Nineteen years old when she died."

Dan leaned back in his seat. "Don't tell me she died of ovarian cancer."

"TB. Emerson called her his snow maiden because she died in winter."

"Oh Mike, for Christ's sake."

"What?"

"Where are you going with this? Didn't Maddy die in February?"

"January 28. Anyway, Emerson went to Ellen's grave all the time. Communicated with her regularly. He wrote about it in his journals." Balducci watched Dan's face for a moment. "You know, Dan, for a while I did that with Maddy. Talked to her like she was still in the house with me. I had real moments when I felt like she was actually sitting there listening."

"I'm not sure, but do we think that's healthy?"

"Maybe not. So, there's Emerson, at Ellen's grave every day, speaking to her, feeling like she's still with him, and then one morning he goes there, walks into the family mausoleum, and opens her coffin."

Dan put his mug down. "Mike, you gotta stop this."

Tipping his beer mug up to finish the last of it, Balducci said the words he'd been thinking about for years. "I've had moments when I've been half tempted to do the same."

"Open Maddy's coffin? Jesus." Dan pulled out his cell phone and dialed. "Julie? Set another place at the table. Mike's coming for dinner."

"Oh don't do that."

"Come on, Mike, the boys will love seeing you again. Julie made vegetarian lasagna. She's on a health kick. It's not bad, really."

A home-cooked meal with Dan's family would be refreshing. Just then his cell phone buzzed. The caller ID read Adam Brooke.

* * *

Minutes later Balducci ran up the stairs of the Brooke home while two police officers searched the grounds. He scanned the bedroom, which was covered with ashes, twigs, and a solid blanket of dried-up leaves. He picked up a handful, took a sniff, then slipped the stuff into a plastic evidence bag. All the windows were closed and locked. The ceiling had dark streaks from corner to corner. Ashes clung to the sailboat wallpaper; the bed sheets were twisted into a knot. Toys, pillows, trucks, game pieces, and Henry's baseball caps littered the floor. Even the blue lampshade had been blown off its sailboat base, which stood on end.

"What are you thinking, Mike?" Adam said. "What caused this? Hatch is still in custody, right?"

Balducci sucked in a long breath. *Trust the instinct to the end, though you can render no reason . . . by trusting it to the end, it shall ripen into truth. . . .* Emerson's words reassured him to take his time, let it evolve, watch, be ready.

"Has that woman Catherine done this? Like the lilies at the rectory?"

While Balducci couldn't find any practical explanation of cause and effect for this whirlwind wrecking the boy's room, the shocking reality drove him to think metaphysically. Hell, traditional science didn't have all the answers. "If it is Catherine, by whatever means she's using, it's pretty clear that she's making a statement."

"Meaning?"

"She's sending dead leaves and ashes."

"And the message is . . .?" Antonia came into the bedroom.

Balducci saw she'd been crying, eyes swollen, cheeks streaked red. "Dead leaves and ashes aren't exactly lilies suddenly growing in the grass, are they?"

Antonia's eyes were wide and glassy. "You don't think she's trying to tell me . . . my son is . . . ?"

Balducci bit his tongue.

* * *

Later that night, at Hatch's cottage, Balduccci stood among crusty old trunks, broken furniture, empty picture frames, and rusty tools hanging from the attic rafters. In one of the trucks, he found a ragged newspaper clipping inside a scrapbook. Quickly he scanned the French text and stopped when he saw the name Christopher Javouhey. He tucked it inside a plastic evidence bag along with a few old letters, also in French, and climbed down the attic ladder. With another scan of Hatch's living room, the half-opened desk drawer drew his attention. As he went through the drawer looking for those odd sketches Hatch had made of stick men—the ones he called *thought-forms*—a clatter from behind startled him. He turned. Nothing. Except for the distinct aroma of chocolate.

He examined the floor, thinking he might have stepped on a candy, but found nothing. What the hell, it didn't matter anyway. The folder with the drawings he'd seen before had been removed. He slammed the desk drawer shut.

On the top bookshelves he saw the volumes of Emerson's works. He took several down and began leafing through them. Many of the pages were marked with little pieces of paper, some pages with pencil notations. He came across Emerson's essay on "Experience." He scanned Hatch's check marks on some of the lines. At the front of the essay, underlined in black ink, he found the nugget.

> *The lords of life, the lords of life,—I saw them pass,*
> *in their own guise, like and unlike, portly and grim.*

Balducci sat down for a moment. *Lords of life?* In the plural?

* * *

Frank and Josie Wilson brought Laura home at ten o'clock. Adam, greatly relieved that his daughter was home, carried her half asleep up to her room. Before he placed a kiss on her head, he smoothed out her long strings of curls on the pillow.

Morning opened without sunshine. Adam tied on his robe and went to take a peek at Laura. The door was locked. He gave a knock.

"Hey, Blondie, you up?"

"Yeah, Dad."

"Why is the door locked?"

"I'm getting dressed."

He went downstairs and found Antonia packing Laura's lunch for school.

"You're awfully late today," she said.

"I called in. Barbara will cover for me." He poured himself coffee.

"Why?"

"Because I'm so damn rattled after what happened last night, that's why."

"Well, don't stay home on my account. Because I'm not."

"You're beat up, Antonia. You were tossing all night."

"Why should I stay home today? For what? Wait for Mike to find Henry? Mike can't find Henry. This is beyond Mike's skills, and I think it's time we recognize that—especially after what happened last night. Don't you think?"

"I wish I could think." He wanted to blurt out that he had felt Henry's hand inside his, but he didn't. It would only end up haunting her like it was haunting him. "Mike took a specimen of the debris for the lab. I don't know what he expects the results will tell him."

"I'll tell you what it's going to tell him. Nothing. You know what I think this is? It's like Plato's illusion on the cave walls."

"The cave allegory?"

"I think we're looking at shadows on the wall. We need to turn around and look at the puppeteers. The truth is hidden, Adam."

"You mean Hatch is hiding something?"

"I mean Catherine, or whoever . . . or whatever she really is. We expose Catherine, we find Henry."

"What about all those leaves and ashes? That was no illusion."

"Maybe. But if those ashes were a trick to make us think Henry is dead, it didn't work. I know one thing. Henry is alive. He was in that room last night and he was calling us. You felt that too, didn't you, Adam?"

"I did. Absolutely. Henry was there." Adam tossed his coffee into the sink, his stomach already churning with acid. *Henry was there and he was reaching out to me.*

"I'm going to the town records department and see what information they have on the name Catherine Javouhey."

"I'm sure Mike has already done that." Adam took her into his arms. Her hair was in black flirty waves, still wet from her shower, her complexion squeaky clean, and she had a wild gypsy look in her eyes. He held her face in his hands, kissed her. It was a gentle kiss, barely touching. "We'll find Henry. I can feel we're closer to him. We'll find him and bring him home."

She drenched him with kisses. "I've missed you. I love you, Adam."

"I love you more."

Laura came down the stairs with a spring in her step, dressed for school. She stood before her parents, her thick blond hair braided and tied with white ribbons. With a quick spin and all smiles, she set the braids flying out.

"Are these cool, or what?" Laura sang out.

"Wow," Antonia brightened up. "Did you braid your own hair?"

Laura giggled and did another spin. "I'll never tell."

Chapter Sixteen

Balducci made sure he was prompt for his appointment with Dr. Phillippa Allan. At the Baldwin Research Center in Manchester, just as he walked the path to the brick building, he spotted Adam.

"You didn't answer my calls this morning," Adam said, falling into the same strides. "I'm out of my mind after last night. I called Dan, and he told me you were having that skull analyzed. What are you expecting to find? Something about Hatch? Or Catherine?"

"Adam, you've really got to let me do my job. This is my investigation."

"I'm sorry to barge in. I just need to know what you're thinking. What do you expect me to do, just sit by and wait and wait?"

"Yeah, yeah, I know what you need. All right. Come on."

They entered the building together and after the initial introductions, the three sat in Dr. Phillippa Allan's office with two small windows that overlooked the parking lot.

To Balducci, Phillippa's style resembled a punk look straight out of *Vogue:* spiked streaky ash-blond hair, a glowing complexion, and the lightest brown eyes he'd ever seen— practically topaz. No wedding ring, either. He expected an academic stereotype with pinned-up hair and buttoned-up blouse.

"Maddy mentioned you to me often, Phillippa. I'm embarrassed to tell you, I don't recall meeting you. But I do remember that she had only good things to say about you." His eyes skimmed over her red blouse with the pointed collar turned up at the back of her neck. The third button was open and white lace skimmed her cleavage. He straightened up, focused on the issue at hand. "So, what's your opinion about this skull?"

"Extraordinary sculpture. I just love it," she said brightly. "I examined it under the microscope. It's authentic quartz crystal. Did you know that?"

"We suspected."

"It's made of the purest silicon dioxide. Extremely hard substance, seven on the Mohs scale, only slightly softer than a diamond."

Balducci scanned the background notes from Pam Peterson. "A diamond? Really? I don't know much about science, but quartz crystal has piezoelectric properties? Is that right?"

"Quartz stores energy. Amplifies energy. Converts energy—which is why quartz is used in computers and clockworks."

"And in radio tuners?" Balducci glanced up from his notes. Adam was tapping his foot in a distracting rhythm against the wood floor. Balducci put his hand out as a signal to calm down. Adam didn't get it.

Phillippa did, though, and gave Balducci a smile and shrug to indicate it was okay.

"When external radio waves enter the quartz chips," she said, "the radio waves become stabilized. Resonant affinity is what we call it."

"So this quartz skull has piezoelectric energy?" Balducci wanted to confirm.

"What is that, exactly?" Adam leaned toward Phillippa.

At least the tapping stopped.

"Piezoelectricity happens when stress is applied to the quartz. If I hit a piece of quartz with a hammer, there would be a charge." Phillippa addressed Balducci. "Now, this quartz skull is really unusual because it appears to possess its own vibrational properties, without mechanical pressure."

"How does it do that?" Balducci asked.

"Not really sure. I can tell you that its electromagnetic field is uncharacteristically strong. Went right off my Gauss meter." She swiped a shock of hair from her forehead. Her sweeping topaz eyes settled on Balducci.

He liked being in her gaze. She was bright and sassy and staring right into him. "Off the Gauss meter, huh? Is that good or bad?"

"Most would call it supernormal. All I can tell you is that the skull's field exceeds our known standards for quartz. This skull was likely carved from one solid piece of high-quality quartz, probably a large sphere. That might contribute to its high vibrations."

"Is it heat?" he asked. "Because we have witnesses who felt heat coming from it in the crime lab."

She frowned. "I didn't find any heat quality going on. Was it exposed to direct heat?"

"I don't think so, why?

"Because when quartz is heated, it will discharge electrons that can sometimes enhance the field. That's why it's a component in digital thermometers." She paused with a slight pucker to her lips.

Mike felt a throb in his belly. *Oh man.*

"You know, Mike, my ex-husband had a quartz crystal ring, a big clear emerald-cut. Whenever he wore it to the beach, in the sun, he'd have to take it off because it would burn his finger."

Amused, Balducci raised an eyebrow. *Her ex.* He remembered now Maddy had said Phillippa was married to a musician.

"Anyway . . ." She opened a file on her desk. "Here's what I found when I examined it." She tossed on a pair of glasses. "The skull weighs eight pounds. Six inches high and six inches wide. At least four inches is solid rock crystal. No veils, no inclusions. Inside, it's concave with a prism behind each eye socket. Extraordinary interior prisms! The cranium surface is just a hair uneven, cheekbones arch accurately to human shape, and the jaw and teeth are practically perfect. What you have here is an exact replica of the human skull in shape and dimension. And I do mean an exact anatomical work. Even the eye sockets are slightly misaligned just the way a human's are. Very impressive sculpting, whoever did it." She closed the file. "So, is it a valid *archaeological objet d'art?* That I cannot tell you."

"Is it an occult object, do you think?" Adam asked.

"Oh, sure—Lord of Doom, extraterrestrials, life after death and all that. Some Native American tribes believe quartz crystals are the brain cells of Grandmother Earth. I kind of like that one myself. I've got Cherokee in my ancestry. Would you like to see the specimen? I've got it soaking in the lab across the hall."

They entered the small lab, lined with microscopes and mechanical objects Balducci couldn't identify. Green shades over the windows darkened the room. On the black rectangular table was a medium-sized glass fish tank filled with water. Phillippa did a drum role with her tongue and a dramatic spin of her hands.

Balducci went close to the glass.

Adam walked around it, peered in close. "Are you sure it's in there? I don't see a thing."

"Oh, I'm sure. Hey, Zoe?" she called out. "Zoe's been helping me with this." Then she whispered through a cupped hand, "The director's daughter. The nepotism in this place would make your head spin. But what she lacks in skills, she makes up in enthusiasm."

A young woman walked in. Balducci guessed she was maybe nineteen years old—had the face of a cherub, a reddish ponytail, and wore an MIT sweatshirt.

"Hi, I'm Zoe, the genius assistant."

"Zoe, didn't we put the quartz skull inside this saltwater tank this morning after our preliminary exam?"

"Yes, we did. Can you believe it? It completely disappeared. I was so amazed, I almost screamed."

"And here's your evidence that it's actually submerged in there." Phillippa pointed a high-powered flashlight on it. "See it now? Honestly, I can't figure out why it's invisible inside this water tank. Salt water is just a neutralizer."

With latex-gloved hands, Phillippa lifted the skull up. It glistened with the streaming water.

"What a beauty, huh? Look closely and you'll see the prisms in back. Zoe, open the shades, please."

The sun flooded the laboratory.

Balducci leaned in to see the prism just as the sunlight hit the top of the skull. The hollows flashed at him like searchlights. He reeled back. Adam caught his arm.

"You okay?"

"Yeah. That's some glare."

"The sun must have shot through that prism. Keep that in mind.

No sunshine for this baby." She handed the skull to Zoe, who placed it down on the tabletop.

The window light bathed the cranium, which took on a bluish cast with red around the jaw. Balducci thought he could see the thinnest of pink tongues behind the teeth.

Zoe began drying it off. She curled up her shoulders with delight, petting the skull, murmuring sweet things to it. "You are absolutely beautiful. . . ."

Balducci grinned when Phillippa rolled her eyes at the girl's drama.

"Thank you, Zoe. Mike, if you need historical info on crystal skulls, I know an archaeologist in London, Eva Sugarman. She's a good friend. I'll give you her number."

"Thanks. I'll need to call her today. How old is this skull, do you think?"

"We can't carbon date quartz, so there's no way of knowing. This skull could be thousands of years old, but if carved by a machine or modern tools, it could be as young as twenty-five. I don't have the expertise in diamond rotary saws to recognize the markings." She peeled off her latex gloves.

"Phillippa, does Baldwin do a lot of research with quartz?" Adam asked.

"No, but I've been hooked on experimenting with quartz for years. In one of my first experiments, we placed a slice of quartz underneath one of two milk cartons side by side, same temperature, same light, in order to test bacteria counts. The milk with the quartz base didn't spoil until twenty-seven days, but the carton without the quartz base spoiled in the normal seven to ten days."

Balducci admired the line of Phillippa's slim hips as she leaned against the window sill, both hands tucked into her navy trouser pockets. She was tall but not quite as tall as he was. Eye level was perfect. And at the moment, those topaz gems were smack on him.

"We did some fun tests with water elements back then. When water is spun in a right-handed spiral around a quartz crystal, the spinning creates a spiral energy field. And that field interacts with the quartz. A resonant vibration is created, and the field from the quartz is transferred directly into the water."

Now that he could see Phillippa in the bright daylight, he wondered about the golden tones of her skin. Tanning salon? Island vacation, maybe?

"The result was restructured water that had the exact same energy values as the crystal. Pretty amazing, huh? Spiral energy fields are getting a lot of scientific attention these days."

Balducci liked the way she tilted her chin to him just then, her bronzy lips curling up, those amazing eyes lighting on him. And that exotic hair. He wanted to touch the streaks, especially the loose wisps that framed her face.

"Spiral energy fields?" Adam repeated.

"Yes."

"There were blue spirals spinning in the cemetery and last night—"

"Blue spirals where?" Phillippa said.

Balducci turned with an expression that a five-year-old would have understood. This time Adam got it.

"Nothing. I was just thinking out loud."

Phillippa's lips parted as if to speak, but then she stopped. Balducci's cell phone buzzed, and he saw it was Dan Hersey calling. "Excuse me a sec." He walked out to the corridor and spoke softly into his phone, pacing, head down.

* * *

Adam watched Mike's expressions for a moment; the man was clearly disturbed. Adam tried to listen, but he couldn't hear anything and grew distracted by Phillippa's chatting about crystal energy fields, "some as wide as six feet and more." She went on and on, and he half-listened to her at the same time watching Mike's reactions. Was it news of Henry? A sighting of Catherine?

"Adam, did you know that frequencies of 100 kilohertz can stimulate the human nervous system? Look at that," Phillippa pointed.

Adam tore his eyes away from the detective. A sunbeam through the window slapped a ray across the skull's face. The forehead suddenly shrank into ridges; the cheek sockets sagged with jowls and creases. Adam swore the eye sockets began to close as if the sun was too bright.

"We need to get that out of the sunlight, Zoe. We don't want to create any problems. Put it in the black box, please."

Balducci walked back into the lab. "Do you mind if I smoke, Phillippa?" He pulled a pack out of his pocket.

"No smoking in this facility, as if you didn't know."

He raised the cigarette slowly to his mouth.

"Don't you dare light up," Phillippa whispered under a laugh. "You like breaking the rules, don't you?"

"Me? Never." He rolled the cigarette inside his hand. "Phillippa, you've been terrific. Thank you. If I think of anything else I need, may I call you?"

"Anytime. I'll give you my home number. I live in Lexington. Oh, and you'll need Eva Sugarman's number too." She grabbed a sheet of notepaper and scribbled. "Zoe?"

Zoe came forward with the black box and laid the skull inside. Adam watched her latch the top. She pulled off her latex gloves.

"I would just love to bring this home to Dad. He'd get such a kick."

"This is police work, Zoe. Strictly confidential. We discuss it with no one, not even your dad," Phillippa said.

The girl flushed. "Oh, of course. I know. I'm sorry. Absolutely."

When Phillippa handed the box to Balducci, she gave it a pat. "Take good care of her. Let me know what Sugarman thinks."

"I'll do that. Wait a sec. Her? You think the skull is female?"

"You know, initially when I first examined it, I thought I saw something feminine in the face. Then the more I worked with it, the more the skull just felt like a female. But we really can't tell gender from something like this."

"So, you don't have any scientific evidence that the face was modeled after a female?"

"Nothing evidentiary I could write on my fact sheet."

* * *

After saying good-bye, Phillippa walked back into her office. From across the hallway she heard Zoe let out a wail. "What now, Screaming Mimi?" she muttered and headed to the lab.

Zoe was braced against the wall. "Look at the tank! Phil, look at the water tank where the skull was soaking."

An image of the skull floated inside the tank. Silvery fluid outlined the cranium, every cavity shining with detail. Even the hollow eyes gleamed like smooth ice balls.

"Do you see it?" Zoe's voice cracked.

Phillippa couldn't believe her eyes. "Yeah, yeah, I see it."

"How can it be in there? I put it in the black box. Didn't I?"

"Of course you did. I saw you. We all saw you."

"And Detective Balducci took it with him? Right? He left the building with it."

Phillippa walked around the table in slow motion. "Yes, he did. Jesus, what the hell is this?"

"Oh Phil, did I do something wrong?"

"No. The first thing you've got to know if you're going to be a scientist is to remain calm. Everything has some mechanism of action that causes the result. Hand me the camcorder."

Zoe grabbed the camera. "But why couldn't we see it in the water when it was there? And now that it's *not* in the water, we can see it?"

"Good question. What's your first guess?" She took the camera from Zoe and began shooting while she circled the tank.

"Oh, I don't know. . . . Water's a conductor of energy, right?"

"Good, but not quite an answer. How about some kind of magnetism? You think?" With each step, she zoomed in. "Zoe, grab that notebook and write down everything I say."

"What? Why?"

"Just do it. I can see the frontal bone. . . . Look at that, Zoe, I can see the coronal sutures." She moved in closer. "The glabella is very clear . . . and supraorbitals. Nasal spine and concha are present. Zygomatics. Stunning, what cheekbones, I mean, really! Are you getting all this?"

"As fast as I can."

"I see the occipital bone, and . . . and yes, there's the maxilla . . . the ramus . . . and mandible. My God, Zoe, this is an exact image of the skull. It's inside the water molecules, just like a photograph."

"The maxilla . . . the ramus. Geez, don't go so fast."

"And what do you know? Look at this, there's the prism. Zoe, it's not at the back of the eye sockets at all. It's at the roof of the mouth. How extraordinary." Phillippa zoomed in again. "I see one . . . two . . . three . . . four facets in the prism. And . . . yes, four on the other side. That's eight facets, Zoe—what do you think of that?"

"I'm afraid to think!"

"See that Petri dish on the counter? Hand it to me. I want to get a sample of this water."

She ran to the counter and back. "Here."

"And go into Lab C and open the freezer door."

"What are you going to do? Oh God, you're not going to freeze it?"

"Of course I am. See how smart you are? Go on. I'll be right behind you."

* * *

As Adam and Mike walked to the parking lot outside Baldwin Research, Adam tried to calm himself with gulps of fresh air. He leaned for a moment against the Jeep parked next to Mike's sedan. Maybe he should have told Mike about Henry's holding his hand last night in the bedroom. He could still feel the slightest tingling sensation lingering on his fingertips. Remnants? Or just nerves.

Mike opened the sedan trunk, placed the black box inside, slammed the hood, and lit up his cigarette. The detective seemed deep in thought.

"Mike, what was that call you took before?"

"Crime lab. They tested the debris from Henry's room. No surprises. Wood-burned ashes."

"And what about the white figure I saw outside Henry's room, on the back lawn? Any ideas?"

"What, you think it was that old woman you saw in the cemetery?"

"Maybe. I didn't get a good look."

"The gates to the cemetery were open last night when we arrived to do another search. So, somebody else out there besides Hatch has got the keys."

"Catherine?"

Mike didn't answer. Or wouldn't answer. "Mike, how are you going to find Catherine? She's our link to Henry. And if Hatch is right about . . ." He studied the detective's face. "You think this is some black magic ritual raising of the dead? All this supernatural phenomenon going on."

Again, no answer.

"Christ, Mike, where is Henry in all this?"

"Right now, there's too much happening. I've got to learn more hard facts about Catherine if I'm going to locate her."

"Can I do something? What leads do you have?"

"I found some old letters written by Christopher Javouhey, in French, in a steamer trunk in Hatch's attic. I had them translated. I didn't believe Hatch at first, but he was telling the truth about Catherine Javouhey burying the skull in Old Willow. Christopher mentions the skull in this letter. He called it the *Lord of Life*. Apparently the Javouheys transported the skull to America when they sailed here in 1880."

"So?"

"So, it corroborates Hatch's statements. Christopher married Catherine in Paris in 1880 and brought her here within days of their wedding. Emerson's wife Lydian even gave them a small wedding reception at their house. Look, Adam, this case isn't average by any counts. But I don't quit because I can't explain events. One thing is clear. If I hold on to the facts too tight, I'll fail. If I hold on to the unreal too loose, I'll fail. I've got to examine both sides equally."

"Both sides?"

"The evidence and reasoning. And the images and intuition."

"The images. You mean like an illusion?"

"We think illusion and reality are opposites. But the transcendentalists, people like Hatch and Catherine, they know illusion to be a part of the reality, inside the same world."

Adam sighed. "Mike, what can I do? Give me a task!"

"Go to work, Adam. Just do your job and I'll do mine."

"Getting my son back *is* my job." He fisted his hand so he could feel that same tingling more intensely now. "And I can't explain what happened in his bedroom last night, but Henry is alive somewhere and he—"

"No, he's not, Adam."

Adam lost a breath.

"Adam, somebody in all this is trying to tell you that your son is dead."

He flinched.

"That's right. I think your boy is dead. What, you want to come at me? Go ahead, Adam, take a swing."

It was tempting. Then it suddenly dawned on him. "That call you got before, it wasn't from the crime lab at all, was it?"

Mike looked down at his shoes, then back at Adam. "It was Dan, from Old Willow Cemetery. He's a good chief to do my job today. We exhumed Catherine Javouhey's coffin."

Adam felt his adrenaline surge. Something snapped and he grabbed Mike by the jacket lapels, slammed him against the car door.

"You tell me my kid's in that coffin, I'll fucking kill you!"

They were eye to eye when a siren shrieked. They jumped apart. The alarm grew louder with every screeching repetition and within seconds streams of people came running out the Baldwin exits. Some employees ran as far as the main street, which was over a hundred yards away.

Mike dashed across the parking lot, raced through the throngs of people, and was just beyond the grassy entrance when a deafening blast shook the building. Adam saw him hit the ground with the impact. Suddenly there were mobs of people screaming and running in every direction. Adam lost sight of Mike and tried to make his way against the crowds to the building. He got as far as the grassy entrance just as the detective was scrambling to his feet.

"Mike! Are you hurt?" Adam helped him up, but the poor guy was doubled over gasping for air.

"Jesus," he managed. "What the hell? Was that a bomb? Look! At the side of the building."

A gaping hole puffed white smoke with shards of glass and bricks strewn on the grass area and curb.

"Where's Phillippa?" Mike said. "And that girl?"

Adam searched the faces of the crowds but didn't see her or Zoe.

"There she is." Mike took off toward the smoking building.

Everyone swarmed, shouting, calling on cell phones. Within a few minutes fire engines sounded. A line of police cars came barreling in, followed by an ambulance and emergency vehicles with red lights circling. A hell of a lot of dust flew around, which sent people coughing, but Adam didn't see any serious injuries. And he didn't see any flames, either. He spotted Phillippa in the distance by a rocky hill with Mike, so he threaded his way through the crowds. The ER crews were handing out bottled water, and he grabbed a couple and brought them to Phillippa.

"Oh, thanks." She drank down half a bottle. "Is that Zoe over there?" She squinted against the sun. "Thank God she's okay. That girl is quick on her feet. It if wasn't for her, we wouldn't have gotten everyone out before it blew."

"What blew?" Adam said. "You're okay, right?"

"I am now." Then she gave Mike an exasperated look. "My lab exploded. And here comes the fire chief. He's probably looking for me. How the hell am I going to explain this?" She tugged on Mike's arm and whispered in his ear, "That crystal skull caused the explosion."

Adam listened in.

"Phillippa, the skull is in my trunk."

"It was the water tank that blew." Phillippa lifted her video camera from under her arm. "I'll show you, but not right now. I have to take care of Zoe. Damn, look at her! She's crying." She dashed toward Zoe, then turned back. "Mike, wait for me? Don't leave."

Chapter Seventeen

Antonia spent hours at the Concord Free Library and then the Hall of Records going through ledgers, files, and microfilm. Christopher and Catherine Javouhey had lived at 5 Webster Street in 1880. Birth and death records documented a boy and two girls: Joseph, Suzanne, Cosette. The house on Webster Street burned down in 1893. No Javouhey descendants. No other Javouhey names recorded in Concord or even in the State of Massachusetts. With no family history to trace there, she drove straight to the Concord Historical Society, hoping they might have something. There Antonia met Mrs. Abernathy, a woman in a starched cotton dress.

"Catherine Javouhey? Not anyone well known in our Concord history. But I'll look in our database. May I ask why the interest in this woman?" she asked as she clicked away, searching keywords, dates, and address.

"As odd as this might sound, the history of this woman may actually help find my son. I'm Antonia Brooke."

She stopped tapping the keys. "Your son is Henry Brooke?"

"Yes. A woman using the name Catherine Javouhey may have abducted Henry. It's much more complicated than I can explain. I'm looking for any information about her life here, anything that will give us a lead."

"Oh, I'm sorry. I didn't realize." Mrs. Abernathy surged into a rigorous keyword search but after exhausting everything she could think of, she came up with zero. "Sorry. I can keep looking through our data index. I'll play around and see if anything surfaces. I'd be happy to give you a call later."

"You're so kind. Thank you, Mrs. Abernathy."

"Please, call me Jo-Beth. Oh now, wait a second. Miss Mae just came in and she's been working here practically forever and knows far more than I do. She's our associate director. Come meet her."

Miss Mae was about eighty, with baggy blue eyes and the most endearing smile. Her stunning grey hair was gathered at the back of her neck in a stylish knot held by Japanese painted hair sticks. She sat at a small drop-lid desk in an office the size of a broom closet.

"No window. You'd think after fifty years here they'd give me an office with a window." She smiled up at Antonia. "What can I do for you?"

Jo-Beth explained the details. Miss Mae began pulling a battered logbook from a shelf filled with dozens of them.

"Not in the computer system, huh? Should I be surprised?" She scanned the pages under J, slowly turning page after page of handwritten ledger sheets. "No Catherine listed here, but I see one entry for a Christopher Javouhey."

"That would be her husband. I think he was a minister."

"Jo-Beth, check the church indexes in my file room. Row C. My personal indexes are better than that silly old computer every time."

While they waited for Jo-Beth, Miss Mae chatted with Antonia: the warmer weather, the Brooke Bookshop, the traffic on Main Street. Antonia launched into a new subject the second a lapse appeared. "I don't suppose you know anything about Elias Hatch at Old Willow?"

"Elias? He and I went to elementary school together. Very shy, he was. Bookish. I know he studied at the University of Keele in Staffordshire and is quite proud that he's a thanatologist like his parents were."

"Thanatologist?"

"Years ago that profession was about rituals of death. Today it's more for the care of the dying. But Elias is so antisocial, I doubt he's ever practiced the profession. Strange old goat."

That was putting it mildly. "A bit odd, yes," she said to be polite.

"The whole family was odd. His mother, Hannah Hatch, was quite a gabber, as my mother used to call her. Does Elias still light candles in his windows or has he succumbed to the modern light bulb?"

Antonia laughed, and it felt good to release some tension. "Yes. Economy, I guess."

Miss Mae chuckled. "The truth is, Elias is so cheap he squeaks. He inherited that habit from Hannah." She leaned in and whispered as if Hannah might be listening. "This is a tad gossipy but . . . Hannah would fill the cottage with candlelight and then claim to peel the shadows from the walls and bury them in Old Willow, insisting the dead needed to sleep."

"You're not kidding me, are you, Miss Mae?"

"Gossipy, like I said. What is true about Hannah is that she had an unusual fascination with death. She once told my mother that when we die, 'we merely shed the body as we would an old shoe.'" Miss Mae wrinkled her nose. "Now, how do you suppose she knew that one?"

Jo-Beth stuck her head in the doorway. "Miss Mae, I did find a cross code for Christopher but it doesn't fit our computer sequences. Does the code FSE798 mean anything?"

"FSE? Famous Signatures Exhibit we had in 1992 is coded as FSE. But I don't think Christopher would be in that exhibit. He wasn't famous, was he? Check it. I'm betting it's another indexing error."

A cup of coffee and ten minutes later, Jo-Beth returned. "Found something but I doubt it's anything significant. The 798 is a correspondence from Mr. P. Curie to the Javouheys on Webster Street. But it's written in French." She showed Antonia a plastic sleeved letter. "No good?"

Antonia gave a shrug. "Maybe." French. She hadn't translated any French in years. "Can you make me a copy? I'll see what I can do with it."

"It's not what you need, though, is it?" Jo-Beth said, disappointment clearly in her tone.

"What I need seems quite impossible these days."

Miss Mae patted her arm. "Perseverance, my dear, perseverance."

* * *

Antonia picked up Laura from school and drove home, anxious to get started translating P. Curie's letter to the Javouheys. Miss Mae confirmed that this was the scientist Pierre Curie, husband to Marie Curie, the famous turn-of-the-century physicist who discovered radium. The historical society had displayed Pierre Curie's letter in their 1992 exhibit of Famous Signatures.

At the kitchen table and with her French-English dictionary at hand, a long yellow-lined pad and pencil and erasers, she began what she feared might be a daunting task.

"Mommy?"

"What, hon?" She answered without lifting her eyes from the page.

"I'm going out to feed the birds, okay?"

"Didn't you feed them this morning?"

"I did. But the feeder's empty now. I guess we have hungry birds."

"Uh-huh. Don't leave the yard."

"I know. You don't have to say that every time. I'll be on the swings."

"Uh-huh." Antonia dove into her task with all her concentration as Laura slammed the back door behind her.

* * *

Beyond the linden trees.

Laura and Emily sat on a woody knoll, giggling at a fat brown rabbit with her babies scampering off.

"I love the linden trees here," Emily said. "I used to eat the leaves, but they're not as tasty as ash tree leaves."

"You can't eat tree leaves," Laura said. "Can you?"

"Linden flowers make a lovely tea. You should try it. Aren't the tree hollows in the trunks fun? When I was little I used to crawl inside them. I'm too big now."

"I'm too big too. Is that where the passage is? The one you told me about?"

"No, silly goose." Emily tugged on one of Laura's braids. "How did your mom like your hair? You didn't tell I did it, did you?"

"You're my secret friend! I'll never tell. My mom can't figure out how I did them myself—but I know she thinks they look good. Emily, why won't you show me the passage? I let you hide in the eaves in my room this morning."

"You might get scared."

"I won't. I'm very brave. My dad tells me that all the time. Is it magic? Is that why you won't show me, because it's a secret trick?"

"I guess it's a little like magic. Do you know who Phylira is?"

"No."

"In the storybooks, they turned her into a linden tree. I would love to be a linden tree. Then I wouldn't have to go away from here."

"I never read that storybook. Why do you have to go away?"

"We all go away. When Auntie Loretta decided to go away, she left her pearls in the grass for me."

"Why?"

"That's how I know she left the passage. See?" She pulled out a thin strand from under her collar. "Auntie Loretta called them champagne pinks because the pearls are so small, like champagne bubbles. Aren't they just divine?"

Laura examined them. "My mom has pearls too. My dad gave them to her."

"If I were a linden tree like Phylira, then I could stand here and look at your house all day, and I could watch you feed the birds. I could let the wind blow my branches up and down and ask the birds to sleep in my arms."

"Why do you want to look at my house?"

"You ask a lot of questions."

"Yeah, so what? Tell me why you want to be a tree and look at my house."

"Because . . . see that window up by the chimney?"

"Yeah, that's Henry's room."

She cupped her hand over Laura's ear. "That used to be my room."

Laura rolled her eyes. "You lived in my house? Just wait till I tell Henry!"

"No telling. If you tell, I won't be able to come here anymore."

Disappointed, Laura sank back against the tree trunk. She pulled a few cookies from her pocket. "Chocolate chip, Mrs. Field's. She makes the best. Emily, can you please show me the passage? I promise not to get scared."

Emily munched her cookie.

"I swear I'll never tell."

"If I show you, you have to sit very still, and you can't scream or yell or call me."

"I won't scream. Oh, I love magic tricks."

"All right. I'll show you very slowly."

Emily got up and smoothed her dress down. Standing straight, she inhaled a deep breath and closed her eyes.

Laura kept her eyes on Emily. "What are you doing?"

"Shhh. I have to think really slow so you can see it."

Emily dropped her chin into her neck. Her hands fell loosely against her sides. Light moved around her body like pockets, tempting Laura to reach out and touch one. Emily's head swayed. Her nose went blurry. Her arms dangled. Feet and legs shrunk into white sticks. Her whole body twirled. First, green ripples. Then brown crinkles. Then silver sparks like stars.

Without a sound, Emily vanished as if someone had blown her out like so many birthday candles.

Laura's hands flew to her mouth, eyes blinking, breath held. A little mist swept up to the tops of the linden trees, then fell down like raindrops. Laura inhaled the scents of clover and green grass.

Something gushed from behind. What a splash! She turned around.

Emily emerged through the clear air. She shook the sparkling droplets from her body and opened her arms with a grand bow.

Laura screamed with delight and applause.

* * *

At the kitchen table, Antonia spent a full hour translating the letter from French into English. She was surprised how quickly she remembered her French. She leaned back in her chair, quite pleased with herself, and read over the letter.

March 12, 1880

My dearest Catherine,

Nothing gives me more pleasure than news of you. I am happy to know you have made the sail successfully and are well and settled in Concord in your new life. Let me take this time to congratulate you on your marriage to Reverend Javouhey. I wish you both every happiness. You must tell me of your transcendentalist friends there, especially of the famous Mr. Emerson. It must be a great pleasure for you to live so near to your favorite poet.

I have been passing some time in solitude, walking our stony hills. The spirit of nature continues to soothe. I shall keep as a treasure our childhood memories in the woods, the lilies of the valley every spring, searching for odd plants and insects to bring to my father for his research. Remember that joyous cobweb we examined for hours and the lovely frogs that made you giggle? We were so spellbound as children, weren't we? I cannot help recall the fine words we spoke during our last night together. "One must make life into a dream and make the dream into a reality." These words have become richer than ever for me now. You are such an inspiration! Women of genius are rare, my lovely Catherine. I do miss you.

I've accepted an appointment as head of the laboratory at the new School of Industrial Physics and Chemistry. Paris is chilly tonight, streets all soaked. I recall how you adored Paris in the rain. I miss the countryside fiercely but

I still enjoy the museums and art galleries here.

Recently, since proving Gabriel Lippman correct regarding quartz piezoelectrique, our experimentations have yielded more publications in the Bulletin of the Mineralogy Society. I shall send you some reprints. You will be happy to know Jacques and I are fast at work. You know how I prefer to devote myself to discovery and I am indeed lost in my research again. At present, we are investigating nature's symmetry. Like the symmetry in the bloom of a flower or the exquisite snowflake, the symmetry of quartz crystals is everywhere in my eyes and absorbing all my time. But, we are also on to something else quite exciting. We are exploring the magnetic properties of bodies at diverse temperatures. Crystals heated with fire can attract ash. What amazing magnets they can be!

Now I am testing ferromagnetics, some iron and nickel, and investigating magnetic "field lines" as Faraday called them. I shall keep you informed of our progress in these magnetic fields and quartz crystals, as I know you are truly fond of the study of physics.

Jacques has become very much occupied with spiritualism these days and, as you know, I too am interested in the paranormal. He has befriended Mr. Henry Sidgwick of Cambridge University, president of the Society for Psychical Research in London. They investigate spiritualistic phenomena. This psychical research will become the new science, since it is becoming clear to many of us that some aspects of these phenomena are related to physics. Our new acquaintance is Balfour Stewart, Professor of Physics at Queens College who desires to publish a book on these supernatural investigations. Their temporary title is *Phantasms of the Living*. More on that to come.

I know we have promised to remain great friends and to that goal, I shall be your loyal pen companion. Please express my deepest gratitude to Christopher for his timely gift. When I mentioned my interest in reading the published *Book of Enoch,* I never expected he should send the book to me. What a thoughtful husband you have. Enoch's passages on crystals, if true and accurately translated, are shocking. Undoubtedly, a heaven built of crystals would fulfill my highest dreams. I wonder if Christopher might know which museum owns the chrysolite tablets that he mentioned to us. Jacques and I would so love to view them.

Do write again soon of Concord and your new home. I shall forever be, your devoted friend,

P. Curie

Antonia reread a line to be sure she'd translated it correctly. *Women of genius are rare, my lovely Catherine.* Was Curie in love with her? Certainly sounded like he was more than just a friend. No doubt, Mike would want to see this. She dialed his cell phone, left a quick message and then faxed him the copy of Curie's original letter and her translation. When she checked on Laura in the backyard, she didn't see her on the swings or by the bird feeder. She put a foot out the door and quickly scanned the patio, the side hedges, the linden trees. Wood-birds folded their wings hurriedly. Heart-shaped leaves stirred with feathery breaths. "Laura?"

The front doorbell rang. Had she locked the front door and Laura couldn't get in? She rushed to the foyer. Antonia swept open the front door, expecting Laura to be standing there with her gleeful little face.

Jo-Beth Abernathy from the Concord Historical Society stood

on the step, all smiles. "Antonia, hi! I'm so excited I found something for you."

"Oh! Jo-Beth. What a surprise." Antonia poked her head out the door. "You didn't see my daughter when you pulled in, did you?"

"Maybe. I just saw a girl running by the hedges to the back. She's adorable. I love her braids."

"Yes, that was her. She likes to torment me at front and back doors sometimes. Come in."

Jo-Beth stepped inside the foyer. "Miss Mae to the rescue, as usual." She waved an envelope. "You're not going to believe what we found. Oh, look at the time. I'm on my way to pick up my son from the gym, but I wanted to get this to you right away. We located a photograph of Christopher Javouhey."

"You're kidding."

"A group shot taken with Ralph Waldo Emerson in 1881 at the Massachusetts Historical Society."

Antonia took the photo out of the envelope. Jo-Beth pointed to the figures.

"There's Emerson and Lydian, his second wife. And Emerson's son Edward. We don't know who all of them are in the picture, but Miss Mae says that's the Reverend Christopher Javouhey standing to the left of Emerson." She turned over the photo. "See, we have some of the names verified on the photo label."

Antonia read the blurry handwriting on the backside.

"Miss Mae checked with the Society and they told her the occasion was listed as a poetry reading of Emerson's works. Someone had written down the program on the back. That list must be the titles of the poems that were read."
"Concord Hymn. The Amulet. Illusions."

"Wow, you're good. I had a tough time reading that handwriting, and it's so faded. Miss Mae said at that time Emerson was no longer lecturing or reading his poems in public because his health was failing. She thinks probably his son Edward did the readings."

"What do the letters C.J. mean at the end of each poem's title?"

Jo-Beth took a look. "Must be initials for Christopher Javouhey. Perhaps it was Christopher and not Edward who did the poetry readings."

She turned it over and examined each face in the photo, stopping at the woman with long wavy blond hair that streamed down her chest. And such dramatic eyes, she could hardly pull her own eyes away.

"Who is the woman standing next to Edward Emerson?"

Jo-Beth leaned over Antonia's shoulder to see. "Oh, Miss Mae thinks that's probably Edward's wife, but she wasn't able to confirm it as I was rushing out. If you want, she can research it for you tomorrow."

Antonia looked closely at the woman's hands. Although blurry, the bunches of lilies of the valley were unmistakable. "That's not Edward's wife. That's Catherine Javouhey."

"It is? How do you know?"

"Because I know what she looks like."

Jo-Beth frowned. "You do?"

"Well, I . . . I have a description. And that's her. Not a doubt in my mind."

"Oh, for heaven's sakes. So, if the woman you're trying to find is a descendant of Catherine's, then maybe Miss Mae could help you trace a family history to present day."

Antonia shook her head. "There are no descandants from Catherine. Her babies died."

"Oh. I'm sorry, Antonia. Then this photo is of no use?"

"Probably not. I'll send it on to the detective and see what he says."

"I did my best."

"I know you did, Jo-Beth. I'm very grateful."

Jo-Beth gave her a hug. "I've got to run. Let me know if you need anything else."

Antonia shut the door, leaned her head against the frame for a moment. If she had the energy, she might have burst into tears. She choked them back and read Emerson's poem titles again from the back of the photograph. "Concord Hymn, C.J. The Amulet, C.J. Illusions, C.J." Letting her mind float, she pictured Catherine, recalled the tone of her voice, the lilt and sway of her distinct words.

"C.J. Was it you, Catherine Javouhey, who read Emerson's poems that day at the Massachusetts Historical Society? I'll just bet it was."

Suddenly it struck her. "Laura!" She dashed through the kitchen barely able to draw a breath until she spotted Laura happily playing on the swings, braids flying, an adventurous grin on her face. "Time for homework, Laurie. Come inside, please."

Sitting at Adam's desk, Antonia began reading some of Emerson's poetry that she had on her bookshelf, and his essays. Over an hour passed before she tossed off her reading glasses. She needed a cup of strong tea. The phone rang, and she glanced at the caller ID. The message machine picked up.

"Antonia, Father Jim, here. I just wanted to remind you, well, actually invite you again to our novena at noon tomorrow for Henry. Our little group has tripled over these last few weeks. Your friends are very dear and loyal. Please come and share St. Helena with us."

Antonia pressed delete and headed into the kitchen to make tea.

Interlude

NIGHT IN THE ETERNAL CITY A.D. 328 ROME

THE SHADOW LENGTHENED. Helena's days declined. Like a desert owl in the wilderness, she cried out, "If day is done, do carry me off, Lord."

He brought up the refreshing mists and the cliffs of rain. Her crabbed hands spread out as lightning flashed within, her sight fully restored for the moment. The Lord scattered crystal's of ice over the city, and she followed His path under the veil of sky. Twelve ice angels floated over her with their *Song of the Arrow*. Helena walked the path, following their hushed rocking voices into a white field.

Snowy winds came down. The wind curled and spun an opening into the dark earth. Helena knelt. Nearby, a little bird hurried to its nest, and she took this as a sign to work quickly lest someone see her as the sun rose. With her bare hands, she dug up handfuls of deep loamy soil. And there, buried under a bed of unfolded roses, the treasure she found drew out her breath.

Helena raised up her old arms. In her hands she held the angels' holy ice, letting the sculpture shine brilliantly with the flooding dawn.

Chapter Eighteen

At headquarters, Balducci secured the skull inside the evidence room and hurried back into his office where Adam and Phillippa were waiting. Phillippa talked on her cell phone, leaned against his desk, whispered, her eyes darting and excited. He sat down at his desk, just as she clicked off.

"Okay, are you ready?" Phillippa held her camcorder.

Balducci had this dreadful cramp inside his stomach. Was this some kind of moment of truth? "What have you got?"

"I've got a fact that I can't explain. I taped this after you left the building with the skull in the black box. Watch." She pressed the play button and positioned the screen for both to see.

The sound came on scratchy and muddled, but Balducci was able to see the skull's image clearly inside the water tank. He actually veered back in his seat.

Phillippa's voice came over the video:

> "I see the occipital bone, and . . . and yes, there's the maxilla . . . the ramus . . . and mandible. My God, Zoe, this is an exact image of the skull. It's inside the water molecules, just like a photograph."

Balducci blinked. Impossible. Was he really seeing this accurately? He watched with intense eyes, listening to Phillippa's instructions and Zoe scream, "I'm afraid to think!"

"Now, Mike, watch this part. Can you see it, Adam? I'll slow down the motion so you get it all."

Zoe's voice came on slurred:

> "Oh Phil, you'll never get that thing in the freezer. Look what it's doing!"

The tank took on a brownish color, then shot up grey steamy coils, but the skull's image remained completely visible.

> "Jesus! It's bubbling up. Zoe, go pull the fire alarm! Get everybody out of the building. Go. Now!"

Dark water boiled up.

Phillippa tapped Balducci's arm, and he nearly jumped. "Mike, watch the surface of the water in the last scene here."

The surface water waved up, transforming the skull's image into a gigantic ball, expanding like a blackish balloon as it rotated, spilling murky water over the edges of the tank. The balloon rose up, the skull's face outlined brilliantly with the water and . . . the screen went fuzzy with zig-zagging lines—then blank.

"What the hell?"Adam said.

"Unbelievable, right? Did you catch your breath yet?" She gave Adam a tug.

"What? How did? I don't even know what question to ask." Balducci ran his hands through his hair as if that might clear his confusion.

"Yeah, well I do know what questions to ask, but who to ask is the key. I called a colleague of mine and he's puzzled as well but he had some theories. Let's start from the observation. First, this skull appears to have transferred its image into the water. Two, the image inside the water appears to have caused the explosion."

Balducci shook his head. "That's not even possible. Is it?"

"We like to think nothing is impossible and keep all doors open. Improbable versus possibilities, that serves science far better. It's true, at this moment, I can't identify chemically or physically how this happened. But I'll tell you this, it was like some cannon ball shooting straight through my lab. Ka-pow! And get this. It was all dry combustion. There's not a drop of water left inside the lab or outside, so I can't even test the elements of the water now. Pretty smart, this thing is, huh? Evaporating itself like that."

"Wait a minute, don't explosions happen in labs routinely? I mean, you haven't seen this sort of thing before?"

"Never."

"Run those last frames again for me."

Adam watched like a kid with his nose to a TV screen.

Balducci scratched his head at the end frame. "How do you explain an image causing an explosion?"

She blew strands of hair off her face. "Damn it, Mike, I can't even explain how the damn image formed inside the water, let alone how it burst through the brick wall!"

"I'm sorry. I didn't—"

"No, I'm sorry for snapping at you. I'm more upset that I can't figure out a cause."

"And your colleague couldn't help?"

"Actually Jackson did have a theory. He suggested, maybe, and this is a big maybe, the image that formed in the tank is actually a morphogenetic field, a pattern of the skull."

"I don't follow," Adam said.

"Morphogenetic means origin of form. It's a field. And it carries the structure of the organism. Think of it as, let's say, a blueprint. So, the skull left its blueprint inside the water. How or why, I can't fathom."

"And how does this field function?" Balducci asked.

Phillippa clucked her tongue. "We know zip about how morphic fields function."

"But you've seen them before, right?"

"Never. As far as we know, morphic fields are not visible to the human eye."

"Then how can we see this one?"

"Maybe we're wrong. Maybe we can observe them under unique conditions. If this is a morphic field, then it's the most remarkable one ever! And I'd like to learn more."

"Wait a sec," Adam said. "Didn't you tell us that the quartz skull had a field that went off your Gauss meter? So you *can* test the field?"

"We test electromagnetic fields, which are physical fields, atoms, protons, etcetera, produced by electrically charged objects like the crystal skull. We test objects with Gauss meters. We test electromagnetic fields in humans with EEGs and EKGs."

"And morphogenetic fields are different?"

"They are different because they're biological fields. A morphic field carries the exact form of a living thing. And carries memory of behavior."

"Can't test it with a Gauss meter?"

"We have no instruments to test morphic fields. We have to observe behavior to verify." She twisted her shoulders in a confident little turn. "But we have every indication that morphic fields are the primary source for all other fields."

Balducci gave her a slow nod. *She's really cute when she shows off like that.* "Primary source? Meaning?"

"Meaning they evolve within nature and are first elements. Trees, birds, sea urchins, animals, crystals, human bodies all have morphic fields as their primary energy source. But don't ask me for absolute proof. It's still a working theory according to Rupert Sheldrake, a biologist in Cambridge, famous for this kind of work."

"My body has a morphogenetic field?" Adam asked. "Henry's too?"

"We all do. Every single one of us."

"Is Sheldrake a reputable scientist?" Balducci put in.

"Highly. He's been published all over the place."

"Mainstream scientist?"

"Not quite mainstream, but let's remember that it was Einstein who discovered the field concept, so we're in good company."

"I don't get this morphic field." Adam's voice had an impatient snap to it. "I mean, if I put my hand in a tub of water and remove it, I don't leave the image in the water."

Balducci snickered.

"What? I wasn't being funny."

"That's not what Phillippa meant, Adam."

"It isn't?" He turned to her. "Explain how a morphic field works in a human."

"I can't. But I can give you an example of how it works in a mouse. Sheldrake surgically removed muscles from lab mice. He ground the muscles up into tiny bits and pieces and surgically put the mixed substances back into the mice. What do you think happened?"

"Dead mice," Adam said.

"Not at all. Those same ground-up muscles became normal working muscles again."

"The mice weren't crippled?" Balducci felt his eyes go wide.

"Not in any way. The morphogenetic field of each mouse, this inherent memory field, redirected the muscles to restructure themselves back into the correct pattern to perform normally. All the mice were fully restored. Now, isn't that just fucking amazing?"

"Fucking amazing," Adam said.

"Sheldrake suspects that morphic fields may exist on a grander scale within nature. They may have the power to gather outside the living body, or object, and vibrate across vast areas. Around the entire planet, is what he says."

"Hold on," Balducci gestured. "You're not saying that this quartz skull might have the ability to vibrate its morphic field to, say, Australia?"

Her smile seemed to reach across the desk. "Can you imagine! But why not? All energy attracts. The planet earth is a gigantic magnet. We don't know what boundaries morphic fields have, if any at all."

Balducci toyed with the pack of Camels, flipping it over and over on its side until he had a steady rhythm going. He let his mind go blank for a moment. This was a lot to absorb. He imagined a clean sheet—no words, no thoughts. The slap of the cigarette pack flipping soothed him and a question surfaced. "Phillippa, earlier you said the image was 'pretty smart.' Why did you say that? You don't think this skull, or its morphic field, is intelligent, do you?"

"Well, look at what happened here. My intention was blocked. I couldn't get the water samples fast enough into the freezer. That damn thing blasted itself out of my lab. The little stinker."

"Why would it do that?" Adam sat forward abruptly. "Are you saying it knew you were examining it?"

"Well, no, not exactly. On second thought . . . possibly."

"Are morphic fields intelligent?"

"We suspect they must be. But we don't know to what level. You have to figure that the actual skull is the primary source of the intelligence."

Adam nodded with a smile. "Well then, why don't we see just how smart that skull really is? I mean, if it's smart enough to leave its morphic field inside a water tank, and then blow itself away so you can't test it, maybe it's smart enough to reveal something about its history . . . about Catherine. After all, Catherine owned the skull. She must have handled it when she buried it in Old Willow. What do you think, Mike?"

"Forget it. I'm not fooling with that thing."

"No, Mike. Wait." Phillippa was on her feet now. "Adam might have something here. My analysis of the skull was only for properties and structure. I can't scientifically explain what happened today. I don't know why the readings went off my Gauss meter. I don't know why we couldn't see the skull inside the water tank."

"Maybe it was hiding," Adam offered.

Phillippa looked straight at him. "You may be right, Adam. I'll tell you what. We drastically altered its environment and definitely disturbed its state. I should take another look at the specimen. Go get it, Mike."

"What do you want to do to it?"

"Let's explore, rather than examine. Oh, come on, don't look at me like that. Clearly, this is no ordinary piece of quartz. I'll be cautious. Go get it."

"Yeah, Mike, go get it," Adam chimed in. "You're not scared of that thing, are you?"

He didn't move. He thought about Jake Kras. Why did the skull radiate heat? Had Jake mistakenly exposed it to heat? Was it hiding? Was all this a warning of sorts? "The skull stays locked up, in the dark, and nobody is going to explore it or examine it."

Phillippa flopped down into the chair. "I think you're being ridiculous. This piece of quartz exhibits inexplicable powers. It would be irresponsible not to investigate further. Adam's right."

"Good, then. Adam's right. And I'm being ridiculous." He leaned back in his chair, put his hands behind his head. "Anybody want coffee?"

"You're afraid that thing has some kind of supernatural power," Adam said. "Well, what about Henry? He's the one who revealed where the skull was buried."

Phillippa frowned. "Henry? He did?"

"Damn straight he did. Grave site number twenty-four. Admit it, Mike. You wouldn't have dug up that site if it weren't for Henry's twenty-four."

"I was just following a lead."

"And here's another one, right in front of you. I want to find out what Catherine's skull can reveal besides its face in a goddamned water tank. Go fucking get it!"

Balducci looked at Phillippa. "This meeting is over. Thank you for your help, Phillippa, you're free to leave."

Phillippa sat there, blinking her eyes for a moment. She looked at Adam. "Guess that's my order to exit." She grabbed her camcorder and proceeded to the door. "I'll call you later . . . Adam."

The door closed behind her.

Balducci stood up. "We're done here, Adam."

Adam remained sitting, his cobalt blue eyes hard on him. "Not until you tell me what Dan found inside Catherine Javouhey's coffin."

Balducci tossed his pen on the desk. "Go home, Adam."

"He obviously found something or you wouldn't be hiding it."

"He found nothing."

"Nothing."

"Not a damn thing."

Adam didn't blink. "Meaning . . . empty? No remains?"

Chapter Nineteen

A BLACK AND VACANT SKY settled over the saltbox-style framed house in the rural town of Lincoln. Mike Balducci had been up most of the night reading, reviewing, examining his notes. First, a few beers, then a few shots, now cups of black coffee. On the bed, he laid out copies of Pierre Curie's letter, the English translation, and the photograph of Ralph Waldo Emerson with Catherine and Christopher Javouhey that Antonia had faxed him. While this information was informative, it didn't provide any real leads to locating Catherine or Henry Brooke. Indirect routes made him edgy and impatient, but experience told him to press on. One thing in that photograph struck him: the lily of the valley in Catherine's hands. Was this whimsy or cunning? Can forces from a determined personality persist after death? Hatch seemed to think so.

Two hours of questioning him at headquarters produced only more frustration. The little bastard sat there, mouth clamped shut, eyes cast to the floor, hands folded tightly on a Bible. Where did the old guy get such nerves of steel anyway?

When Balducci brought up the subject of disinterment of corpses, Hatch didn't even blink. If Hatch was surprised by the news that Catherine Javouhey's coffin was empty, he kept his cool head, or he wasn't surprised at all.

Body snatching was hardly a modern-day crime. But in the nineteenth century, body snatching was more than just a ghoulish activity. These crimes for the purposes of anatomy dissection for medical information were not uncommon in the 1800s, and Massachusetts was one of the first states to enact laws against such practices. Dan Hersey had an ancestor back in the 1770s, Ebenezer Hersey, who donated money to Harvard to hire a Professor of Anatomy. Dan and Mike often debated if Ebenezer was a member of the secret society known then as the Spunkers, who obtained fresh corpses for their anatomical studies. After a few beers, that debate could get very heated.

But Balducci knew that Hatch's family history might be in play here, so he asked him outright, specifically avoiding the term body-snatcher. "Was anyone in your family a resurrectionist?" All he got was a shake of the head. Before Balducci walked out of the cell, Hatch spouted a single warning: "The *Lord of Life* is at work here. Be smart, Detective, and leave it be."

Leave it be? "'*The lords of life . . . I saw them pass,*'" he read aloud from Emerson's book. "Did you really?" While Emerson was extraordinarily forward-thinking when it came to science and nature, did Concord's sage know that Catherine had buried this quartz crystal skull in Old Willow in 1880? Did Emerson know about electromagnetic fields and quartz piezoelectricity? Catherine certainly knew, and she knew it from Curie, the very scientist who'd discovered it.

"Who are the *lords of life,* Waldo?" In his essay, *History,* Emerson wrote about *using the secret virtues of minerals.* In another essay, *We have quitted all beneath the moon, and entered that crystal sphere in which everything in the world of matter reappears, but transfigured and immortal.*

Crystal sphere? Transfigured and immortal? But that was just poetics—Emerson's famous talent for the metaphor. Or was it his mystical and metaphysical speculations? Balducci rubbed his eyes. Exhaustion took over. He read more passages, paged forward until he couldn't see the lines of text any more. Sleep, that's what he needed. And he surrendered, letting the books fall from his hands, his last thoughts that he needed to improve his aptitude for metaphysical deductions.

When dawn broke through the windows, he could barely open his eyes. He avoided looking at the clothes heaped on the chair, overflowing ashtrays, and files scattered everywhere. The bottle of Tennessee whiskey (the kind his old man used to drink) sat on the dresser.

Had way too many of those last night.

He showered and dressed, fumbled with his tie at the mirror. Nearly seven o'clock. Dan Hersey was likely at Old Willow already. He yanked off the crooked tie and pitched it into the clothes pile. And with that sweep, sent the bottle of whiskey over. It splattered across the carpet.

Maddy'll kill me if she sees this—

He stopped the thought right there. His eyes wandered her dresser, the perfume bottles, her silver hairbrush with the blond strands still tangled in the bristles. Even her white robe hung expectantly on the hook in the closet. "Hey, Babe. I'm losing this case. My God, Maddy, I may never find this kid." He sat down on the bed, head in hands. "I'm missing something . . . something big. Remember, Babe, when you used to be my sounding board? You always asked just the right questions."

Emerson's biography fell off the bed. "For all the help you are. Fucking *lords of life.*" He flung the book across the room. On the floor, streaked with fresh whiskey stains, lay the notepaper with Phillippa's phone number. The biologist's husky voice swam inside his head. *This piece of quartz exhibits inexplicable powers. It would be irresponsible not to investigate further.*

He picked up the phone, dialed the number, then hung up before it connected. He hated second thoughts; sometimes they could really screw up the best instincts. In the kitchen he reheated stale coffee. Again he picked up the phone and dialed. This time he punched the numbers without hesitation, knowing he had to move ahead despite the dangers.

"Good morning, Dr. Allan. This is your wake-up call. Courtesy of Mike Balducci."

"Oh, I remember you." She made a sleepy laugh, rustling the bed covers. "You're the guy with the brisk manner who shooed me away yesterday."

He winced. "My apologies. Can I buy you lunch?"

"And why would I have lunch with you, Detective Balducci?"

"I have something . . . in mind . . . that I'd like you to consider."

A short pause while she thought that over. "Does it involve that charming skull you're so fond of?"

"Yes, you win."

She must have thrown the bedsheets clean across the room from the sound of it. He wondered if she wore lacy silk to bed or tight little T-shirts and boy shorts.

"Where? What time?" She said breathlessly.

* * *

The Bobcats were in position at Old Willow, the crane hauling up buckets of dirt and stone. Clouds threatened rain—probably a storm coming—ah, what the hell, no turning back now. There was truth in the air. He could smell it.

"You didn't need to come," Dan said. "I told you I'd take care of this."

"I know you did. And I appreciate your taking care of yesterday's exhume, but I'm here now. As I should be. Who's first?"

"The grandparents, Ezra and Sophie Hatch. Damn nasty business. How the hell did you get Hatch to agree to exhume his family members?"

Balducci squinted toward the gates. "Where's the photographer?"

Dan froze. "Oh, Jesus. You didn't get authorization?"

"Who'd you get to do the photography?"

"Fat Devon. What the hell, you didn't get Hatch to sign the release? Christ, Mike, I'm not happy with this!"

"Me neither." And he walked away.

It took them a half-hour to dig down to the coffin of Ezra Hatch. They secured chains around the wood and hauled it to the surface. Balducci ignored his racing heart and the rattle in his bowels.

Cynthia "Fat" Devon showed up just in time, camera in hand. She wore a white plastic rain hat with pink hearts on the brim. Devon fiddled with her photo lens. "Hey Mike, are these guys union gravediggers?"

"No. Why, you got a problem with that? You always got a gripe, Devon. Can't you ever say anything jolly?"

"You want jolly when we're hauling up coffins?"

The men pried open the lid with crowbars. Decayed wood crumbled off. Balducci wanted a smoke, anything to drive out the sour saliva filling his mouth.

With a *crack,* they lifted the lid. Devon zoomed in and snapped. "Oh, for Christ's sake, another one with no remains? What is this? Want a snap for your wallet, Mike?"

"Knock it off, Devon."

"Hey, wait a sec." She refocused her camera. "I saw something reflect in my lens again. Just like yesterday, Dan. Is it jewelry?"

Balducci bent down and with a plastic-gloved hand scooped up a handful of dirt. "Looks like sand to me." But there was something shiny in his palm.

Dan leaned over his shoulder. "Same sandy elements we found yesterday in Catherine Javouhey's coffin. Odd, isn't it? I took a sample for the lab."

"Looks like the smallest diamonds in the world," Devon said. "Maybe they *are* diamonds. Maybe people were sprinkled with diamond chips in their coffins back then. Like the pharaohs in Egypt were buried with—"

"Shut up, Devon. More likely mica washed in from soil erosion." Balducci slipped the sandy substance into an evidence bag.

They exhumed three more coffins. Balducci puffed Camel after Camel, walked away, stared at the grey sky, the mud, the pockets of water. The crew pried open Sophie Hatch's coffin. Balducci kept his distance but could see that it was empty too. Then Hatch's parents, Hannah and Gideon Hatch. The interiors contained dirt, spider webs, and some of the same glittery sand. But not a dry bone nor a single article of clothing.

"You're under oath, Devon," Balducci reminded her. "No disclosures to anybody."

"Yeah, yeah, yeah. I'll have the prints for you tomorrow. See ya."

"Wait a minute. Where're you going?"

"What, we're not done? Dan told me four coffins today. One

from yesterday, that's five. I'm outta here."

"I've got three more."

"What three more?" Dan shouted. "You got court orders for three more exhumes?"

"Brady granted me three more."

"Whose graves?"

"Catherine's children."

"What do you want those for? For Christ's sake, Mike, isn't this enough?"

"Brady signed the orders." He slapped them into Dan's hands.

These three coffins proved much easier to unearth than the others. The crew opened the lids, and Dan scooped the gravelly substance into evidence bags. "Same as the others, Mike. What the hell? 'From dust to dust' as they say, huh?"

Balducci felt something drop into the well of his stomach. He remembered a phrase he had read from last night. *Grain of dust? Stones to dust? Crystals to dust?* An urge to rush home hit him.

"Close everything up here. Catch up with you later, Dan."

He sped off to Lincoln.

When Mike pulled into his driveway, he banged open the front door and rushed straight to the bedroom. He tore through his Emerson collection, checked the yellow note stickies, skimmed the highlighted printouts, ran his finger down indexes and tables of contents but couldn't find the passage. He was sure Emerson had written something about the body's crystal dust and meridians, or was it in relation to the brain? "Or maybe not. Goddamn! I'm losing it."

He needed more coffee, needed to refocus. In the kitchen, when the phone rang he almost didn't answer it.

"Mike Balducci? London calling, Eva Sugarman here. I got your voice mail and email. Is this a good time to talk about your crystal skull?"

"Perfect time, Eva." He sat down in the kitchen chair and searched for a pen.

"I just emailed you about twenty files. Where is your skull from, do you know?"

"That's what I'm hoping you'd be able to tell me. This skull was apparently brought here from Paris in 1880."

"Give me a second to open my file and I'll read you what I have on that. Let's see now, 1880? Here it is. I have notes on a crystal skull at the Musee de L'Homme in France. The records indicated that a French soldier sold a crystal skull to the museum sometime around 1840. The description reads a 'gleamy surface.'"

"This skull we have here has a gleamy surface."

"Many of them do. Did Phillippa mention my work scouting the famous Twelve Ancient Crystal Skulls from around the world?"

"She didn't specifically. There's twelve of these guys?"

"There are. And they are highly acclaimed. Now here's a characteristic of the French skull. No moving parts. A number of frauds out there have moving parts."

"Like what, exactly?"

"The jaw, my good man, the jaw. This is not a talking skull."

"Glad to hear that one."

"Aha! Have you shown it to anyone who can determine if it's one of the famous Twelve? Frauds are abundant from New York to Melbourne. For myself, I've identified several impostors."

"Only Phillippa has examined it."

"Then you'll need Document 8012 from the International Archaeological Society. It describes the famous Twelve along with each site of origin. I've emailed it to you."

"Who put this document together?"

"Dr. Emilio Perucca, with the European Archaeological Society. He attempted to locate the famous Twelve skulls but never succeeded. He compiled this list from historical data, archaeological reports, logbooks, letters, and journals from hundreds of archaeologists. And word of mouth as well, which is not very reliable, but he did a fine job with it anyhow."

"So you know Perucca?"

"I did, yes. Perucca wanted to know what crystal skulls were reportedly in England at the time and if I could lay my hands on any of them. He shared some of his files with me. I found him to be a compulsive fact checker."

"Are there any pictures of these skulls?"

"Not a chance of that. Perucca does have a note about a daguerreotype of the Twelve skulls exhibited at the first World's Fair in London in 1851. That was at the Crystal Palace in Hyde Park. That's how they became known as the famous Twelve Ancient Crystal Skulls from around the world. But that daguerreotype was never located."

"1851 in London? Eva, hold on a minute." He rushed into the bedroom, picked up the Emerson biography, and paged to Emerson's timeline. Yes, his memory was accurate. Emerson had attended the World's Fair in 1851 in London and visited the Crystal Palace while he was visiting geologist, Charles Lyell.

He grabbed the portable phone. "Eva, did you say all twelve skulls were exhibited?"

"All twelve, yes, lined up in a room draped in black velvet and lit by candlelight."

Balducci was accessing her emails on his computer screen as they spoke.

"And what's the story behind the use of these skulls?"

"Occult rituals, healings, eternal youth, curses, the list goes on. Stories abound from the Aztecs to the Mayans. And then there was a story going round that if the secret of the crystal skull is revealed to you, you die. Perucca mentioned only one case that he claims was verified."

"Who died and how?"

"Two men who came in contact with the Lipton-Wolff skull died on the spot. Suffocation or heart attack. The medical reports were conflicting. Their names were Jonathan Benequist and Eugene Wheeler. The suspicion was that they wanted to misuse the skull's powers. At the time, the skull was owned by the Lipton-Wolff family. Of course the family denied the deaths had anything to do with the skull. That would be skull number six on Perucca's list. Perucca was convinced the Lipton-Wolff skull caused their deaths."

"Do you know if any of these skulls radiated heat?"

"No reports on that."

"And where are these famous Twelve skulls now?"

Her peal of laughter made Balducci wince. "Who knows? After the 1851 World's Fair, they were presumably returned to their respective owners. Perucca never got his hand on a single one of them, poor chap. He claimed he was commissioned by the Society to assemble the famous Twelve skulls and display them at an upcoming World's Fair. Lofty ambition to say the least."

"Thanks, Eva. You've been very helpful."

"You know, it's likely you have an imposter. I'd be astonished if it turned out to be one of the ancient Twelve. Anyway, I'd send you a couple of names of people who can examine it for you, but none are in the United States at the moment. How about you bring it along to London and I'll have a go of it myself? Would love to."

"Not possible. I don't suppose that French skull is still in the Musee de L'Homme in Paris today?"

She practically hooted. "Sorry, that skull was stolen from the museum in 1879. It's anybody's guess where the old devil lies now."

After hanging up, he read over Dr. Emilio Perucca's bio, dated 1994. The Italian, trained at universities in Toronto and Cambridge, had spent years researching crystallography and mineralogy in Scotland, the Middle East, Honduras, Italy.

Quickly he read through the first page of Perucca's Document 8012.

> Skull #1 Australia. [description: clear quartz] Documentation: letter. Willem Dampier (1689) reportedly obtained skull from the Wurundjeri, the Aboriginal people of the Kulin nation, who occupied what is now Melbourne. Aborigines claimed skull was beamed down into the earth from the stars (verbal report). Owned for a short time by Melbourne Museum (1880), documentation verified. Current owner unknown.

> Skull #2 Sumba Islands (Sandlewood) Indonesia. [description: amethyst] Reported by a Portuguese sailor. Skull buried with wood sculptures and masks of Marapu

clan (verbal report: unknown date). At one time owned by Major David Dinsmoor (led expedition to China for Boston Museum of Fine Arts in 1936). Documentation: published bulletin in Indo-Pacific Prehistory Association. Fate undetermined. No known owner.

Skull #3 India: Bombay. [description: small rose quartz, some jade] reported to have been excavated from Bombay, possibly Elephanta Caves, Gharapuri. Six Brahmanic caves, carved 8th cent. (documentation is letter fragments of Sir Charles Stokes of Harvard University, 1841). Current owner unknown.

He skimmed down to the Lipton-Wolff skull.

Skull #6 Belize in British Honduras, Central America [description: weight 8 lbs, clear gleaming quartz, interior prisms] Location of excavation, old city of Lubaantun, outskirts of city of Belize. Discovered by Edward Lipton-Wolff in 1849, during excavation of collapsed Mayan altar. Documentation verified. Owned by Lipton-Wolff family. Unconfirmed reports the skull was returned to descendants of Mundo Maya tribe for burial.

"Eight pounds? Interior prisms? Shit."

Chapter Twenty

At Vincenzo's Restaurant in West Concord, Balducci asked for a quiet table in the far corner near a Van Gogh print of "The Café." Phillippa walked in twenty minutes late. She wore a little black dress that revealed a lot of leg. Flushed, breathing heavy as if she'd been running, she sat down and ordered a glass of red wine with lots of ice. He settled for a club soda.

"On duty, huh?" Phillippa tossed her napkin in her lap.

"Almost all the time with this case. Red wine with ice?"

"I love it that way. The old Romans drank snow-chilled red wine. So, where *is* the little sweetheart? In your trunk? I can't wait to get my hands on her."

"*She* is at headquarters, locked in the black box. Shall we eat first?"

Phillippa opened the menu, barely looked at it. "That grilled romaine salad sounds good." With a slap, she closed the menu. "So, this is what I plan to do. First, I want to use an ultraviolet light source on it and—"

"Hold on a minute."

"What?" She played with the rim of the glass against her lips.

"When you said you wanted to explore the skull, what exactly did you mean? We have to be very careful here. I need details."

"Of course you do. One, I want to examine it under different light elements. Two, I want to get it to shed its morphic field again so I can test it. That is going to be very exciting! Three, I want to try some Kirlian photography, which might show unseen energy. I'm taking a leap with the Kirlian, but what the hell."

Balducci took a slug of his club soda, picked up the menu. "I think we should order."

"I gotta ask you, Mike. I've been thinking half the night about this. Why did Adam say he thinks the skull might reveal something about Catherine Javouhey?"

Balducci tightened his grip on the menu. "No idea. And don't try testing me. How about that shrimp and swordfish special? They prepare it for two."

She took the menu from his hand. "I had a very detailed talk with Adam last night."

He gave her a chilly look.

"And I spoke to his lovely wife, Antonia, too. Can you prove Catherine and Hatch are conspirators in Henry's kidnapping? Do you even have—"

"I didn't come here today to discuss the Henry Brooke case with you."

"So we're here because . . . ?"

"I'm betting that instinct will triumph over reason. Taking a goddamn leap that I don't mind telling you, I'm more than just a little uncomfortable about."

She gave a cute smirk. "Aha, digging up that warrior within, are you? Works for me."

"So you want the shrimp and swordfish special?" he said. "It's charcoal grilled."

"Mike, to be fair, I have to tell you. I just now spoke with Eva Sugarman on the way over here."

Oh for Christ's sake. "The fish is topped with black olives."

"I told her about what happened yesterday at the lab."

"Capers, roasted tomatoes too. What the hell did you do that for?"

"I told Eva about Henry. About Catherine Javouhey. Told her everything."

"Phillippa," he said a bit too loud, "don't get clever and try to meddle in my case."

"Ohhhh, getting brisk again, are you?"

"Confidential police work, remember that?"

"You're right. I'm sorry. But Eva knows everything about these skulls, and I needed her opinion before I start testing. I had to give her the whole picture and the details of my exam. You know what she said? She suspects you might have the Lipton-Wolff skull from Belize."

"Did she?" He tried to say matter-of-factly.

"Did you know they estimate the Lipton-Wolff skull to be some 3600 years old?"

"Really," he tried to keep his tone flat.

"And used by Mayan high priests as an instrument of death?"

He closed his eyes tight for a second. "Don't tell me any more. And anyway, you're a biologist, what do *you* care about the supernatural stories?"

She lifted her chin, cocksure. "Look here, I know plenty of worthy scientists who've validated supernatural events. I don't mind dabbling in such a challenge. And I wouldn't mind being on the edge of a metaphysical discovery that breaks the barriers."

"Keep your agenda out of this. And don't you dare go dabbling in the Henry Brooke case! Brisk enough for you?"

"Brrrrrrr."

The waiter came over, put down a basket of bread. "Ready to order?"

"We certainly are," he said. "And you can bring me a nonalcoholic beer."

"Could you give us a few more minutes?" Phillippa said, ever so politely. She placed her cell phone on the table. "Jackson's waiting for my green light. We're going to use his lab." She could hardly sit still. "I told him to set up to do x-ray diffraction experiments on the skull."

"Jesus, you can't stop, can you? What'll that prove?"

"It produces a three-dimensional picture of the density of electrons in the quartz."

"Say again?"

"Whatever's stored in that crystal might very well show up as a pattern. Get it? A face? A body? A location? Oh, man, I couldn't eat a thing right now. Can we just go!"

Twenty minutes later, they were both at police headquarters. Phillippa waited in Balducci's office while he fetched the skull. When he walked in with the black box, she grabbed it without a blink and unlatched the lid.

"Just wait until Jackson gets his hands on you, baby. This is going to be some ride." She scooped up the skull.

"Let's keep that thing inside the box, if you don't mind. When does Jackson expect us?"

"I'm waiting for his call back now. Within the hour, I think. You know quartz is ageless, don't you?" She slipped the skull back into the box. "What's that smell?"

"I don't smell anything."

"It's like . . . wet ropes or something. And salty." She sniffed both her palms. "Oh, Christ, it's me."

When she stretched her fingers out, Balducci saw a thick icy glaze form over her skin. The ice webbed her fingers into stiff bent claws. Trembling, she curled to the floor in pain. "Mike! Help me."

He grabbed her hands and banged them against the desktop. Chunks of ice flew.

"Get it off!"

Again he slammed her hands. More ice shattered over the carpet. She cupped her fists into her lap and screamed through clenched lips.

"Sit down. Put your hands under the desk lamp." He began rubbing them, melting the ice with his own body heat.

"Ohhh . . ." She let out a sigh as her fingers unclenched.

"Christ Almighty, Phillippa. You had to touch it, didn't you?"

"Oh, that's better. Thanks. I touched it yesterday a dozen times. And Zoe, too. But, we were wearing exam gloves."

After a minute of rubbing, he stopped and looked closely at the insides of her palms. The skin bubbled up raw as meat.

"Where are those ice chips, Mike?" She scanned the floor and desk.

"Your skin is damaged."

"Can you get an ice sample so we can test it?"

"This must hurt like hell." He didn't see any chips anywhere. Had they all evaporated?

"I'm okay. There, Mike, I see one near the doorway. Put it in the freezer. Hurry!"

He scooped it up with a piece of paper and hurried it off to the kitchen freezer and ran

back to his office. "Happy now?" he said walking in. "You should have a doctor take a look at your hands."

"I'll be fine. Doesn't hurt much now." She kept her palms under the lamp light, then lifted them for him to inspect. "This was my fault, Mike. I should never have handled it like that."

"Christ, was it reacting to human touch?" Balducci got up to latch the black top over the skull. He froze. The skull appeared to be trembling, shivering like some old car motor. He veered and turned his head away abruptly.

"What is it?" Phillippa jumped up to see.

Cracks splintered over the cranium. Droplets of black ice dripped down the back like thin hair. Spotty dark patches spread at the sides, deforming the head into a bright pink oval. As he closed the lid, the jaw flickered with fuchsia sparks that began to buzz.

Balducci snapped the lock on. "Did you see that?"

"It's shape-shifting. Fucking amazing! Maybe it'll calm down now that it's back in the dark box."

"Why did it turn you to ice like that?"

"I can only guess . . . self-protection. But Mike, what mechanism did it use to do that? What kind of energy is this?"

"I don't think I want to know. Call Jackson. Cancel the tests."

"Oh Mike, don't get all—"

"If Eva Sugarman suspects this is the 3600-year-old Lipton-Wolff skull that caused the suffocation of two men, and if you think I'm going to let that kind of danger have the advantage here just because you and Jackson want to go exploring, you can waltz out that door right now."

"This isn't about me. I thought this was about using your instincts over reason. What kind of warrior are you? Running scared?"

"Sometimes, Phillippa, there's strength in strategic retreat!" He walked the black box to the evidence room, a string of Emerson's words ringing in his head: *Always do what you are afraid to do.*

Not today, Waldo. I can't be that hero today.

Chapter Twenty-One

ANTONIA CLIMBED THE STAIRS to Laura's room and placed the stack of clean laundry on the bed. A mess of sweaters lay on the floor. Just the sight exhausted her. And a headache brewed behind her eyes from spending hours discussing the events of yesterday with Adam (exploding water tank, empty coffin, skull images, morphic fields). How could a morphogenetic field of energy—whatever that was—make itself seen? She tried to picture it but failed. Adam couldn't stop talking, couldn't stop examining all the theories. He insisted they find more information from the Internet about magnetic and morphic fields until she felt so overwhelmed she'd finally had to close her eyes and not listen anymore.

Until Dr. Phillippa Allan called. Their conversation went late into the night. The idea of that crystal skull having scientific powers—electromagnetic or piezoelectric or otherwise—shook her to the bone.

She threw open Laura's closet door with a bang.

At the top of the closet, Henry's shoebox marked with the *H* sat on the shelf, the top askew. Without hesitation she reached for it, flipped the top off. Her eyes went wide. "Adam? Adam!"

Her feet barely hit the stairs down into the library, where Adam sat at his desk examining the photograph of Catherine Javouhey from the historical society.

"Take a look at this." She placed Laura's drawing before him. "How do you suppose Catherine managed this? Her picture is completely mended."

Adam grabbed it and ran his fingers over the surface of the paper.

"Has that woman been here, in the house, Adam?"

"Oh, Jesus, don't even say it." He put it up to the window light. "Did Laura draw another picture? You know how persistent she can be sometimes. Maybe—"

"No, Adam, this is the original. Look at that same odd curve on the hood. I remember the heavy mark. It looked like her arm skidded on the page with the crayon. Catherine did this."

"I'll call Mike."

"This is a message, Adam. Catherine's telling us she's been here in this house. Don't you see what's going on? She's taken Henry because she's lost her own children. Her boy Joseph was five years old and her two girls were under three when they died. Well, she can't have my son. I'm going over to that cemetery. She came to me before. Maybe she'll come to me again."

"Annie, let me. This might be—"

"You stay here with Laura. This is between Catherine and me." She tossed the drawing at him, snatched a shawl from the kitchen hook and ran for the cow path.

By the time she got to the cemetery gates, she realized they'd be locked. And they were. The rock walls looked pretty steep. *Of all days to wear a long skirt.* Just the same, she found a slip of ledge and wedged her foot onto it, hoisted herself up, grabbed on to the branch of an accommodating hemlock, and lifted herself to the top of the wall. In the process, she caught her skirt pocket on a jagged edge, which ripped across the front. The hemlock branch snagged her shawl, making her fight with the branches to get it back. She slid down the wall on the other side, scraping the inside of her forearm on a sharp rock. The gash ran from her elbow to wrist and gushed blood. Blotting the blood with her skirt, she shivered from the raw throbbing pain.

Unsure of exactly where Catherine's grave was located, Antonia wandered along the paths. A deer sculpture didn't look familiar, nor did the statue of St. Agnes, but eventually she found the main path. The Hatch family graves had fresh dirt over them. What was going on? Was Mike digging up more graves? Catherine's empty coffin wasn't enough? She rounded the bend, passed the ivy patch around the root cellar, shovels and rakes abandoned on the grass. Her arm stinging, she absorbed more blood with her skirt.

At Catherine's grave site, the sooty dark sculpture looked taller than she remembered. "Catherine? Catherine Javouhey!" A flock of birds tittered in the trees, then flew off. "I know you're here, Catherine." Something raced behind her. Nothing but a few squirrels. "Catherine? Why do you weep?" she repeated the words that had brought Catherine forth before.

Antonia sat on the bench under the cloudy sky. Pressing her skirt firmly against the searing cut, she hoped it would stop bleeding soon. A triple call of a whippoorwill in the oak tree soothed her. A blue jay pecked at a twig. The jay freed the twig from the branch, flew up to the statue where it landed on the shoulder. The dry twig floated down, past the statue's full chest, down along the folds of the cape, and landed at the delicately carved toes. Antonia picked it up and saw that it wasn't a twig at all but a single purple violet among a stem of green leaves. Violets didn't grow in April.

She recalled the lines she had written on that Friday afternoon, March 20th. *I walk naked into your arms, like the faithful violet . . .*

From far off, she heard the sucking sound of water on rocks. She lifted her eyes to the statue. "No doubt, my poetry is not as illuminating as Emerson's. His 'Illusions' is quite amazing. Did you like his poetry, Catherine?"

Only the breezes stirred.

"One thing is certain . . . faithful I am. Henry wants to come home. Do you hear me? I've come for my son."

The jay, still perched on the statue's shoulder, cast his beady eyes upon her. Not a feather ruffled in the sudden wind that blew Antonia's dark hair. The bird gave a hearty *caw-caw,* then zoomed off.

"I understand you perfectly, Catherine. Shall I come to you, then?"

She followed the bird's flight to the ivy bed. At the root cellar, thin braids of white smoke escaped through the slatted doors. Behind the hill, an old woman stood in a long white gown. Her black bonnet sat low on her face, the ribbons snapping in the wind.

Was this the old woman Adam had seen in the cemetery?

"Hello."

The woman jumped at the greeting and ran off, the white of her dress streaming out thinly among the headstones.

"Wait! Please." Antonia dashed forward, that blue jay zinging by her face and making her stumble. When she lifted her eyes to the headstones, the woman was gone. The blue jay sat like a sentinel on the slats of the root cellar.

Is Catherine tempting me? Or trying to confuse me? Trusting nature, and the sharp eye of the bird, she made her steps toward the root cellar. When she reached the double doors, she opened both sides as the blue jay flew circles above her head. She descended the stone stairs, holding on to brick walls, her bloody wet skirt cold against her thighs. At the last stone—the cellar roof near touching her head—she crouched under the damp dome and stepped inside.

A flat cone of sweet-smelling light swayed before her eyes. "Catherine? Catherine, are you here?" Cups of shadows, hollow and deep, circled at eye level. Slowly the two cups lifted, hollows examining her face and body in long sweeps. With a step back, palms on her chest, she willed her heart to slow down. That slash in her arm felt raw now, like a flame burning the flesh; she winced with pain.

More shadows swirled around her. Suddenly drowsy, she struggled to stay alert. Vibrations of soft words drifted into her head. *The feeling is dark. The shadows protect. It scans us wide. We don't die.* Such dreamy thoughts, all blue-washed and thatched. But they weren't her lines.

Shadows transformed into a studded arch, like a double strand of squared pearls, tempting her to touch them. Her breath grew light as a series of pinwheels fanned her; she scarcely breathed at all. From the dirt floor, vertical cords shimmied up warm and soft—she might have floated on the watery shafts.

The feeling is dark. The shadows protect. It scans us wide. We don't die.

Was that Catherine's voice? She was here, inside these shadows. "Catherine?"

Winding circuits spread out in a circle, pulsing with meridians across her face, oscillating into her belly, up her legs and down both arms. Toes, fingers, even her scalp tingled. The luminous web tightened around her. Something rotated at a point on the back of her head—like a current spiraling her spine and flooding her skull. Her vision spread out into a starry noosphere, points of light rolling toward her. In a second she might melt into the dizzying webbed light. Eyelids dropped. *Bang!*

Antonia gasped and fell to the floor. With her hands breaking the tumble, she curled her body and scrambled up. The old woman stood at the half-opened cellar door. Those monkey eyes, narrow with grim determination, blinked erratically. With a twitch of her head, she batted the other door with a shovel, closing out all light and air.

"No. Don't!"

Only the weak blur of the webbed light remained. It pulsed there in the dull shadows, then shrank into a tiny flame-like skull. Slender. Crystal clear. The face wore a thin gossamer gleam with its gaping mouth, teeth, and hollowed eyes. Silently, hanging like a dewdrop in the thick air, the skull image slipped into the darkness.

Antonia felt her way through the pitch-black cellar toward the steps. She called to that old woman. "Let me out!" A shovelful of dirt hit the doors. She found the stone steps, crawled up one by one. Another shovel of dirt hit, some sifting through the slats. Dust and dirt flew in her eyes and nose. She began screaming, hoping someone would hear her. Would Adam think she was gone too long and come looking for her? Would Mike come by the cemetery? Another heap of dirt came down; this time bits shot into her mouth.

On the top step, she pushed against the doors with her head and hands as if she were a wedge. She could only budge them an inch. Lying across the top step on her back, she shot her feet up at the doors. *Bang, bang, bang.* More dirt came through the slats. She kept beating at the doors with her feet, twisting and pushing, until she lost her balance and fell down the steps.

Again, she inched her way back up, feeling for the walls and steps, this time thinking that the old woman wouldn't have the strength to shovel much more dirt on top of the doors. *Stay calm! The door is right there.* She felt for loose stones at every level and found a wobbly brick. It took some skill to maneuver it free. In her determination, she beat the brick against a rotted wooden slat. Some of the wood fell off. She jammed the brick into the slit at the center of the doors. A sliver of light gave hope. Again on her back, on the top step, she manipulated the brick, and with both feet and one violent thrust—and a wild scream that tore at her throat—the doors shifted apart. One more thrust and she pushed open one side of the doors.

Antonia squeezed through the opening and dragged herself to the grass. She coughed up dust and dirt, spit out bits of gravel and somehow found the strength to stand. The air was heaven and she took in great gulps.

That old woman stood with a vagabond whitewashed cat only a few feet away.

She walked to the cellar and sent the door clanging shut with her shovel. "We must seal the doors. That's what she told me. Seal the doors."

Antonia steadied herself. "Who are you?"

She gave a little grin. "Who are you?"

"Antonia. Please, what's your name?"

She whispered with cupped hands. "You can call me Miss Dorotheus."

"Miss Dorotheus," Antonia said. "Where do you live?" She had seen only one mausoleum in the cemetery and she wondered if the woman was finding shelter there, batty as she might be.

"These are secrets."

Dorotheus pushed the shovel into Antonia's hands. "She wants to bury the entrance."

"She?"

"Just do it," Dorotheus picked up a rake as if to strike. "Hurry."

Antonia didn't have the strength to oppose her, so to placate the woman she began shoveling dirt over the doors. Dorotheus sat in the grass, petting the cat with her bony hands, and counting out the shovelfuls like a child playing a game. Antonia pretended to finish;

a boom broke the sky. Thunder?

"Rain on the way. I love the rain!" Dorotheus said and wandered away with her cat.

Antonia followed her on the paths through the cemetery, but kept a safe distance. Grey and alone, Dorotheus made her frail steps. She turned quickly at a huge blackthorn tree. Antonia followed the turn. But all she saw was the wet wind flowing over the gardens. On a nearby headstone with a winged skull, she read the epitaph: *Here lies Dorotheus Von Ruysbroeck, 1893.*

* * *

Adam waited on the front step impatiently. When he saw Antonia coming down the cow path, relief didn't set in immediately. She was covered in dirt, hair flying, shawl shredded and falling off. *Is that blood all over her skirt?*

"What happened? I was just about to put Laura in the car and go over there."

"I went inside the root cellar."

"What for? Annie, you're bleeding."

"It's nothing. I cut my arm on the rock wall." She extended her arm.

Adam examined both arms. "Where? There's no cut here." Her face had smudges of dirt and sand, and a few small scratches, but nothing that would cause half her skirt to be soaked in blood. "Did you cut your leg?"

"No, my arm." She raised both up, feeling the smooth flesh of her forearm with her fingers, not a single drop of blood anywhere on her. "It's gone. The gash."

"Come into the house," he reached for her. "You're bleeding."

"I'm not bleeding, Adam. The gash is healed."

"Your skirt is soaked in blood!"

"It's healed! It mended my flesh. Look."

"What did?"

"The thing. Inside the root cellar."

Adam took a step back. "What thing?"

"It was all over me, Adam. Like a ghost. Shadows and light. The skull. I saw it."

"You saw the crystal skull?"

"I saw its field." She grabbed his arms and shook him. "I want that skull. It has powers, Adam, and I want to use that crystal power. Call Phillippa."

* * *

Three hours later Adam sat waiting in Balducci's office. Fifteen minutes went by. He shifted in his seat, ran his eyes around the room, crossed his leg, uncrossed it. He checked his cell phone messages and saw a missed call from Phillippa Allan. "Adam, I am discussing your plan with my colleague, Eva Sugarman. One thing we agree on: If Antonia thinks the crystal skull's field in the root cellar communicated thoughts to her, you can assume this force field possesses highly charged particles, creating optical and auditory stimulation. Which means . . . the inherent frequencies of the actual quartz skull can be highly dangerous for you to access. You can't do this alone. Call me."

Adam calmed his nerves. He knew he had to be completely rational when he explained Antonia's experience in the root cellar to Mike. He went over the words in his mind for the third time when the detective came through the door.

Walking briskly, tossing a file on the desk, his face in a defeated frown, he muttered, "Bad news, Adam. I don't have enough evidence for an indictment. We have to release Hatch tonight. I'm sorry, we—"

"You can't release Hatch! It can't happen. Not tonight!" he blurted out too anxiously. *Remain calm. Remain rational.*

"I know this is not how you expected this to go but—"

"Mike, something has happened. I need you to hear me out." He placed the restored picture of Catherine from Henry's shoebox on his desk. "Catherine did this. Restored the picture, just like she said she would. And there's something else."

He related Antonia's experience with Dorotheus Von Ruysbroeck in Old Willow. Then he described, as logically as he could, Antonia's experience inside the root cellar with the field of energy. The detective remained standing, wide-eyed and pale. Adam gave him a few seconds to absorb everything.

"Are you shocked, Mike?"

"Nothing about this case shocks me anymore. Although, yeah, at the moment, I am stunned."

"Antonia is convinced the skull's field healed a gash in her arm half a foot long. Her skirt was covered in blood."

He sat down in his chair, slowly feeling for the metal arms as if he wasn't sure the seat was actually beneath him.

"And, Mike, this field . . . it communicated with her."

"Communicated?"

While Balducci listened to Adam elaborate the details, he knew the detective would be skeptical. A force field relating thoughts, actual words? He read aloud the lines from a piece of paper that Antonia had written, but stumbled on the words *we don't die.*

"That proves nothing, Adam. Doesn't Antonia write poems?"

"Antonia is certain these were not her lines. She thinks they were Catherine's words or . . . or whoever. There's communication here! Listen, we know now what we have to do to find Henry."

"You think so, huh?"

"Yes, I think so! We want the crystal skull, Mike. We want to use it tonight inside the cemetery."

"Jesus! Don't go getting any wild ideas, Rambo."

"Just let us have the skull for one night." He heard the begging in his tone. It took every ounce of restraint to keep his voice steady. "We think that if we can directly use the quartz energy waves, we might—"

"Adam, you don't know enough—"

"Just let us have the damn skull! Tonight!"

"Nobody touches that skull. Not tonight, not tomorrow. Its stays in the evidence room, in the dark where it can't injure anybody."

Adam was on his feet. "You are not going to—"

"Look, I've got a twenty-four-year-old lab tech in a coma since he handled that skull. The kid went into cardiac shock and he's still unconscious."

Adam shook his head. "Well, Phillippa handled it, and she's all right. Zoe too. Don't try to scare me off, Mike. If Hatch is right about the skull restoring Catherine, and if that skull possesses powers to release a morphic field that can bust through brick wall, heal torn flesh in minutes, then maybe we can use that same power source to locate Catherine, and my son!"

"How, exactly?" Balducci crossed his arms over his chest.

Adam chose his words carefully. "We create our own field of power. We amplify the skull's energy waves over Catherine's grave site. Over the whole damn cemetery if necessary."

Mike blew out his breath.

"Phillippa said heat makes quartz discharge electrons, enhancing its field, right? If we expose the skull to a measured element of heat, the skull's field will magnify. Magnify enough electromagnetic energy to produce Catherine on the site."

"You plan on manifesting the dead?"

"If that's what it takes!"

Balducci had no response. The squeak in his chair grew louder as he rocked back and forth.

"Christ, Mike, Hatch may be right. Maybe *we don't die.* Who knows that reality for sure? Do *you?*"

Something in his eyes went far away. Almost hopeful. "Mike? Are you with me on this? Look, I know there's danger. I'm not stupid or being foolish here. Accessing the frequency-field response curve will attract the magnetic ions so—"

"Oh Christ Almighty, listen to you. Phillippa's got her fingerprints all over this."

Adam tossed up his hands in an admission. "Yes, okay. She's with us on this, one hundred percent. And I know, and she admits, we're skating on thin ice but—"

"You got that right."

"You got a better idea on how to get my son back? What plan of attack do *you* have? You've got zip, Mike."

"Adam, I've got a report that two people died suddenly while trying to use a crystal skull's powers. And this afternoon, the damn thing reacted to Phillippa touching it. Did she tell you about that?"

Adam held his breath for a second. "She told me. I'll wear gloves."

"Two people died!"

"I hear you. I want my son back! Catherine has him. Nothing you can say will stop us. Here's what you do. Stall off releasing Hatch. Just keep him here one more night so we can get into the cemetery. Tonight, you bring that skull to the house and—"

"Adam, this is—"

"Don't you dare say no! I'll wait for your call."

On his way out the door, Adam nearly knocked down the assistant coming into the office.

"Oh, sorry," the assistant said. "Here's the lab report you wanted, Mike."

Chapter Twenty-Two

BALDUCCI CLOSED HIS DOOR and read the lab report. Blown away for a second, he dialed Phillippa. "Glad I caught you in. I hear you've been talking with Adam Brooke."

"Yes. Antonia called me, Mike. I'm just doing what I can to help her. My God, if this were my kid missing all this time, under these circumstances? I'd go to hell and back to find him. Their will to find their boy is greater than their fear, or the risks. That skull exhibits power. None of us can deny that. And you can't stand in the way of their only option to find Henry."

"I know you want to take control here, but this is my case, my responsibility. Phillippa, I need you to take a look at something." He fed the report into his fax machine and watched it send. "Check your fax. I'm sending you a lab report. I'll hold on." He heard ice clinking in a glass and her footsteps. The coffee on his desk had gone cold but he sipped it anyway.

"Geez," she said after a few moments, "your lab identified magnetite crystals in exhumed coffins?"

"Does that surprise you?"

"Well, I wouldn't have expected them to be actual remains of the dead. But magnetite crystals *are* in human brain matter. We discovered that fact back in the 1980s."

Balducci couldn't inhale his next breath. "Quartz crystals in brain matter?"

"Yes. And in the inner ear, there are crystals that exhibit piezoelectricity. Bone matrix is a crystalline solid as well. Brain magnetite crystals are organized into linear, membrane-bound chains. About eighty crystals per chain."

"What do the chains look like?"

"Prismatic particles. Pyramidal. And they are not just in humans. Fish and birds too. They navigate by them. Homing pigeons' brains are saturated with magnetite."

"This is going to sound like a stupid question, but why do human's need magnetite?"

"A study done some years ago verified the crystals operate as a spin point, which can trigger formation of blastema . . . cells for regeneration."

"Cell regeneration? I'm practically falling off my chair here. Like healing a flesh wound?"

"The research analyses are ongoing. I recall a report last year on reaction kinetics using quartz crystal microbalance. Biomineralization and nanotechnology are the cutting edge now. Heal flesh wounds? If not now, down the road certainly. By the way, you still owe me a lunch, Detective Balducci."

"And these spin points? They do what exactly?"

"They transmit energy signals to the body. Some scientists suggest this transmission acts as a link to our self-awareness."

"You mean a link to consciousness in the brain?"

"Oh, please. Not a single study in a hundred years has proven that consciousness resides in the brain. Let me enlighten you. Consciousness lies outside the body, flowing in the human morphic energy field. You want to do lunch tomorrow?"

* * *

Balducci hung up and leaned back in his chair. He couldn't get that idea out of his mind. Consciousness flows in the human energy field outside the body? What, like some kind of aura? He thought of Hatch's stickmen drawings with the thought-forms like a cage over the bodies.

Should he trust his instincts to Adam a second time?

He pulled out Perucca's Document 8012. Which one of these twelve skulls might have ended up in Paris in 1879 and into the hands of Catherine Javouhey? If he was going to let Adam tap into the powers of this skull, he wanted some idea which one of the twelve might be sitting inside the evidence room. And he hoped to God it wasn't the Lipton-Wolff skull from Belize that sent two men to their deaths. *Eva Sugarman, please be wrong.*

Start at the beginning. He grabbed a map of the world from his shelf and spread it out. From Perucca's list, he drew black circles around all twelve sites of origin. Viewing the whole picture, he counted six sites in the east, six sites in the west, four in the north, four in the south, four at the middle of the map. Visually, several sites appeared to be equally distant from each other.

Wait a minute. He counted them off again. One skull in Alaska, one in Greenland, in North America, Central America, South America, Africa. Two in Europe. Two in Asia. One in Russia. One in Australia.

A skull discovered on each major land mass region around the globe? What kind of coincidence was that? And all twelve sites nearly equally balanced north, south, east, and west. How was that possible?

It's not possible. Could Perucca's Document 8012 be faulty?

He flipped through Eva's emails, looking for a phone number or email for Perucca. In the back of the stack he found a single sheet.

> Dr. Emilio Perucca, Italian archaeologist, died of sudden heart failure on October 31, 2005.
>
> Buried in his hometown, Greve, Italy, he is survived by his wife, Lola Perucca.

Isn't that just dandy. He read over the document again, this time looking for a description of a skull that would match the one in the black box. He found five descriptions: the clear quartz skull from Australia, found by the Aborigines; the clear and gleamy Lipton-Wolff skull in Belize; and three others.

> Skull #7 Alaska: Barrow. [description: clear quartz] Said to have been buried by "sky people," according

to Iñupiat Eskimos (1822 report). Was once property of Iñupiat Heritage Museum. Documentation: letter fragment. Classified as lost.

Skull #8 Canada: North Battleford. [description: clear quartz] emerged among rocks in "fighting waters" of Battle River, property of Blackfoot tribesmen (verbal report). Became property of Museum of Anthropology, Vancouver, British Columbia. Documentation Report #U885. Current owner unknown.

Skull #11 Italy: Rome. [description: clear quartz] Discovered in ruins of Rome (verbal report); preserved by Benedictine monks (documentation fragment Benedictine logbook). Became the property of the Duke of Ratibor (1846). Fate undetermined.

Just at that moment, Dan Hersey appeared in Balducci's doorway. "Hatch has got a lawyer," he announced.

Balducci didn't lift his head from the list. "Hatch declined a lawyer," he mumbled.

"Not any more. His attorney just showed up. Insists on supervising an immediate release. Like right now, Mike."

Balducci lifted his head. "I need a delay."

Hersey sat down. "Look, I know dropping the charges on Hatch is a crash for you, but you've done everything to find that boy. Canvassed the whole town, hospitals, the Internet, offered rewards, searched all the databases . . . exhumed more coffins in Old Willow than I'd like to know about. And we've been scouring the whole town for that wacky woman in her blue cape. You gotta release Hatch."

"I need a stall. I've got—"

"You've got nothing!" Hersey put his head down for a moment, then looked up. "They've moved Jake Kras out of the ICU. He's stable and showing signs of consciousness. Thank God! I hate this fucking case." Hersey walked out and called Hatch's attorney into Balducci's office.

"Roman Cavallo." The lawyer extended his business card. "I'm here representing Elias Hatch. I understand you're dropping all charges because of lack of evidence and releasing him today?"

He spoke every word as if it were snipped with a sharp scissors. Balducci gave the lawyer a quick scan: elderly, thick white hair straight as a poker, silk suit, chained medals at the neck, no tie. *Shyster.*

"Chief Hersey says he's ordered the release documents."

Balducci said with a half smile, "That'll take a while."

"And this is a list of Mr. Hatch's personal items that were confiscated at the time of arrest?" Cavallo lifted a copy of the police form.

Balducci nodded.

The attorney took out a legal document, opened it. "This is a court order, signed by the Honorable J.P. Prentice, county of Middlesex, Cambridge, for the release of an artifact, one crystal sculpture that was seized from Old Willow Cemetery by the Concord Police Department under search warrant UC5542." He laid it on the desk. "This is a valuable piece of art that needs to be secured in the vault at the Cambridge Trust Company, as instructed and agreed upon by Mr. Hatch. I assume you will be releasing the sculpture at the same time you release Mr. Hatch?" The attorney looked at Balducci from above his eyeglasses, which sat low on his nose.

"We have the sculpture registered in our evidence room."

"What evidence? You just confirmed that all charges were dropped because of lack of evidence."

Balducci looked over the court order from Judge J.P. Prentice in Cambridge. He needed to call Judge Brady right away.

"Detective Balducci, how is the sculpture evidence? You don't have the missing boy's fingerprints on it, do you?"

Balducci gave a short shake of his head.

"Then the sculpture is not primary evidence."

"It's classified as circumstantial evidence."

Cavallo smirked, pulling off his glasses. "Now, that's quite a leap, Detective Balducci. From my understanding of this case, you've taken quite a number of leaps with my client."

"When did Mr. Hatch become your client?"

"I believe that's confidential."

He looked at the man's card again. "Marc St. Blane, Attorneys at Law, Boston? Never heard of you guys."

"Guess you don't get around much."

"Excuse me a moment." Balducci took a walk out. He made long easy strides down the corridor, hoping the slowness would have a calming effect. In Deputy Paul Owen's office, he dialed Judge Brady, at the same time faxing Prentice's court order.

Brady's clerk answered the call. "Hi Gina, it's Mike. I just sent a fax for Norman. Is he available?" Balducci's stomach did a double flip when Gina told him Norman was in chambers and couldn't be disturbed. "It's urgent. Tell him it's about the Brooke case. I'll wait for his call."

* * *

In the library, Antonia found Adam in his desk chair with his face toward the window. She came up from behind him, slipped her arms around his shoulders. "Don't look so gloomy. Let's just focus on getting that skull tonight."

He swiveled in his chair to face her. "Annie, Mike had to drop the charges against Hatch. They're planning on releasing him tonight."

She let out a defeated sigh. "How will we get into the cemetery if Hatch is there? And what about the skull? Will Mike have to release that to Hatch too?"

"I don't know."

"I'll tell you one thing. Nothing is going to stop this plan. Adam, call Mike and find out what's going on."

* * *

Balducci saw his phone light up. The ID read Adam Brooke. "No way, not now, pal." He drummed his fingers on his desk and let voice mail pick up. Cavallo was waiting with Hersey outside his door in the corridor. The lawyer wore a big smile. Hersey did his usual head dunk and toothy grin. Why were they being so chatty?

Paul Owens poked his head in. "Hey, Mike, they need your signature on the Hatch release documents. Front desk."

"Be right there."

The desk phone rang and he grabbed it. "Norman?"

"You've got problems, Mike. I've got no cause or authority to override this court order. You're going to have to hand over the goods."

"Can I stall? Just overnight?"

"You got probable cause?"

"None that I can create."

"Then you are out of options."

"Who are these guys at the firm Marc St. Blane? You know them?"

"Nah, but I'll see what I can find out about Cavallo. Get back to you later."

He wanted to throw the phone down. But he needed to act cool and confident. He walked out, feeling Hersey's eyes on him as he stopped at the front desk. He picked up the pen and hesitated.

"We're all set," Hersey said, ridiculously loud. "Detective Balducci is signing the docs now."

He scribbled his signature and went back into his office. From there he watched Hatch escorted to the front desk. The officer handed Hatch a plastic bag with his wallet and personal items. Cavallo hovered over him, spoke quietly to him, patted him on the shoulder, checked off everything on the list.

"And the sculpture, Chief Hersey?" Cavallo said.

Paul Owens walked over carrying the black box. "Right here."

Cavallo took the box. He whispered something in Hatch's ear to which Hatch shook his head vigorously.

Cavallo opened the lid just a sliver. Satisfied, he closed the box. "Thank you for your cooperation, Chief Hersey."

Balducci watched the two men enter the parking lot. Cavallo placed the black box on the floor of the back seat; Hatch got in the front. A few seconds later, Cavallo's cream-colored BMW X-6 sports coupe pulled out onto Walden Street.

He heard Hersey's footsteps approach from the hall, but before he reached his office door, Balducci slammed it with a wicked kick.

Chapter Twenty-Three

ROMAN CAVALLO DROPPED ELIAS HATCH at his cottage and drove out of Old Willow Cemetery driveway with a horn blast, the headlights shining through the dark. In a second, Elias was inside the cottage. He put kindling and logs in the wood-burning stove and struck the match. He lit candles in every window and on the tables until the whole cottage glowed with the flickering light. Settled into his rocking chair by the window, he took his Bible, paged to Ezekiel 28, a favorite, and read aloud. "'In Eden, a garden of God, you dwelt, adorned with gems of every kind: sardine and chrysolite and jade, topaz, cornelian, and green jasper . . .'" He paused to catch a breath.

A bad case of the shakes overwhelmed him for a few seconds. He reached to the phone and dialed. After three rings, the answering machine came on. "Father Jim, I'm at home now. They've dropped all charges, a great relief. Thank you for coming to see me. It was a great consolation to see a friendly face under such circumstances. May I bother you again? Please, will you come by tonight? I need . . . to talk. I'll wait up for you." Hatch put his head back, his hands clutching the Bible.

* * *

The cream-colored BMW sped along Concord Turnpike. From a side street, the Concord police car pulled out and began tailing the coupe. Balducci couldn't resist a smile.

"Give him a sec, let him get over the speed limit," he told the officer at the wheel. When Cavallo accelerated, the officer hit the siren and flashing lights. The coupe kept up its speed until the flashing lights glared into the rearview mirror, then slowly edged to the highway's shoulder. "Looks like he's on a cell phone, too."

Balducci watched the officer walk up to the coupe and knock on the window.

"Out of the car." The officer yanked open the door. "Out!"

"Officer, I'm . . ."

"I said get out of the car. Right now, sir."

Cavallo hesitated. The officer grabbed his arm.

"Do you know who I am?" Cavallo yelled. The officer propelled him twenty feet away to a spot on the shoulder in front of the coupe.

"I do, sir. Face down."

Cavallo squirmed and threatened.

Balducci got out of the patrol car, opened the BMW's back door without a sound and searched the back seat with a mini flashlight. Carefully, he lifted the lid of the black box and rolled the skull into a heavy black pouch. The briefcase on the seat was too tempting to pass up. He quickly examined the contents and withdrew the leather travel organizer with an airline confirmation.

Another patrol car pulled up. Balducci placed the skull in the trunk, got in, and within seconds they were cruising past Cavallo, who was still face down on the ground.

Balducci punched in Phillippa's number. "I'm on my way to the Brooke's. I've got the skull with me."

"You know I'd do anything to be there with you."

"I can't—I won't—Phillippa, put you in harm's way a third time. Besides, I don't think *she* likes you very much."

"Little ol' me? What, you think I'm threatening?"

He laughed—it felt good to lighten up. "Look, we'll handle this. I've got your instructions. I'm clear on all your precautions and warnings."

"Good. I have a message from Eva. Be sure to read Perucca's handwritten notations in the files."

"Why, is there something in particular she wanted me to check?"

"As a matter of fact. She said, beware of the white fire."

"White fire? Meaning?"

"She didn't know exactly, but Perucca mentions it in his notes."

* * *

Antonia was at the front door before Balducci had a chance to knock. She knew he'd come through. Everything was going to fall into place, one, two, three. Balducci came in with arms full: a small monitor, wires, briefcase, bags of rock salt.

"Can I set up in the kitchen?" he said, heading there without an answer.

"Yes. We have three high-beam flashlights. Phillippa said that would do."

He started connecting all the gear. "Adam, you remember to keep the fire low in the grate beneath the skull. Just kindling will be enough. You only want embers. Mix the rock salt and water and submerge the skull into a glass bowl that can withstand heat. Oh, and Phillippa said quartz is rotary polar so it will rotate the plane of light that passes through it, amplifying the electromagnetic field outward. Let's be smart. Keep your distance."

"Yeah, she went over everything with me. Twenty-five feet," Adam said.

With gloved hands, Mike handed the sculpture to Adam's gloved hands.

"Make sure you bring this baby back here. That skull has to mysteriously turn up by tomorrow or I'm in violation of a court order. Understand?"

Adam gave him a shot in the arm. "Rambo never fails. And what about the keys to the cemetery locks?"

Balducci pulled out a ring with four keys on it.

"And the combination padlocks on the gates?"

"Taken care of. You'll find them busted but hanging on the posts."

Adam shoved the keys in his pocket. "Annie, are you okay with keeping Hatch occupied while I set up in the cemetery?"

She grinned. "I know exactly what I have to accomplish with

him." Hatch knew more about that skull than anyone did and keeping him talking about it was her key objective.

Adam gave her a puzzled look. "Just keep him distracted and occupied. That's all you have to do."

"Leave Elias Hatch to me."

"Give me thirty minutes, Annie. Then you come into the cemetery."

"Thirty minutes."

* * *

Evening sulked with a brindled moon over the cemetery gardens. An odd woodpecker persisted with hollow knocks making Adam all the more jumpy. He listened to it pecking as he placed the crystal skull, submerged in a saltwater bowl, on the grate over the fire embers. He positioned it directly on the cement footing belonging to Catherine's grave. Then he aimed the three high-powered flashlights directly into the crystal skull. The light inside the skull rotated, splashing out the eight prisms in crisscrossing patterns. The shafts of lights created perfectly shaped V's, two of them spreading out on both sides and the thickest V shooting out the top of the skull.

Moving back twenty-five feet, as Phillippa told him, he sat down on the ground. That was it. Let the energies flow and expand. Observe the forces converge. *Watch. Be ready.* He reassured himself that Laura was safe asleep in her bed. *Who better to stay with her than Mike and an officer stationed on the second floor? Two police cars nearby. One in their driveway. Everyone ready at hand.* He stared at the skull, the head looking swollen now. A silvery color, like an aura, waved out.

Man, what if the skull explodes? No, it won't. No one was hurt at Baldwin. Not a single scratch on anybody. And anyway, it wasn't the actual skull that exploded. He glanced at his watch again. Minutes ticked by slowly. *Here we go, Annie.*

* * *

Antonia rapped at Elias's door. With her ear to the wood, she listened to his footsteps across the floor. He opened the door a crack.

"Hello, Elias."

Stunned, he stood there, unable to speak.

"May I come in? Please?" Gently she brushed the door open enough to pass into the cottage.

The amount of candlelight flickering everywhere gave Antonia pause. Shadows rocked across the walls and bookcases as she stepped into a puddle of darkness on the carpet.

"Antonia, is there . . . ?"

"Yes, there is, Elias. You don't mind if I sit, do you?"

He remained at the door, cane in hand, face aghast. "This is not a good time, Antonia."

"Oh, I'm sorry." She sat on the sofa. "I just wanted to speak with you for a few minutes. It's important. I wouldn't come here if it wasn't."

"What do you want?"

"I have something I'd like to ask you. Just you and me. No detective, no police, no accusations." She settled in, her hands folded in her lap. On the ceiling, grey darklings twitched from so much candle smoke. Was something breathing? Behind her. By the window. She could hear the suck and hiss of deep breaths. She turned but saw only the dark glass. *Stay calm. Stay focused.*

"Please close the door, Elias."

He did so reluctantly.

"I want to ask—" She thought she heard something in the kitchen. "Is there someone else here?"

"No. Why?"

She walked to the kitchen doorway. A row of votive candles lined the countertops. At the cellar door a waft of smoke dissipated. She waited a few moments, then walked back into the living room. Sitting on the sofa, she planted her feet together and in her strongest, clearest voice she said, "I want to know about Catherine. I want to know everything, Elias."

He gave a sigh.

"Catherine has my boy, Elias. Do you know what it's like to lose your child? To wonder night and day where he is? Is he safe? Is he warm? Is he hungry? Is Catherine being kind to him?"

His eyes seemed a bit gentle.

"I ask myself every day, where is she keeping him?"

Elias sat down in his rocker by the stove that was hot with wood and ash. How glassy his eyes became as he stared into the fire. Then he lifted them to the window behind her, gazing into the darkness beyond.

She watched him for several moments while candle wax overflowed onto the tabletops. Elias slumped in his rocker, his arms hanging like a marionette's cut from its strings. The creases on his face seemed etched with charcoal. She had never seen anyone look so vacant. "You're just the image of silence, aren't you, Elias?"

"I think you should leave, my dear."

"Oh, Elias, don't send me away." Antonia ran her pinky over the metal armillary sphere on the coffee table. "Isn't it odd that you have the exact same armillary my dad has in his study? His in Umbria, so far away from me, and yours here in Concord, right next door. Do you think that makes us related, in a poetic sort of way?"

That got a little smile. "A lovely thought. I can see you miss your father."

"I do. He's been lost to me for a number of years, in and out of hospitals since I was little." She held the sphere in her open palms. "You know, Elias, you're a bit like him. Quiet, soft-spoken. You have tenderness in your eyes, like him."

"You flatter me. I'm just a simple old man."

"Oh, no. I can see that you're a brave man. Reverent. Even a dash mysterious." She widened her grin, then lifted the metal sphere up higher. "'The crystal sphere of thought is as concentrical as the geological structure of the globe.'"

His lips turned up. "You've been reading Emerson."

"Yes, his poems mostly. I've always admired his work. And his essays. You did say that Catherine was a transcendentalist, didn't you? And fond of poetry?" She ran her pinky around the metal again. "'Crystal sphere of thought.' What did Emerson mean by that?"

"Emerson was being figurative, no doubt."

"Do you think Catherine knew what it meant? Catherine was his student?"

"Emerson had many students. Waldo and Lydian endeared Catherine, I'm sure."

She placed the armillary sphere down and moved to the edge of the sofa. "Elias, tell me about the crystal skull."

"Your face is just ashes. Do you know that? I'm sorry for all your suffering, Antonia. There is nothing to tell." He picked up his Bible. "God Bless Roman Cavallo. By now, he has certainly locked the skull up at the Cambridge Trust Company. At least one thing has been resolved in all this disruption." He turned his head to the window again. "One cannot unring the bell. So much has been exposed. But the *Lord of Life* is safe now. And for that I am deeply grateful."

Antonia let her shoulders drop to relax, rested her wrists on her knees so she could check her watch.

"Yes, of course, I'm sure. So, does Catherine come to you often?"

"I'm afraid Catherine comes and goes at her own will. Such is the privilege of the . . . I hate to say the *undead,* because Catherine is far more than that."

"Meaning what, exactly?"

"You're afraid of her, aren't you, Antonia?"

"Yes, in a way I am."

"I know how frightening it is to see someone like Catherine in the flesh. Believe me, this whole idea has frightened me for years. But not so much now. One does learn to trust."

"Tell me about her."

"Ah, now I see what this visit is really about. You want to know how Catherine died? That's what's troubling you, isn't it?"

"Everything about Catherine troubles me."

"You're thinking it was a violent death?"

"Was it?"

"It was suicide. Chloral hydrate. Not an uncommon drug in those days. She had what they called at the time *melancholy.* That's what my grandmother Sophie said. Losing three children, one could hardly blame her."

"Suicide. How dreadful."

Elias shook his head. "Death doesn't have to be such a dark hand. My mother, Hannah, died fully conscious of the death process. I watched her die. Her eyes were wide open. She was smiling, looking straight at me, taking a last breath, like a little bird letting go of her wings."

Antonia wanted to say how sad that sounded. Instead she just nodded, leaving him to continue.

"Dying is a great event, you know."

"Really."

"The body curls up as the consciousness detaches from the flesh. Death can have invincible beauty!"

"Death, a form of beauty? How odd to describe it like that."

Ashes from the stove shimmied out, flecking the air with tiny sparks. The shadows in the room grew thinner now, slipping into the cracks and cubbies. Except for one smoky shape that seemed to linger by the front door.

Antonia kept her eyes focused there, trying not to blink.

Chapter Twenty-Four

On Eastwick Road, Balducci sat at the Brooke kitchen table, his eyes on the monitor of the video relay inside Old Willow. The night vision was blurry, but he was able to see a wide portion of the cemetery with a view of Catherine's grave with Adam sitting nearby. Plenty of backup officers were just a block away with a fire engine on call, and an ambulance ready. He reassured himself everything was under control.

He kept his eyes on the monitor most of the time, but he wanted to finish reading Eva's electronic files. Perucca's data remained overwhelming with so many accounts and descriptions. He had a time sorting through so many pages on-screen. He found one scanned handwritten reference to white fire but Perucca didn't have any details except that he had something scribbled next to the notation. Balducci enlarged the view: *Libro di Enoch.*

"*Book of Enoch?*"

He scanned page after page in the file for another reference. Another scanned handwritten sheet listed meridian latitudes and longitudes next to each skull's site of origin with notes on the earth's magnetic field: *current flows north/south at 7.83 hertz per second.*

Why would Perucca care about the meridians of the sites? Or, the flow of the earth's magnetic currents? The numbers stuck to his eyes. 144, 120, 72, 60, 36, 12, 156, 108, 48, 44, 9, 88. Like a kid exploring sums, he toyed with the numbers, mentally subtracting and dividing the numerical coordinates. Was there a common thread Perucca wanted to find?

As he calculated, he found that these numbers were variations of the number twelve. Each skull's site of origin a variation of the number twelve? How odd is that.

Except for Cape Farewell at 44 instead of 48 degrees, Lisbon at 9 instead of 12 degrees, and Belize at 88 instead of 84 degrees, these were just slightly off by a few degrees. But these three locations were recorded on Perucca's list as *in the vicinity of* or *outside of,* so for all practical purposes, they were close enough to be a variation of twelve.

"No way." All twelve skulls discovered at sites that were multiples of the number twelve on the longitudinal meridians? Impossible. Perucca's document was either just plain faulty, or it was a total fake.

Balducci checked the monitor, checked the time, checked in with his backup. He walked over to the kitchen door to check one of his men positioned out back and gave a thumbs up. At the sink, Balducci helped himself to a glass of water and noticed a familiar blue glass angel ornament on the windowsill. He took a whiff of the bunch of lily of the valley. Smoky sweet. His cell phone buzzed: Hersey. He'd already missed two of Dan's calls earlier, so he picked up.

"Mike, where the hell are you?"

"Tracking a lead."

"What the hell have you done? Do you know who Roman Cavallo is!"

It really wasn't a question. "Come again?"

"This is the most transparent sleight-of-hand you've ever pulled! I'm not covering your ass on this one."

The phone clicked off and he saw he had voicemail from Judge Norman Brady: "Hey Mike. That Marc St. Blane you asked about? Bogus law firm. And Roman Cavallo? International clients from here to kingdom come. Big shot, licensed in Rome."

Mike blinked with the sound of the phone's click. In a little panic, he dug out Cavallo's leather travel case. From the side pocket, he found a black velvet pouch. He opened it and removed a heavy iron key. The shaft was thick with a jagged bow.

He flipped open the other side pocket that held the airline confirmation. He opened it and read Boston to Rome. Folded inside was a limo confirmation from Leonardo Da Vinci Airport to the

Piazza San Pietro.

The Vatican. Balducci remembered now where he'd seen the *Book of Enoch.*

He quickly called his backup patrol car, gave instructions, and phoned Alitalia Airlines.

* * *

Adam grew uncomfortable in the cemetery. The skull glowed brighter; the air seemed to shudder. His heart pounded as he paced around. In the elm tree, he spotted a leg hanging down with a large black boot. Then another leg. He could make out a hunched back curled in the crux of the branch. The man wore a straw hat and tiny round spectacles, but Adam couldn't see features. Tempted to say something, he nearly yelled out but then recalled Mike telling him to stay focused and keep to the plan.

On the rock border that curved along one of the paths, a girl in a white and blue dress walked the rock wall. Gingerly, she placed one foot before the other. Her braids with white ribbons hung at her waist. Something was familiar about her.

A flock of owls with glistening feathers perched in the cluster of birch trees, their hoots like muffled cries. Below the owls, three men stood sporting stiff white collars and dark waistcoats. They ignored the group of women huddled together wearing white headcaps and long dresses with aprons.

Christ, what have we done here? Adam stepped back into the shadows. And he waited. Near a row of headstones at the far corner, a nun in black veils held a large white conch. She seemed to look straight at him for a quick second, then raised up her conch and trumpeted out a long cool note.

His cell phone vibrated.

"Adam, you okay?" Mike said.

"Yeah. Are you getting this on your monitor?"

"Fairly clear. How many people are there?"

"About twenty or so. Are these . . . ? I don't even know what to call them."

"Don't make a move. I'm sending in backup."

"No, don't. They look pretty harmless. Let's not disturb anything. Catherine might show any minute."

* * *

Hatch's cottage grew dry with the smoky flames from so many candles. Antonia put on her best smile. "You're so smart about these things, Elias. After Catherine died, did your grandmother Sophie say how the crystal skull restored Catherine to life?"

Elias put his head back. His eyes wandered off again.

"Please tell me."

He rearranged his hands on his Bible.

"I suppose this is a secret? The crystal skull's powers," she pressed.

"It is a great secret. My family has protected it for over a hundred years. Passed on from my Grandma Sophie, to my mother Hannah, and on to me."

"And who will you pass it on to, Elias?"

"What do you mean?"

"Who will guard the secret here in the years to come? I mean, if I were your daughter, would you pass the secret on to me?"

"If you were my daughter . . . I like that," he gave a small laugh and patted her hand. "But these secrets are not for the apprentice."

"Were they for someone like Catherine, who liked to study physics?"

He didn't answer.

"Or for a prolific writer like Emerson? Did he know that Catherine buried this skull in Old Willow?"

"I couldn't say."

"But Catherine knew the secret of the skull, didn't she?"

Elias made a little bow of his head. "I expect you are right."

"Did Emerson know the secret?"

"I understand that Catherine and Waldo were of the same mind, and excellent friends."

"Emerson wrote about the crystal skull, didn't he?"

He sat forward. "If Waldo did, we must remember that everything was emblematic for him."

"Was he being emblematic when he wrote 'Sleep is not, death is not; Who seem to die live'?"

Elias's face lit up, and his eyes drifted to the blank wall. "That's from his poem, 'Illusions.' 'When thou dost return, on the wave's circulation, beholding the shimmer, the wild dissipation . . .'" He seemed to slide away with the words. "I will tell you this much, my dear." His voice went very soft. "At death, after the last breath is expelled, the consciousness can choose to remain here in this world. Now, isn't that remarkable?"

"Choose to remain here?"

"For a minute, days, years for all we know. This form of energy never ceases . . . 'the wave's circulation.'" He closed his eyes as if he had just spoken a prayer.

"The wave, like an electromagnetic wave of a field?"

"Mmmm. Grandma Sophie said it is like a transparent marble light." He smiled proudly. "Of course she never actually saw it, but that was her idea. Kind of poetic, don't you think?"

"Yes. I can almost see it."

"But none of us can actually see it. Not unless the consciousness chooses to be seen. As Catherine chose to be seen in the cemetery that day with you."

"And exactly *how* was she able to be seen?"

"Oh, my dear, the crystal skull has unfathomable powers."

* * *

In the cemetery, Adam observed the people standing about. These were Old Willow's residents, like Catherine. One of them crept to a bush to hide. Others whispered among themselves. They seemed almost frightened by the exposure. He decided to approach one of the men but as he did, the man faded into the dark. The women scattered.

Where is Catherine? Dare I ask one of them?

Hissing from the skull drew his eye. Instantly it shot out sparks, one very long one that nearly struck his legs. He made one small step forward and the skull threw balls of light rolling across the cemetery like an ocean wave. The skull was heating up and throwing light on the headstones and trees. That little girl with the braids still walked along the rock wall. "Look at me, I'm Emily, the linden tree." She jumped off and joined a group of children who suddenly appeared on the grass. Four boys and three girls were in some kind of game, clapping hands, earnest at their play, all full of laughter.

Adam searched their tiny faces through the flickering shadows. "Henry?" he whispered.

* * *

Antonia saw lights flicker out the cottage window. The far end of the cemetery looked ablaze. She turned back to Elias. "When Catherine's body was restored, did she have to come in direct contact with the skull?"

"Oh, no," Hatch said. "Her thought-form is the ignition. Just as Emerson illustrated . . . 'the crystal sphere of thought.' The conscious alignment of Catherine's thought with the crystal skull's energy fuels the physical manifestation."

Antonia walked to the desk, concealing her anxiousness. Something was happening in the cemetery and she wanted to flee but knew she couldn't until she got Elias to tell her everything she needed. "So the energies of the crystal skull and the person attract? Kind of like magnets?"

"This is much more complicated than that, but yes, you have the main idea. Can't you just picture it? Shafts of invisible energy forming molecules and cells, bones knitting and femurs curling, flesh, muscles, veins. Quite magnificent!"

"Elias, if I wanted to . . . if I needed Catherine to be *seen* in a certain place at a certain time, what would I need to accomplish that?"

"*You* cannot."

"Catherine has my child. I have to find her. There must be a way."

"My dear Antonia, I honestly don't see how you can force Catherine to come to you. It's always at her will to be seen."

She went to him, knelt on the floor and reached for his hands. She squeezed his rough knuckles as they rested on the black leather Bible. "What if I aligned my thoughts, my will, with the crystal skull? Would that bring—"

Elias grabbed her arms and shook her. The fear on his face turned his skin to chalk. "Don't even speak of it! Why do you think this skull was buried? The dark protects its power, and us."

"But—"

"And anyway, it's locked up. Tomorrow it is being hand delivered to an archaeologist who has pledged to return it to where it was excavated. He will bury it there and that will be the end of it. I thank God the skull is out of my hands! I have been afraid of that thing since I can remember."

"But if the skull can receive thoughts of the dead, then it can receive my thoughts too, couldn't it?"

"This conversation is pointless. You don't have the skull."

"And if I did?" She twisted away from him.

His faced dropped like a curtain.

His beady eyes scanned the room and out the window, which gave him a view of the illuminated cemetery.

"You foolish girl!" He gripped his cane and stood up. "Don't you dare try such a stunt."

"Why? What would happen if I did?"

His lips trembled. "My God, you'd never survive it. The white fire."

Antonia made a dash to the door. But as she reached for the knob, a bony hand clutched hers.

"Dorotheus!" Elias called.

Antonia pushed the old woman away and ran out the door.

She ran the main cemetery path, the whole time stealing looks back to see if Elias had come after her. When she reached the hill near Catherine's grave, she found Adam among a circle of children and men and woman wandering about. "Adam, are these people...?"

"I think that skull has produced everything in this cemetery except Catherine," he said. "I can hardly believe it. She isn't here."

The children continued their hand-clapping game with giddy singing and finger-snapping. "They're adorable. Like little angels with rosy hands. Aren't they beautiful, Adam?"

"I thought Henry might be among them, but . . ."

Antonia wanted to tell him everything she learned from Elias, but all she could think about was Henry. "Where is Catherine!"

"I don't know. I wish—"

"Henry? Henry, I'm here," she began walking in circles. "Henry, can you hear me?" She inhaled deeply. "He's here, Adam. Henry's here."

"Where?"

"All over me." She spun in a circle with her arms wide. "Right here!"

Everything glowed, the wood violets at her feet, the insects humming the elastic air. Even the stars dropped low enough so she could see their brilliance. Knowing she didn't have much time before Elias would catch up with her, she set her eyes on the skull. Can I find my way to do this? *Can I align my thoughts with this power? Who can help me now?*

A voice cried out, weak and fluttery like a baby's call. "That's Henry. Do you hear him?" She cupped her hands over her ears, savoring his voice "I'm here, Henry." She looked at Adam. *Will you understand that I have to do this? Will you let me go? No matter what happens?*

Henry called again. This time his voice echoed inside her belly, reminding her of when she'd carried him. Those little poohms and gentle kicks. "I'm coming, Henry. Right now, Henry. I'm coming." She walked toward the skull.

"Annie, don't. Stay back."

She tore away from him. "I'm going to get our son back."

He pulled her back and looked into her eyes. "Jesus, don't look at me like that, Annie. What are you going to do?"

"Leave this to me." She pushed him away.

Antonia listened to the trees vibrate like thudding drums as she approached the skull. With each step, the weeping willows twisted in an ancient wind. Birds drew into their nests; she could hear their feathers close like tiny fans.

One eye socket of the skull rotated. She stood directly in its path.

I'm here. Do you see me?

The skull shot alive with colors. Deep blood reds washed over her. The hollow eyes burned into her throat. As she positioned her body before the skull, she put all her thoughts to focus on the crystal sphere.

Vicious crackling spun from the skull's head. The glass bowl burst, the fire smothered into purple and brown smoke. White electrical charges flared out.

Adam called, but a snapping bolt sent him to the ground.

Henry cried out again.

I'm coming, Henry. Another step. *Catherine, do you see me?* Thoughts of Catherine's translucent face and those tear-drenched eyes filled her mind. She imagined Catherine's hands, moving delicately against the blue cape. She pictured her golden curls on her shoulders, could almost see her tiny feet coming across the grass.

The skull sent white-hot charges at her. A fizz of lightning streaked with the smell of hot ash. Antonia felt her heart shift heavily in her chest. Blood beating, her pulse zoomed. The throbbing roared into her ears. She recited the poem's lines. "Catherine . . . Listen. 'When thou dost return, on the wave's circulation, behold the shimmer, the wild dissipation . . .'"

Jagged arcs flared.

" . . . 'out of endeavor to change and to flow . . . the gas become solid . . . and phantoms and nothings return to be things.'"

Her vision narrowed. Eight dazzling snakes of white fire waved from the skull's prisms. They missed her by inches. Her head and neck dropped, pulled forward by the hot skull. Each breath jerked into little gasps. "Catherine, 'when thou dost return . . . return . . . return.'"

White-hot tentacles nearly touched her head when a thunderbolt came spinning straight for her chest. Her heart stalled. Her breath fell. She struggled to open her lungs . . . dizzy, all light fading, her chest collapsing . . .

"Stop!" Catherine appeared in a vaporous light between the skull and Antonia. The thunderbolt passed through Catherine's body, diminishing into a spiral of sparks. "I shall not have your death upon my soul."

Dazed and trembling, Antonia did not take her focus off Catherine for fear she would dissipate. Her breath restored, she felt Adam's arms around her.

"I've underestimated you both," Catherine said, her voice soft and deep. "Quite the illustrator of human power, aren't you?"

"Release Henry to me, Catherine."

"I have no power to do this. He belongs to another now."

"Henry belongs to me."

Catherine's eyes blazed. "How excellent is your love."

"Where is Henry?"

"The child is here. Even at this moment, he still calls for you."

"Show me, right now, that he's here!"

"You wish the joy of his physical presence restored? Even if only for a short time?"

"I want my son."

She turned. "Dorotheus? Bring the boy."

From the dark thickets, she came. Dorotheus carried Henry in her arms, his legs dangling, an arm limp at his side, his head dropped back from a wobbly neck.

Antonia ran and took him from the old woman. His body felt warm, his muscles tender in her arms. She immediately recognized Henry's fresh sugary aroma. "Henry, my sweetie, I'm here."

"You can rely that he will awaken when ready." Catherine stroked his head.

Adam pushed Catherine back. "Get away from him."

The hood of her cape fell, and with palms up, she swiped at the starlight. In that sweep, she fetched what looked like a tiny star and decked it at the side of her hair. The rays streamed out.

"I will carry this for Henry . . . for when the hour comes for his return."

"Stay away from us, Catherine," Adam shouted. With his arms

around mother and child, he hurried them down the hill to the cemetery gates.

"Antonia!" Catherine called.

She turned back.

"You will find him much altered, in the twinkling of an eye, at the last trumpet. Did you not hear it?"

Chapter Twenty-Five

BALDUCCI HAD AN OPEN LINE to his backup crew, ready to give the order as he watched the actions on his monitor. And it wasn't easy to hold back—all he really wanted to do was descend on the lot of them with sirens and officers—but he feared he'd be standing in the midst of headstones and trees, no Catherine, and worse, no Henry Brooke. Nothing was worth that risk.

Minutes later, the front door flew open as Henry Brooke came home.

Balducci followed the family upstairs to Henry's room where Adam laid his son down on the bed.

"Henry? " Adam kissed his head. "Henry, look at me. Henry?"

Antonia was all over him with reckless sobs when Henry opened his eyes. The boy didn't seem to recognize her and stared out blankly for a second.

"It's okay, darling. We're here." Antonia rocked him. "You're home now. You're safe. This is your bed in your room. Remember?"

Adam held his hand. "Hey buddy? You okay?"

Those big brown eyes wandered the room, from the pegged baseball caps on the wall to the action men lined up on his desk, to the wallpaper of sailboats.

Adam snatched a T-shirt from the dresser. "Remember this?"

Henry looked at the Snoopy shirt and gave a weak smile.

Adam pulled off Henry's shirt and examined his chest. Balducci knew he was looking for that star-shaped birthmark. Satisfied, Adam gave a thumbs up to Mike. Then Henry popped his head through the Snoopy nightshirt with a peek-a-boo laugh.

Antonia searched his head. "I don't see anything here." She

parted his hair with her fingers. "No cuts, no bruise, no scar. Is your head okay, Henry?"

"I'm hungry," Henry said, falling into Antonia's arms. "Where's Laurie?"

Greatly relieved to hear the boy speak and recognize the family, Balducci felt the urge to applaud.

Laura awoke on a dime with a joyful shriek. They tumbled in hugs all over the bed. Laughter filled the house as they ran downstairs, Laura leading the way to the Cheerios box in the kitchen.

Balducci let out a long sigh of relief until Adam signaled him into the foyer.

"Mike, I forgot to get the crystal skull. You said to bring it back but—"

"I've got one of my guys on it. Adam, nothing's more important right now than Henry." The cell phone buzzed and he walked into the library to take the call.

* * *

When Adam returned to the kitchen, Laura was dishing up a bowl of ice cream smothered in maple syrup for Henry. Within minutes, he polished it off. Adam gave him a fake punch in the chin and Henry erupted with laughter. *He's safe. He's unhurt. My God, thank you.* Adam scooped up his son and spun him around like an airplane.

"Hey, Daddy, can I have a bath? Can we play with my boats? Can I?"

"You can do anything you want," Antonia said, and they all climbed the stairs to the bathroom.

"Adam?" Balducci called from downstairs.

Adam descended the steps feeling a real spring in his step.

"Adam, I've got something that needs my attention. I'm going to run but check in with you later."

"Oh sure, Mike. Listen, thank you for everything. Henry looks terrific, doesn't he?"

"He does. You might want to have Dr. Zondervan take a look at him. We could call her to make a house call tonight."

"He's fine. I just want Henry to feel safe at home right now."

"Of course."

"Hey, Daddy!" Henry shouted from upstairs.

"Man, does that ever sound good. We'll do Zondervan tomorrow, first thing. Antonia's got him in the tub."

"Go ahead."

"Adam! Adam, come here! Quick!" Antonia's scream practically shook the walls.

Both men hurried upstairs. The door was slightly ajar with steam wafting out. Adam pushed it open. First thing he saw was his wife dazed, unable to speak, making hand motions. He looked behind the door, into the tub.

Henry stood up, his little feet slapping the surface of the water as if it were puddles on pavement. What fun he was having, walking back and forth, creating splendid waves.

"Give me your hand, sweetheart," Antonia said in a voice hoarse with fear. "You might fall."

"I'm not going to fall." Henry walked on the water, splashing and squealing with delight.

Balducci leaned in to see.

"Henry," Adam said breathless, "how can you do that?"

Henry looked up, grinning. "I learned it."

"Learned from whom?"

"From the boy who walked on water. He taught me"

"What boy? Where?"

"The little boy who lives in the stars."

Chapter Twenty-Six

In the Brooke living room, Henry insisted on sleeping near the fireplace, a request he had often made. "Mommy, can we have a fire?"

"Good idea. Daddy will light it." Antonia held back tears. "Everything is back to normal now, isn't it." She said this with a blinking of her eyes that Adam would recognize as the signal to agree.

Adam piled the kindling and logs into the fire grate, struck the match.

"It's very late, you know. Laurie's gone back to sleep already." She tucked her little boy in and within seconds saw his eyelids drop.

"Mommy?" His eyes opened.

"Yes, Henry, we're here, right here."

He yawned. "Where's Cat? She'll be coming for me soon."

"No. You're home now. No one is coming to take you away."

"Oh, yes she is. She promised." Henry threw off the covers and called out. "Cat? Where are you?"

"Who is Cat?"

"My friend."

"Where did you meet her?"

"She found me when I hurt my head." He rubbed the backside of his skull. "It hurt so bad. She made it all better."

"How did she make it all better?"

"She showed me the passage." He began playing with his toes, a little game of bend and wiggle that Antonia recognized as his favorite.

"What passage? Where?"

He lifted his feet straight up. "I forget. Hey, Daddy, can you wiggle your toes and whistle at the same time?" He tried to blow a tune with his lips.

"I don't know, I'll have to try it. What does the passage look like, Henry? Is it a tunnel?" Adam pressed.

Henry kept up his effort to whistle. "Ummm, I forget."

"Do you know what color the passage is?"

Henry frowned. "Color?"

"Was it red like your fire engine? Blue, like the sky?"

He leaned his head against Antonia's shoulder. "Mommy, what color is the air?"

"That would be, ahh, clear."

"Yep, that's it. Hey, watch this." Henry put his wrists together and made a V with his open hands. He put his face inside the V. Quite proud of this display, he suddenly slapped his hands shut, making both of them jump.

They burst out laughing.

"Where did you learn that trick?" Adam lightly pinched his plump cheek.

"I forget."

"Did you learn that in the passage?" Antonia asked.

He rolled his eyes as if thinking hard. "Nope."

"What happened when you were in the passage? Did you play games?"

"Ummmm, yeah. A wiggle game, like this." He shook his hands. "Cat said to wiggle my fingers . . . and then . . . let go. That was easy. And then she said, let go of my arms."

"And then what?"

"Um, and . . . and then, all the way down . . . and all the way up." He shook his head and made circles with his hand. "I got dizzy . . . inside the passage."

"Who was inside the passage with you? Just Cat?"

He laughed. "Noooo. The little boy was there too."

Antonia exchanged a look with Adam. "What's the little boy's name?"

"It's a secret. Nobody tells." He grinned.

"Oh, sweetie, you can tell me."

"Can't."

"I see. Was Cat nice to you while you were in the passage?"

"Uh-huh. I showed her how I feed the birds with your thimble at my window. And then she showed me how to go to the top of Charlie."

"You went to the top of the willow tree? How?"

He began wiggling his toes again. "Oh, it was like swimming. I just floated up." He raised both his arms. "You've got to try it, Mommy, it's soooo much fun. Tickles."

"What a lovely way to describe it." Catherine spoke from the front corner of the living room, Henry's star nested in her curls.

Antonia jumped up on the sofa and locked her arms on Henry.

Adam was on his feet. "Get out of here, Catherine."

"There is nothing to fear. I cannot take him. My mission is to prepare and to send. Find comfort that Henry's becoming the Splendor of the Stars. A fine choice."

Catherine set her flashing eyes on Adam. "Know this. My Joseph is of the Splendor of the Stars. My Suzanne, the Splendor of the Moon, and Cosette, the Splendor of the Sun."

"I said get out!" Adam moved toward her.

"My departure will change nothing." She turned and addressed Henry. "Sweet boy, rest your eyes. Would you like another dream?"

"A basket of kittens?" Henry said. "And a mama cat with big green eyes?"

"Go quickly and make your dream."

"Can I send my dream to Lucky?"

"Your little doggy? You may send your dreams to anyone you like."

Henry snuggled to his mother, fluttered his eyes, and quickly dropped off.

"You need not be alarmed about our Henry. His safety is assured, Antonia. I have promised to call him when the time comes for his return."

"This is *not* your child! And he's not going anywhere with you. This is *my* Henry."

"In appearance only. Cut the child. He will fail to bleed."

Clefts of light enclosed her as her blue cape grew transparent. All slapped shut until nothing remained of Catherine but a fine mist hanging on the air.

"Fail to bleed? Fail to bleed!" Adam bolted into the kitchen.

Antonia felt a horrible chill that she literally had to shake off. She held her son tighter, kept her eyes on his peaceful little face. *Is he really dreaming of kittens?*

Adam appeared in the doorway, knife in hand.

Antonia stifled a scream. "Are you out of your mind!"

"I want to see if what she said is true. I want proof this is our child."

"No! You can't cut him."

"Antonia, we have to know if—"

"I know this is Henry. I carried him for nine months inside my body and you watched him come out of me. I know my own child."

"Look, either Catherine's changed him, or this isn't our son. Damn it, Annie, our child cannot walk on water!"

She closed her eyes. *No, no, no! None of this is happening. Henry is home. Tomorrow I'll bake bread and make lemon tea with clover honey. We'll have a lovely day, all of us at the kitchen table.*

She opened her eyes. Adam stood before her with one hand held out like a beggar and the other holding the knife.

"You can't do this, Adam, please!"

"Just a tiny cut. It'll be nothing. Then we'll know Catherine's lying." He approached Henry sleeping on his side. "Hold him still for me."

With a hand that trembled slightly, Adam laid the sharp tip of the knife against the soft fleshy padding of Henry's thumb and pressed.

Crackling white fire burst.

The flash bolted Adam off his feet, shot him across the room, and slammed him against the wall. The armchairs spun like tops. At the same time, the voltage snapped the sofa up off its legs, knocking over lamps, books, and glass objects. A picture crashed off the wall.

Antonia jumped up, leaving Henry tossed to the floor. Adam

scrambled to his feet, but had no power in his legs.

"Adam?" She tried to help him up.

He mouthed words until his voice finally surfaced. "I'm okay. Give me a minute."

In the middle of the wreckage, Henry stood in the Snoopy nightshirt, his bright eyes sad like never before. "I wish you hadn't done that," Henry said weakly. Eyes filling with tears, lips quivering, he lifted up on his tiptoes and raised his arms. "My heart hurts. I don't want to hurt you, Daddy." He ran to Adam, who scooped him up.

"It's okay. You didn't hurt me."

The three of them sat on the floor, Henry settling into Adam's lap. Antonia put her ear to the back of Henry's chest.

"I hear his heart beating. Yes, that's it exactly. It sounds just like . . . like what, Henry?"

"Swish, poohm . . . swish, poohm."

Adam examined Henry's thumb, then showed it to Antonia. Not a mark on it.

Henry reached up to her, cupped his hand to her ear and whispered. "I'm not afraid to go. I'm not, Mommy." He tilted his head around to see her face. "And I'll only be gone from you a little while. Then you can come to the garden, too."

"What garden is that, Henry?"

"The one made of stars. In the Splendors."

Antonia let out an impatient sigh. "What stars? What splendors? Henry, I don't know what you're saying."

Henry seemed a little giddy, his eyes bright with anticipation. "You know it, Mommy. Where the little boy lives. I'll bet you didn't know he wears shoes made of starlight."

"Does he really?" Adam said.

"Yep, and when I go to the Splendors, my shoes will be made of starlight too. Stars everywhere. Even the trees! And guess what else, Daddy?"

"What?"

"The little boy is going to let me fly in his secret boat."

"Boats don't fly."

"They do in the Splendors. The little boy showed me."

"Who *is* this little boy?"

Henry giggled behind his hands. "It's a secret. I can't tell." He looked to Antonia. "But Mommy knows him."

"No, darling, I don't know any boy like that."

"Oh yes you do." Henry said it in a singsong.

Adam took Henry's small chin and gently lifted it up so they were eye to eye. "Did this little boy do something to you?"

Henry nodded. "He breathed on me."

A lull fell over them. Antonia felt it. Not exactly soundless—more like a faintness of sound. She saw that Adam felt it too, because he looked expectantly around the room. The fire snapped out a single spark that landed on the stone hearth and rolled as if someone were blowing on it. Like a firefly, it twirled to the center of the carpet.

Henry ran to scoop up the spark. He brought it to Antonia.

She looked at it inside Henry's palm. It wasn't a spark at all. It was a tiny liquid star, soft and pulsing. Henry lifted the star with two fingers and placed it on her face.

It melted into Antonia's cheek in a cool radiance.

Henry whispered, "That's for you . . . from the little boy in the Splendors."

"For me? Why?" She brushed his floppy curls off his forehead.

"Because he knows you. Because of the last trumpet. Cat said you heard it."

Antonia didn't know what to say. She tried to recall Catherine's words. *You will find him much altered . . . in the twinkling of an eye . . . at the last trumpet. Did you not hear it?*

"You remember the words about the Splendor of the Stars, don't you, Mommy?"

Antonia closed her eyes, picturing the words. *The Splendor of the Stars.* Was it from a storybook? Some line of poetry? Some verse. *Splendor . . . Splendor . . .* Her eyes flew open. "Yes, the Splendors."

"What is it?" Adam asked. "Do you know it?"

"'The sun has one kind of splendor . . . the moon another . . . and the stars another . . . and star differs from star in splendor.' Henry, tell me the name of the boy who breathed on you. Please!"

"Oh, Mommy! You know, the little boy . . ."

Her throat tightened. "It isn't . . . it can't be—"

Chapter Twenty-Seven

ANTONIA SAW THE WORDS on the page in her mind: thin pages of text, black and white, columns, numbered verses . . . *Listen! I will unfold a mystery . . . in a flash . . . in the twinkling of an eye . . . for the trumpet will sound* . . . She ran to the bookshelves in her library. Frantically, she flipped through her Bible, the holy card of St. Helena dropping to the floor. "It's in the New Testament, at the end." She found First Corinthians, Chapter 15, and skimmed the lines. With a shaky voice, she read the passage aloud to Adam.

"'Listen, I will unfold a mystery: We will not all die, but we shall all be changed in a flash, in the twinkling of an eye, at the last trumpet-call. For the trumpet will sound, the dead will rise imperishable, and we shall be changed . . .'"

She looked to Adam who failed to draw a breath, his expression frozen.

"'There are heavenly bodies and earthly bodies; and the splendor of the heavenly bodies is one thing, the splendor of the earthly another. The sun has a splendor of its own, the moon another splendor, and the stars yet another; and one star differs from another in brightness. So it is . . . with the resurrection of the dead.'"

She lifted her eyes to her husband.

Adam took the Bible from her hands.

"Adam, our son is . . . That little boy who breathed on Henry is the little boy J—"

He put his hand up to silence her.

Coda of Saint Helena

CYPRUS A.D. 329 OCTOBER

THE OLD SHIP SAILED A STAR-LIT COURSE. At the rail, with Sister Nurse guiding her steps, Helena lifted her face. Her vision gone, airy cups of blue masked her sight. The waves carried a scent of bubbling salt as they slapped the ship's bulwarks. Stout-hearted, Helena hung on against the tumbling surf and imagined great leviathans spouting majestic puffs. And there was a great white moon, too, with sea hawks gliding into shore. This scene she recalled from a voyage years before.

On her first visit to the Stavrovouni Monastery, Helena found the forests to be infested by deadly snakes. The trees burned with a fierce red fire. As she had climbed the mount, she carried pieces of Christ's cross in her satchel. With each step up the mountain, the power of the wood cast the snakes into the sea and suffocated the red fire into ashes. The residents of the island of Cyprus rejoiced that day, making Flavia Julia Helena of Constantinople their own personal saint.

This day, once more, they would soon go ashore and make the long trek up that same mountainside. Though time had written more wrinkles onto her brow, she made this second journey carrying another treasure in her satchel. At sunrise, on donkeys, with her handmaid on the left and Sister Nurse on her right, a platoon of Roman soldiers fore and aft, they ascended the Mountain of the Cross.

The air was flush with autumn. Helena did not see the flanking walls and high turrets of the monastery. Nor did she see Father

Kosmos, the abbot, smiling behind his happy whiskers. When he offered her an armful of lemon leaves, she inhaled the citrus, fondling the tender fruit.

Helena pictured the brothers lined up under the archway as they sang their clearest hosannas to her. She embraced each one against her old soft cheeks and felt a refreshing grace.

In the walled garden, the monastery brothers celebrated Helena's return by creating a solemn feast of baked fishes, roasted plums, and honeyed figs. The bread, fluffy as air, melted in her mouth. Tapers flickered on the ivied walls. Blue herons perched on the turrets with wings as wide as heaven. The handmaid described every detail to Helena.

At the end of the meal, Father Kosmos led Helena into the modest chapel decorated with one silver cross encasing the small piece of Christ's wood. There, on the altar, she gave the good abbot her satchel.

"Pray, dear Helena, may I ascertain your permission to view it?" Father Kosmos asked.

She nodded.

Father Kosmos opened the drawstring, removed the mounds of hay and lifted out a bundle of the finest white linen. When he lifted up the holy ice, Helena heard him gasp at the beauty of the crystal skull.

Helena spoke. "Father Kosmos, my time is near. Because of the breath that passes and does not return, I entrust this and all I have written to your guardianship."

"We most humbly accept, in the name of Jesus Christ and the prophet Enoch."

Father Kosmos took the twenty-four scrolls of parchment from her hands. The monks' evening vespers echoed with molten notes.

These voices filled her heart, and she let go of herself. *If day is done, do carry me off, Lord.* Helena collapsed on the altar floor.

Father Kosmos accompanied her with Sister Nurse on the journey back to Rome.

ROME, HOUSE OF CONSTANTINE

A SLASH OF STARS opened the winter sky with a moon turned to alabaster. Helena's fading breaths were the only sounds in her bedchamber. At her side, her son Constantine stood strong, much like the sword that hung off his hip. In these last hours, her face, still rugged as a rock, grimaced with a spasm. The handmaid lit more candles, burned another pot of incense. Sister Nurse laid jasmine at her feet, lilies at her head, and a holy palm rested over her heart. They attended her dry mouth with oil and water, her wavy grey hair fanned against the white pillow as if she were a bride all silver-ribboned.

Angels raced. Servants breathed psalms. A flock of legless birds settled at her window, cooing like lutes. Constantine knelt, took her hand into his. How mute the spirits of heaven played upon her. Her deep violet eyes, never to open again. No more that melody in her voice. He flexed his back, blinking away tears.

With Helena's breath all but gone, Sister Nurse bowed to the emperor to cue him and pointed to the voluptuous vein throbbing in Helena's neck. Alone in the room, the son watched that glistening pearl snug inside her vein—swell and fall, swell and fall. The pearl became a trembling, then a riffle, almost a blooming in her glide to joy, before her soul looked out.

A thrilling marble light emerged.

Chapter Twenty-Eight

DETECTIVE MIKE BALDUCCI didn't bother to ring the bell at Saint Therese's rectory. The front door stood open, wide enough that he could slip inside. A brown suitcase sat at the entrance. A telephone was ringing in the background. The message machine picked up and Antonia's voice came over the recorder with a desperate plea for Father Jim to come over right away.

Balducci stepped inside. Blaze was descending the staircase with fast steps.

"You going to answer that message?" he asked. The priest halted midway on the staircase, a hand splayed out on the rail. Was that panic flashing across his face? "Looks like you're leaving town, Blaze. Got a plane to catch?"

The priest raised his chin and took the rest of the steps down with deliberate slowness. "Detective Balducci. Something I can do for you?"

"I hope so."

Blaze looked out through the open front doorway. "Detective, I would advise you to call off your patrol cars blocking my driveway." He reached for his suitcase. "You have no legal cause to—"

"Not so fast." Balducci blocked him. "I understand you made a late night visit to see Elias Hatch tonight."

"Hardly a violation of any law that I'm aware of."

"Maybe, maybe not. I'm curious, where do you know Roman Cavallo from?"

Blaze's vision wandered the wallpaper of faded wheat stalks. He gave a huff.

Now there was an admission if I ever saw one. "You a client of Cavallo's, Blaze?"

Blaze cleared his throat, checked the time on his wristwatch. "I'm in a—"

"Hurry, yeah I get that. What's in the suitcase, Blaze?"

"Presumably, my clothes."

An unpleasant pause stretched between them.

Blaze shifted from one foot to the other.

Balducci stood firm.

The priest adjusted his shirt at the clerical collar, stretched his neck.

Oh, yeah, that looks a lot better.

Something puckered inside Blaze's cheek like he was biting it.

From his jacket pocket, Balducci withdrew Cavallo's leather travel case. He opened the front flap. "Look what we found today." He showed Blaze the airline confirmation. "Flight 704 to Rome, departing tonight. Cavello's got a seat in first class. And yours is right across the aisle from his. Alitalia confirmed it."

Blaze blinked.

Balducci flipped open the travel case, exposing the black velvet pouch. "This is a curious thing. What an old key. I'll be damned if I can figure out what it opens."

The priest worked hard to keep a neutral expression, but his hand moved like a magician's in an attempt to snatch the pouch. Balducci slapped the case shut.

"Hey, Joe?" Balducci called to the officer stationed just outside the door. The officer reached in and lifted the brown suitcase.

Blaze dashed to the door with a yell. Balducci grabbed his arm.

"I don't really care what that key opens. I do know one thing. Something valuable is in that suitcase. Did Hatch give you authority to take his sculpture?"

"As a matter of fact, he did."

"Good. So, let me do you a favor, Blaze. Because, who knows why, but, I like you. Hell of a smile you've got. And here you are, on your way to the airport. My car is right outside. I'm happy to be your taxi."

The priest's forehead beaded with sweat.

"Roman Cavallo is not going to make his connection with you at the departure gate. He's been detained. Speeding, driving while on a cell phone. Oh, and his tail light was out too." Balducci opened the front door to its full width. "At your service."

"Detective! What do you want?"

"Just your assurance that you're the good Father Jim of St. Therese's Church and will answer the calls of those in need and distress. Isn't that right?"

"Yes, that's right."

"Then we don't have a quarrel. And you won't mind making a stop before leaving Concord."

"A stop?"

"I think you know where. Your counsel is needed at the Brooke household. We found Henry Brooke tonight. But you already knew that."

Chapter Twenty-Nine

Antonia held Henry asleep in her arms. The bleached silence that hung in the room numbed her. Balducci leaned against the dining room wall; he held her Bible in his hands, reading the passage from First Corinthians. Adam sat at her side; she'd never seen him so stunned. Father Jim Blaze's eyes riveted on the aquamarine crystal angel at the center of the table. He tried to keep calm by gripping his hands together, but they trembled nonetheless.

"Father Jim," Antonia said, her voice echoing inside her head. "You've known about this, haven't you? About Henry."

"My apologies," Blaze said. "My deepest apologies to you both. It was not my intention to mislead you. I didn't know about Henry at first. I admit to having suspicions after I heard about the hit-and-run accident, but . . ."

Adam was on the edge of his chair. "Why didn't you come forward?"

The priest nodded. "I tried to bring you some comfort. Please understand, I am bound by a sacred oath. We are not permitted to speak of this."

"Speak of it now," Adam said. "We deserve to know the truth. And why are you stealing the skull? Mike found it inside your suitcase."

"I have Elias's permission to transport it to safety. The skull does not belong to Elias and should not remain in Old Willow."

"Really? Who does it belong to?" Balducci asked.

"I am not permitted to say. This is not mine to reveal."

"You *are* going to reveal it," Balducci said with a snap of the Bible cover. He placed it on the table in front of him. "What is your role in all this?"

He let out a defeated sigh. "I will tell you . . . I am a member of the Council of Helena in Rome and devoted to her cause. Part of my assignment from that council was to locate and obtain this crystal skull."

"Why?"

"Because of its powers."

"Council of Helena?" Antonia asked. "Was that why you told us about the holy ice, the angels, and Urim and Thummim?"

He nodded. "St. Helena is famous for finding Christ's cross, but some of us know the full story of her life. She was the one who unearthed this crystal skull in Rome in 329 A.D." I can't really say more than that. I will say that I worked with an associate named Emilio Perucca from Greve who knew the skull to be in America. That's why I came to Concord. To continue his work after he passed away."

Gently he lifted Henry's hand. "May I?" Withdrawing a small flashlight from his jacket pocket, the priest targeted the light directly on Henry's hand. Like an x-ray, the light revealed the bony structure, a perfect skeleton of the human hand.

Antonia gasped at the sight. Adam shook his head with disbelief.

"It is true. Henry has visited the Splendors. Flesh and blood do not enter the New Jerusalem. Henry has passed from this life and, like Catherine Javouhey, risen."

"New Jerusalem," Antonia whispered. "You mean the last trumpet? Henry asked me, why didn't I hear it? But the last trumpet means the end of the world, doesn't it, Father Jim? That can't be right. This isn't the end of the world!"

"Oh, no, not at all." He looked to everyone. "Christ comes to us privately now, one by one, in a very personal way. And he, the little boy Jesus, has come to Henry."

Antonia hugged Henry closer, threading his fingers into hers. "And the crystal skull?"

"Just as the earth provides us with bread, water, and sunlight to nourish the human body, the earth also provides us with this sacred tool for our transformation."

"But I . . . never thought . . . I don't think I can say the word."

"I find it difficult to say as well. I think it's easier to say on the exhale. Resurrection."

He said it with such reverence; she dared not repeat it. "I never thought it would require anything material, certainly not scientific. It's supposed to be a miracle, isn't it?"

"The most important miracle. God is a scientist too. When Christ rose from the dead, he set this pattern of energy into motion across the planet, from north pole to south pole. The angels' holy ice is the tool that ensures our resurrection into heavenly bodies."

"Just like that, it happens?" Adam said. "No fire and brimstone? No cataclysmic end to the world? No Satan banished into an everlasting pit of fire as it's written in Revelations?"

"I can't answer about the destructive descriptions in Revelations. I can only tell you what I know to be happening now, and what I've witnessed. Henry is not the first, you know."

"I don't know . . . how to believe this."

"Adam, look at your child. Is he not proof of the miracle? Do you think the Holy Spirit was not a mighty force in this? Earthly energies are nothing—human, electromagnetic, morphic, or otherwise—without the power of God within it. This world, the entire creation, is God."

Adam ran his thumb along his son's nose and lips, along his small chin. "I've never seen him so full of peace, so absolutely perfect."

"Do you know who carved the crystal skull?" Balducci asked.

"No human hand, I can assure you of that. This is the work of the angels."

Henry opened his eyes, observed everyone around the table. "Can I wake up Laurie? When I go to the Splendors, I don't want Laurie to miss it." He ran upstairs.

Antonia's eyes fell. "I can't lose him . . . again." She barely said the words. On her cheek, where the star had melted, the cool radiance still clung.

No one spoke for a full minute. Adam picked up the aquamarine crystal angel and seemed deep in thought. Mike had a puzzled expression on his face as he stared at the floor, rocking on his heels, anxious, tired. Father Jim kept his head bowed, fingered his rosary beads.

The priest lifted his eyes to Antonia. "You need not look at the empty tomb, Antonia. The Father has granted you a gift, a last day to witness the joy of eternal life in Henry. Would you deny Henry this?"

Would I deny Henry this?

When Henry returned to Antonia's lap, his small body felt so creamy warm, flesh-fragrant. She kissed the crown of his head. Henry would always belong to her no matter where he lived. "I haven't lost you. Not really. You've always belonged to eternity." She reached out a hand to her husband. "The Father is asking . . . asking us, to let the absence bloom. Can we do this? Adam?"

* * *

Catherine Javouhey appeared in the arch of the foyer doorway, Henry's star still fastened in her hair. She gave Henry a pinky wave to which he immediately waved back. Adam looked deep into the woman's tear-filled eyes. For the first time he checked the hour: after five o'clock. Morning soon. He took Henry up on his lap.

Catherine observed everyone from the doorway and Adam observed her. Catherine had lost her three children. *How is it she hadn't gone with them into the Splendors? Why does she stay here?* Catherine's vision fastened on him suddenly as if she heard his thought. He glanced away.

"Dad?" Henry playfully poked him in the ribs. "What about the tree house?"

"The tree house. Yeah. What about it?"

"Those papers with the lines? Inside your desk. What did you call them? Blue pins?"

"Blueprints."

"Blueprints!" He snapped his fingers, a skill he hadn't quite mastered in the past but seemed quite good at now. "Will you still build the tree house? For Laurie?"

Fighting back tears, he ruffled the brown curls. "I'll build it, just like we planned."

Henry tilted his head. "With a roof? Just like the picture. Can you?"

"You got it. With a roof."

"When, Dad?"

"I have to buy the lumber first." Adam saw the urgency in Henry's face. "I'll go to the lumber yard tomorrow."

Henry threw his arms around him. "Everything's going to be great. You know that, don't you, Dad?"

Adam answered with a voice that broke. "Yes, Henry. I know that."

"Look outside. It's still nighttime. Let's go outside, like in *Nightdances,* and run through the trees in the woods. Can we, Daddy? Will you come with me?" He didn't wait for an answer. "Can everyone come? Hey, Laurie! I'm going to the Splendors. Come on!"

Adam was the first to stand. *Would I deny Henry this?*

Laurie came in with sleepy eyes. When she recognized Catherine in the archway, she gave a gasp. Henry ran to his sister and pulled her away. He whispered into her ear. Laura flushed and giggled.

"You can do that, Henry? How can you do that?"

"All the children in the Splendors can do it."

"What's that, Henry?" Adam asked.

"Send happy dreams."

"You dream in the Splendors?"

"Anything I want!" He spun around, jumped with both arms in the air, and clicked his fingers. "Happy, snappy dreams."

Laura imitated Henry's spin, then planted a kiss hard on his cheek. "I can't wait to see this," she said. "This is soooooo exciting!"

"*Au revoir, cherie,*" Catherine called to Henry.

Henry looked back. "Cat, will you be coming to the Splendors?"

"I cannot enter yet."

"Where is Miss Dorotheus? I liked playing her clapping games. Is she coming?"

"I must wait for Miss Dorotheus to choose her splendor. When she does, I will take her hand as I have taken yours." She turned to Adam, and placing her warm hand on his, she whispered, "We are all called to the things of this world. Draw your breath deeply, Adam. Your Laurie has great need of you."

* * *

The sky was alive with the clearest stars, all white-hushed with anticipation. Hand in hand, Antonia walked her family over the front lawn, through the path that led into the woods, Henry taking the lead. Father Jim Blaze followed with Detective Balducci.

"Say the words from *Nightdances,* Mommy," Henry said.

"Let's see if I can remember."

"'The sky is dark,'" he began.

"Oh, yes, 'The sky is dark, the house is still. The night is dancing on the hill.'"

Henry led the group into the field of cypress trees. Antonia made a circle with her eyes, admiring the natural canopy. A bird called from the far field. An eagle appeared. It flew across the clearing with thick silver wings that illuminated the whole field of green. Nose straight up, the eagle climbed vertically, then made a terrific power spin down and sailed away into the stars. Five more eagles approached from the east. One belly-landed, showing off with flips. Two flew piggyback into the cypress trees. Others made high-speed passes, tilting their wings to Henry, then fishtailed their landing.

He applauded. They all did.

Laura jumped up and down. "I love them, Henry. Are they yours? From the Splendors?"

"The starbirds belong to all of us."

"Oh, everything wonderful happens to Henry!"

Another eagle made its entrance, this one with bright blue wings spreading out like sapphires. He cruised an easy descent, gracefully tipping the clean air before landing directly at Henry's feet.

A firm breeze urged him forward. Henry let go of his father's hand. Antonia heard him utter a sound just shy of a sob. Then Henry turned. With brave eyes, he opened his arms to his mom.

She fell on her knees, swept up her child. An old lullaby filled her throat. But she didn't hum it. Instead, she unlocked herself and gave her son to the Splendors.

A deep cut of wind emerged. Henry reached out to the great blue bird, both released into the rise of the morning light.

Chapter Thirty

ELIAS HATCH LEANED ON HIS CANE, watching from his corner of the woods. Antonia saw him as the sun climbed the sky. He had observed everything, standing alone there in the shadows. She guessed it wasn't his first time seeing the starbirds. Soft light skidded through the woods, making a promise of a bright day. Elias waved a shy hand. She waved back.

A slip of weightless grey smoothed their path ahead. They all walked together in the direction of Old Willow Cemetery, Elias trailing at the rear.

Antonia stopped and turned to Elias. "Do you have anything to say to me, Elias?"

"About our dear little Henry? No words of my own, I'm afraid. Mr. Walt Whitman says it best: 'All goes onward and outward, nothing collapses, And to die is different from what anyone supposes, and luckier.'"

He reached out and patted her hand. "The secret remains with us all now."

Chapter Thirty-One

VATICAN CITY
Rome, Longitude 12 Degrees East

The air grew hot. Darkness welled. Father Jim Blaze unlocked the first door. Another set of stairs and another door; this one required an eye-scan identification. The second door opened to the Vatican Secret Archives.

He had one more eye scan to pass before entry into the *sanctum sanctorum*. Once inside, he lit a thick yellow candle. The hem of his black vestments dragged down the rough-hewn stone steps for five flights underground. He paced to the corner, withdrew the black iron key, turned it a full rotation to enable the bolt to release.

The hatch snapped opened.

Lying on his stomach, he reached down, hoping to grab a rung of the rope ladder that he was told would be there. He swung his hand against the side but didn't find it. He tried again when something brushed his fingertips, something warm and soft. He slid the candle closer to the opening.

Two sparkling blue eyes met his. He immediately recognized the face.

"So, we meet again," came the craggy voice from the darkness.

"You startled me, Perucca. I never expected . . . to see you again."

"No? *Perchè non?* A lot of years have passed since I let you see me on the banks of the Greve River. What a night that was!"

Indeed, what a night that was inside the dark woods of the Greve cemetery. When Blaze had seen the dead archaeologist, when he examined the physicality of Emilio Perucca's resurrected body, it was an unspeakable shock. And in that moment, all doubts vanished. The perishable was clothed in the imperishable. Instantly, Blaze gave his vow to the Council of Helena to complete Perucca's last commission. Rome dispatched Blaze immediately to Concord.

And now, leaning into the hatch, the priest breathed a great sigh of relief.

"Father Blaze, what have you brought?"

He handed over the black box.

Perucca bowed his head. "*Grazie.* You may lock and seal the hatch."

The priest obeyed the command. He let the hatch fall into place, turned the key a complete revolution to connect to the permanent bolt. Then he pushed the thick marble slab over the hatchway, sealing the tomb.

* * *

Perucca walked the hardened earth floor between twelve stone pedestals. White palm stalks grew up the walls like giant horns, and he touched them affectionately as he passed.

At the first pedestal, he stroked the smoky topaz skull. Australia's Aborigines had guarded it for decades. Perucca had acquired it by way of a desperate nun running away from her convent. Still, she drove a hard bargain, manipulating more money than he was willing to pay.

From the Sumba Islands, the amethyst skull, an Indonesian beauty, once lived at the Boston Museum of Fine Arts. On the third pedestal, one of Perucca's favorites, sat the Bombay rose quartz with its third eye of jade. He delighted in its silvery thatched head.

None of the skulls was as dark as the tourmaline from Mozambique. The elongated cranium drew the eye with magnificent strength. Dr. Tars Zalaf of Damascus University took a bullet in the leg to protect this sculpture he named, Black Milk.

The fifth skull, a milky-white Brazilian quartz, stood a mere three inches and had miraculously survived, in a large teacup, the earthquake of 1935. Number six: the Lipton-Wolff skull, clear and gleaming, pulsed a spectacular white aura with great smoky eyes. After many failed attempts, Perucca had acquired it from the descendent chief of a Mayan tribe who had warned him of immediate death, should he possess it. Perucca transported it on planes and trains without a single incident.

The seventh and eighth holy skulls sat as mirror images and faced each other. Both were citrine with yellow swirls—Alaska and Canada, the Northern Twins, Perucca liked to call them.

From Greenland, discovered on the outer banks of Cape Farewell, the rainbow skull sported a zigzag of colors over its cranium. Perucca had smuggled it into safety under a crate of whiskey bottles, guaranteeing a tasty celebration when it arrived in Rome.

Number ten: Portugal's mesmerizing red jasper eyes in pyrite looked like the sun shined from this skull. In 1989 Perucca had stolen it from a wealthy Texan, an exciting caper with police tracking his trail from Corpus Christi to Amarillo.

By far, the largest skull of all weighed thirty-one pounds. The Russian green adventurine exhibited at the Vernadsky State Geological Museum in Moscow was reported to have projected images of the assassination of the Tsar of Russia, Alexander II, in a snowy fog of bloody horses, carriages, and the Tsar's shattered legs. Perucca spared no expense to secure this sculpture, transporting it to Rome in a steel trunk.

Now, the archaeologist paused to pay tribute to Helena, the brave Disciple of the Redeemer. Her cause became his cause in 1956 during an expedition in Myra, Turkey. During a grueling excavation at the old church of St. Nicholas, Perucca discovered a cranny behind marble sculpted walls. Inside this hollow were twenty-four scrolls, penned by Flavia Julia Helena of Constantinople, mother of Constantine. The translation of the damaged scrolls took nearly ten years to complete. Her journals described the excavation of the Christ's cross, extraordinary healings, and her vision of the crystal angels.

Written in Helena's crabbed script was the crystal angels' *Song of the Arrow*.

Twelve keepers of starlight,
chiseled faces of might . . . holy ice,
a spangled heaven lies . . . the crystal Christ,
swimming in polished skies.
Blue snow on houseless dead, rise up,
twelve secret heads.
Angels of the kisses . . . holding Enoch's keys,
come, sweet children, glide moony beams
and sacred suns
. . . breathing . . . thy splendid resurrection.

Perucca placed the last crystal skull on the pedestal, completing the circle of the twelve skulls under the vast domed ceiling. He turned the holy ice to face the center, and in this movement ignited the ancient air. With hand over heart, he let the clefts of light take him into a choir of voices inside the Splendors.

A single horn exalted.

Chapter Thirty-Two

"The secret of the world is that all things subsist and do not die, but only retire a little from sight and afterwards return again."

– Ralph Waldo Emerson,
Nominalist and Realist Essays: Second Series, 1844

At St. Raphael's Cemetery, Mike Balducci walked the flagstone path. On this clear day, with the sun shedding warm light on his shoulders, he made his way to Madeleine Balducci's grave near an old apple tree that no longer gave fruit but did drop the most delicate pink blossoms. When he reached her granite headstone, he knelt down on one knee to rest a bunch of white peonies on the earth.

Maddy loved peonies. *Beauty breaks in everywhere.* Emerson. Did it break into the grave? *Even the corpse has its own beauty.* Why did Emerson write that? Why did Emerson open his wife's coffin? What did he see? What didn't he see? Mike touched Maddy's headstone as if he could reach into her coffin and touch her.

I want to know. Maddy, is your body in there or not?

Something glinted in his eyes. In the grass, lay a silver chain. He lifted the necklace, the diamond cross he had given Maddy when they married, the one she wore to her grave. He looked up. A pale sea green evanescence swept over her gravestone to fade into the splendor of the sun.

Epilogue

ANTONIA GRABBED A NAIL out of the box and handed it to Adam. "It's a wonderful tree house, Adam. Very cozy." She gave a knock on the roof. "I like the two lamplights."

At the ladder, a sleeping bag was tossed over the top rung. Pillows came flying up, flashlight, thermos, and a bag of cookies.

Laura popped her head over the landing. "How cool is this!" She climbed up and began setting up pillows against the walls.

"What's this?" Antonia asked, lifting a strand of pearls at Laura's neck.

"I found them in the grass, near the linden trees. The girl with the long braids, Emily, left them for me."

"Really? What a lovely gift."

"Champagne pinks. Aren't they just divine?"

* * *

Antonia and Adam sat in lounge chairs on the patio, just as a purple twilight streamed with shadows.

Adam put down his coffee cup and looked through the binoculars at Laura in the tree house. "She's wearing Henry's Red Sox cap, and has all his books with her. I'm a little uneasy about her spending the night alone in the dark up there."

"I think she's okay with it, at least for a few hours."

"What resilience she has with all this." He lowered the binoculars. "I wish I had some of it."

He reached for Antonia's hand, locked his fingers through hers. "She doesn't understand that Henry has died, does she?"

Antonia rested her head against his shoulder.

A deeper twilight spread across the lawn. She raised her eyes to the row of linden trees lush with green. A vibrant streak of white flashed. An antlered crest appeared.

From beyond, she could hear the stag's soft hoofs galloping . . . galloping in through the dazzling darkness.

THE END

Acknowledgments

I'd like to thank the editors at The Editorial Department in Tucson, Arizona, for their enduring attention to *The Dazzling Darkness*. A number of editors there advised me on the story development, but Peter Gelfan took this manuscript in hand and gave it some fine nurturing, and for his talents, I am truly grateful. Renni Browne, Ross Browne, as always, supported me at every turn and offered direction. Teresa Kennedy, who gave the manuscript that final examination, advised the finishing touches—her editing skills are always valuable. Kay Urbant did a first-rate job on the final proofread.

To Jacky Sach, previously of BookEnds Literary Agency, she wrote me the most encouraging letter about *The Dazzling Darkness* when I needed it most. And to my family, Ron, Gina, and Jon-Paul who have endured hours of reads and rereads, my heartfelt appreciation.

Author's Note

The details of Ralph Waldo Emerson's life and quotations have been made available to me through various biographies, his essays, journals, and other sources in the public domain. Although I've included some real events and people from Emerson's life in this novel, all references to his knowledge of crystal skulls are solely mine and fictitious.

About the Author

PAULA CAPPA is a published short story author, novelist, and freelance copy editor. Her short fiction has appeared in *Whistling Shade Literary Journal, SmokeLong Quarterly, Every Day Fiction, Fiction365, Twilight Times Ezine,* and in anthologies *Human Writes Literary Journal* and *Mystery Time.*

Cappa's writing career began as a freelance journalist for newspapers in New York and Connecticut. Her debut novel *Night Sea Journey, A Tale of the Supernatural* launched in 2012. *The Dazzling Darkness* won the Gothic Readers Book Club Choice Award for outstanding fiction in 2013.

She also writes a weekly fiction blog, Reading Fiction,Tales of Terror, on her website: http://paulacappa.wordpress.com.

CPSIA information can be obtained at www.ICGtesting.com
Printed in the USA
LVOW10s0847041014

407163LV00006B/134/P

9 781883 953614